Grandpa and Grace were dancing and the music was turned up loud.

Zoe sat in the Pack 'n Play clapping. How did this happen? How long had he been gone?

His grandpa noticed him. "Oh, Cole, come dance with Grace. I have to sit down and catch my breath."

A slow Ray Price song came on and Grace drifted into his arms. Without a second thought they moved to the beat and sailed across the living room floor. It seemed as if he'd danced with her all his life. Bo's mom had taught Bo and Cole how to dance and they'd stepped on her toes many times. But today he wasn't stepping on Grace's toes.

The music stopped and they swayed together as one.

"The song ended," she said.

"I know. This is nice."

"Yes," she replied in a soft voice.

"Hey, the record stopped. Fix that, Cole."

Sometimes his grandpa was really annoying.

Dear Reader,

To Save a Child is the eighth book in the Texas Rebels series. I went back to my country roots for material to write this story, including a farm, eccentric characters and a folksy grandpa.

Grace Bennett literally crashes into Cole Chisholm's life during an ice storm. She is on the run trying to keep her nine-month-old niece safe from an abusive father. Being a cop, Cole knows she's hiding something. When he finds out, he must decide whether to help her or to turn her in.

Cole tries to forget his past and Grace yearns for a normal family life. Baby Zoe wraps everyone around her little finger, including Cole. And soon Grace and Cole are thinking they might have a future together. But first they have to save Zoe.

I love these characters and I hope you do, too.

With my love and thanks,

Linda

PS: You can email me at Lw1508@aol.com, send me a message on Facebook.com/authorlindawarren, find me on Twitter, @texauthor, write me at PO Box 5182, Bryan, TX 77805 or visit my website at lindawarren.net. Your mail and thoughts are deeply appreciated.

HEARTWARMING

To Save a Child

—

Linda Warren

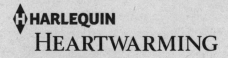

HARLEQUIN
HEARTWARMING

HARLEQUIN®
HEARTWARMING™

Recycling programs
for this product may
not exist in your area.

ISBN-13: 978-1-335-88961-4

To Save a Child

Copyright © 2020 by Linda Warren

All rights reserved. No part of this book may be used or reproduced in
any manner whatsoever without written permission except in the case of
brief quotations embodied in critical articles and reviews.

This is a work of fiction. Names, characters, places and incidents
are either the product of the author's imagination or are used fictitiously.
Any resemblance to actual persons, living or dead, businesses,
companies, events or locales is entirely coincidental.

This edition published by arrangement with Harlequin Books S.A.

For questions and comments about the quality of this book,
please contact us at CustomerService@Harlequin.com.

Harlequin Enterprises ULC
22 Adelaide St. West, 40th Floor
Toronto, Ontario M5H 4E3, Canada
www.Harlequin.com

Printed in U.S.A.

Two-time RITA® Award—nominated author **Linda Warren** has written over forty books for Harlequin. A native Texan, she's a member of Romance Writers of America and the RWA West Houston chapter. Drawing upon her years of growing up on a ranch, she writes about some of her favorite things: Western-style romance, cowboys and country life. She married her high school sweetheart and they live on a lake in central Texas. He fishes and she writes. Works perfect.

Books by Linda Warren

Harlequin Heartwarming

Texas Rebels

A Child's Gift

Harlequin Western Romance

Texas Rebels

Texas Rebels: Egan
Texas Rebels: Falcon
Texas Rebels: Quincy
Texas Rebels: Jude
Texas Rebels: Phoenix
Texas Rebels: Paxton
Texas Rebels: Elias

Visit the Author Profile page at Harlequin.com for more titles.

To Aria, who was the inspiration for Zoe.

CHAPTER ONE

"IT'S SO LONELY, Cora, and the house is empty without you. You were always puttering in the kitchen or complaining about something."

Walter Chisholm shifted in his chair to get closer to the warmth of the stone fireplace. "I guess you know Cole is home. He says he's going to make sure I eat right and take my medicine like I'm supposed to. Can you send him back to Austin and his girlfriend? That's where he needs to be, and I know you can make it happen. But then I know how you are...

"What am I supposed to do now? There's nothing left to live for. I know, there's Cole, but he's a grown man and has his own life in the city. Me, I'm just lost."

The wind howled with groans and grunts. "The devil's having a party night, Cora, like you used to say. It's gonna take a whole lot of faith to get through it. It's November in Texas and the temperature's below freezing, and the wind is mad as that old hen that fell into the water bucket and couldn't get out. Remember that? We couldn't get near her for days." Walt chuckled at the thought. "Don't worry about your animals. They're in the barn, and they're nice and warm. You probably know that, don't you, Cora? What am I gonna do without you?"

His dog, lying by the fireplace, lifted his head and barked.

"What is it, Rascal?" Walt asked. "Are you cold? Get closer to the fire."

The black-and-white-speckled part–Australian blue heeler stood and barked again.

"What's wrong with you?"

Rascal trotted to the front door and barked even louder.

"Rascal, come back in here. I'm not going outside. I have strict orders from Cole."

Rascal continued barking. He trotted back to Walt and then to the door again.

"What's wrong with you, you crazy dog? I told you it's cold outside," Walt grumbled as he got up.

Rascal leaped high on the door, barking his head off.

"Okay, I'll show you." Walt opened the door, and the force of the north wind almost knocked him down. "See, I told you. Get back in the house. This is nonsense."

But Rascal was already on the porch sniffing at something. Walt looked down. What in the world…? It was a baby carrier—with a baby in it.

He raised his eyes toward the sky as tiny shavings of sleet slowly littered the front yard. "Cora, you sent me a baby!"

THE SLEET TIP-TAPPED across Cole Chisholm's windshield as the wipers swished back and forth to keep up, but the sleet was winning. He drove over the cattle guard to his grandfather's farm, his tires crunching on the frozen hard ground. What a night, and it was only seven o'clock. He'd pulled three vehicles out of ditches they'd slid into from driving on the icy roads. His shift was done, and he was now home to take care of his grandpa.

He'd only been in Horseshoe, Texas, a week, but it seemed much longer. His grandmother had passed away three months ago, and his grandfather had stopped eating and taking his medication, so Cole had to come home to make sure Grandpa was okay.

Cole was trying to help his grandfather adjust, but he had just made detective on the

Austin Police Department, and he needed to go back to work. Grandpa had said he would be fine, and when Cole called he said he was fine. Then Cole got calls from the sheriff in Horseshoe and neighbors who said Grandpa wasn't doing so well. Cole came home to find a grieving old man who didn't want to live anymore.

Cole's parents had died in a traffic accident when he was a year old, and his grandparents had raised him. But no matter how close Cole was with his grandfather, the man was the most stubborn, orneriest cowboy alive.

With a push of a button, the garage door went up, and Cole parked beside his grandmother's thirty-three-year-old Buick. It had only thirty thousand miles on it and not a scratch or a dent. Grandpa started it every day to keep the battery charged. Any thought of selling it was met with a big frown. It was the first and only car his grandparents had ever bought new from a dealership. After an old truck had blown a tire and rammed into his parent's car causing a fiery crash on I-35, his grandparents had decided they needed a safer vehicle for Cole to ride in. He grew up knowing that car was extra special, and he never once asked to drive it. That would've been too much hell to walk through.

He pulled out his cell and called Wyatt Carson, the sheriff of Horseshoe. "Hey, Wyatt, I'm in for the night."

Wyatt had asked if he could help while he was in town. Cole couldn't take money for the job because he was already employed by the Austin Police Department, but Wyatt agreed to check on Cole's grandfather every now and then when Cole was away, and Cole was thankful for that. Wyatt was always short of deputies, and Cole had agreed to do some work just for something to keep him busy while trying to help his grandpa adjust to his new situation. He might need a few angels for that.

"Thanks, Cole. Did you have any problems?"

"No, just pulled a few cars out of ditches. The electricity is probably going to go out, so I'm sticking close to home. At least I still have cell reception."

"Me, too."

"Tomorrow's Sunday, and with this weather I'm staying home to make sure Grandpa stays out of it."

"Good deal."

As Cole jammed his phone into his pocket, it buzzed. He looked at the caller ID. Stephanie. It was just what he needed—a breath of fresh air.

"Hey, Steph." He and Stephanie had been dating for about six months, but lately she'd been pushing him for a commitment. One he wasn't ready for. At thirty-four, he didn't understand why. Maybe because he liked his freedom. Ever since he was a kid, freedom was the only thing he ever wanted.

"Cole, when are you coming home? You've been there over a week now."

"I'm trying to get Grandpa back into the groove of living, but he's not cooperating very well."

"You're going to have to accept that he can't live alone anymore. He's seventy-eight, and he needs to be in a nursing home where he'll be taken care of by professionals. There are a lot of nice facilities here in Austin—you can pick one close to us and visit him all the time. That's the obvious answer. I don't see why that isn't obvious to you."

"Come on, Steph. Give me a little more time. My grandpa isn't leaving this house or Horseshoe until he's drawn his last breath. I know him, and I'm trying to find a way for him to stay here."

"I miss you."

"I miss you, too."

"Then come home."

There was that push again. He didn't like being backed into a corner. "I'll be there soon."

He shoved his phone into his pocket with a grimace. He had a foot in two worlds. He wanted to return to Austin and Stephanie and his life. Grandpa was holding on to him with a guilty clutch. Well, not literally his grandpa, but Cole himself. He couldn't in good conscience walk away from his grandfather.

He pushed a button, and the garage door shut out the cold night. As he exited the truck, a slight smile tugged at his lips. His grandmother had had a hard time opening and closing the garage door, so when he came home from the Army on his first leave, he'd installed a garage door opener. At first she was afraid of it and wouldn't use it. Then one day she went into town to buy groceries and the dark rumbling clouds threatened rain. When she reached home, she pushed the button without a second thought. She didn't want rain to get on Bertha—that's what they called the old Buick. From then on, the door opener was the best thing ever invented.

Going into the house, he brushed his winter boots on the mat Grandma always kept there. Then he slipped out of his heavy coat and wool cap and hung them on the pegs by the door. He could hear his grandfather talking. *Oh, no...* He talked to Cole's grandmother all the time like she was in the room, and sometimes Cole had to look around to make sure she wasn't. When Grandpa did this, it was like jabbing a spike on the last nerve Cole had.

"I'm home, Grandpa."

"Come in here and see what your grandma sent."

What... His shoulders sagged with resignation. Every day it was the same thing. Dealing with that mind-set was getting to him, so he braced himself for another round of "what was real and what wasn't." He stopped short as he saw his grandfather sitting in his chair in the den...with a baby in his lap.

He blinked. *What the...*

He glanced around to see if he was in the right house. One time when he was about seventeen years old, he'd gotten drunk with his friends and wound up at Miss Bertie Snipe's house. He had that same feeling now of waking up and being somewhere he wasn't supposed to be.

All the photos on the walls were of his dad. The stone fireplace burned brightly under Grandpa's wood-carved mantel, Grandma's rocker recliner on one side and Rascal in his bed right beside it. And then there was Grandpa, sitting in his rocker recliner...with a baby in his lap.

He took a deep breath. "Grandpa, where did you get that baby?"

"I told you. Your grandma sent her." Grandpa looked down at the baby. "She's dressed all in pink, so I'm sure she's a girl."

He gritted his teeth. "How did Grandma send her?"

"Well, it's the darnedest thing. I was talking to your grandma, telling her how life wasn't worth living. I told her you were home and she needed to talk to you so you'd go back to Austin and your life. Then the wind started howling, and I told her again how lonely it was and how I didn't know what to do with myself. Then all of a sudden Rascal starts barking and barking. He wouldn't stop until I went to the door, and there she was, sitting right there in that." Grandpa pointed to the carrier on the sofa. "What was your grandma thinking? I can't take care of a baby."

"The baby was left on our porch in this weather?"

Grandpa nodded. "Yes, she was. She was all wrapped up, and I took all that extra stuff off her." He gestured toward the clothes and blankets on the sofa.

Cole went to the front porch and looked around. He saw nothing but sleet coating the grass like frosting on a cake. The trees were like stick figures standing boldly against the chilling wind. No one would leave a baby on someone's front porch in this weather. What was going on?

He went back inside and found Grandpa staring down at the baby, who was sound asleep. With barely visible dark brown hair, she had a big pink bow fastened to her head with some sort of band. If she got caught in the wind, he was sure that bow would lift her off the ground.

"I'll put her back in her carrier," Cole said.

"No." Grandpa wrapped both arms around the baby as if to protect her. "She's sleeping, so lower your voice or you'll wake her. There was a bottle of milk in the carrier, and I gave it to her and now she's resting just fine."

"I'm going to check and see if someone had a wreck and brought the baby here for safe-keeping. They probably knocked at the door and you didn't hear them."

"I hear just fine. Your grandma sent this baby." There was grit in his grandpa's voice—the voice he'd heard many times during his teenage years.

Cole sighed. "Grandpa, you know Grandma didn't send that baby."

"Ah." Grandpa waved his hand. "You don't believe nothin'."

"I know that baby didn't drop from heaven."

"I know that, too." Grandpa frowned, the wrinkles on his face as deep as the tire treads on Cole's four-wheel-drive truck. "But she had a hand in this baby being here." Grandpa gazed at the baby. "I think I'm gonna name her Grace. Yeah, Grace. That's what we were going to name Jamie if he was a girl."

Cole groaned inwardly. He couldn't endure another story of his father. "I'm sure she has a name. I'm going outside."

Grandpa waved his hand again. "Go. I'll take care of the baby."

This morning his grandpa had wanted to die, and tonight he wanted to take care of a baby. The man was losing some of his knockers. His grandma used to say that all the time about someone who wasn't quite all there. She had it confused with the saying "off your rocker." He'd figured that out when he was about ten. Grandma had come up with some crazy sayings over the years. Yep, Grandpa was losing some of his knockers. He had to find that baby's mother before Grandpa claimed that kid was his.

Getting back out in this weather wasn't something he really wanted to do, but the baby's mother or father had to be close and likely in danger. Cole grabbed his coat and wool cap and headed for his truck. He'd come home on the county road from the right and he hadn't seen any vehicles, so he took a left going out to Highway 77. If someone had slid off the road, they would probably be on the highway. He drove about a mile and didn't see anything but an empty, cold highway. No traffic. The strong wind tugged at his vehicle and the sleet dusted the tarmac, making it a slippery slide, but it had let up some and visibility was better.

Driving was a hazard, but the all-weather tires on his truck made it a little easier. He drove slow, looking for a vehicle. When he didn't see anything, he turned around and went the other way. Again, he didn't see anything. There had to be someone out here who needed help. That baby didn't drop from heaven. Of that, he was certain.

He pulled the truck over to the side of the road to figure out what to do next. And then his headlights picked up a shimmer of light. He turned the truck in that direction, and that's when he saw it. A blue car had slid off the road and hit a tree.

He pulled the hood of his coat over his head and slipped on his gloves. With a flashlight in his hand, he got out of the truck and ran to the car, being very careful about his steps. The wind slapped at him, and the icy temperature made him glad he had on his long johns.

There were a lot of baby things in the back seat. He looked around at the darkness. Nothing and no one. He had to figure this out and fast. Since he didn't see anyone around the car, they had to have crossed the broken barbed-wire fence and walked straight up the small hill to Grandpa's house. He couldn't figure out why the driver didn't stay with the baby.

He stepped over the fence, shining the light, and saw nothing but ice-covered weeds and grass. The wind stung his face, but he kept walking.

"Hey, anybody out there?" he called over and over with no response.

He could see the light from Grandpa's house from where he stood. The driver had to be close. That's when he saw someone sprawled on the grass facedown. *Oh, man!*

He fell down beside them and tried to find a pulse, but the woman had on so many clothes. She was soaked from the sleet, and he had to get her to shelter. Supporting her neck, he gently tried to turn her over.

She moaned, and relief washed over him. She was alive!

"Can you hear me?"

A fur-lined hood was over her head, and a thick scarf covered her face up to her nose, so all he could see were her eyes, and he couldn't even see those very clearly.

"Can you hear me?"

"O-h."

"Talk to me."

A gloved hand went to her head. "Stop yelling at me."

"Listen, lady, we don't have—"

Suddenly, she sat up straight and looked around. "Where's Zoe? Where's Zoe?"

"She's safe, and now we have to get you out of this weather."

"Where is she?"

Cole got to his feet. "I'll explain later. Right now we have to go. Can you stand?"

She tried, but she couldn't.

"Can you hold the flashlight?"

"Y-yes."

He lifted her into his arms and carried her toward the fence to the truck. She held the light so he could see. When they reached the truck, he asked, "Do you think you can stand?" The wind grabbed his words and threw them into the darkness, but she heard them.

"Yes."

He carefully lowered her to her feet, and they were in the truck in minutes. Turning up the heat, he said, "I'll get your things out of the car."

"Thank you," she muttered through chattering teeth.

He had to get her home and soon. He jammed all of the baby stuff and the suitcases into the back of his truck. He didn't know where she was headed, but she was prepared to stay awhile.

GRACE BENNETT SHIVERED from head to toe. She was so cold, but she had to concentrate. She had to focus. This man had just saved her life and, yet, she was nervous. He had a commanding voice, like he'd been in the military or something. She didn't know him, and she didn't know where he was taking her. Unsettling thoughts floated through her head, and sleep pulled at her brain. But one thing was persistently tapping her consciousness.

"Where's Zoe?"

"She's at my grandpa's house. You can see the light through the trees."

She remembered seeing the light and making the decision to walk there to safety and warmth. But it didn't make sense why Zoe was there and she wasn't.

"How did she get there?"

The man looked at her, and she noticed his eyes were bright blue. "You took her there. What I don't understand is why you didn't stay instead of going back to the car."

She shook her head. "No." Her thoughts became clear. "I didn't make it to the house. I bundled Zoe and myself up and then I started walking up the hill. I slipped on the icy grass, but I had the carrier tight in my right arm. My last thought was I had to keep her safe."

"I think you're disoriented. The baby was left at the front door of my grandpa's house."

"I wouldn't leave her out in the cold at a

stranger's house." The words came out angry between chattering teeth. She was so cold.

"We'll sort this out later. My goal now is to get you someplace warm. I'm sure you have hypothermia, so just sit tight and you'll see your daughter in a minute."

Daughter. Tears welled in her eyes. By fleeing she'd put both their lives in jeopardy. But she couldn't stay in Austin. If she had, they would've taken Zoe away from her. She would do anything to keep that from happening, even butting heads with this take-control stranger.

She just hoped he wasn't a cop.

CHAPTER TWO

COLE MANAGED TO get the woman into the house. She walked into the den and went straight to Grandpa and the baby. They were both asleep with a blanket thrown over them.

"Zoe," she whispered and reached over and kissed the baby's forehead, waking Grandpa.

"What are you doing?"

"This is the baby's mother," Cole told his grandfather.

"Well, be quiet or you're going to wake her."

"Is she okay?"

Grandpa clutched the baby closer. "Fine as a tuned fiddle on Saturday night."

"W-hat?"

"It means the baby's fine. Grandpa talks funny sometimes. You'll adjust."

"Oh."

Cole guided the woman to Grandma's chair. He thought a second before he did that, because the chair was like a shrine and he didn't know how Grandpa would react. But he threw caution to the wind and hoped nothing got thrown back at him.

"That's your grandma's chair," Grandpa pointed out.

"I know, but she's not sitting in it." Cole walked into the kitchen to get his medical kit.

"I don't want to be a bother," the woman said.

"You're not a bother," Cole told her. "I have to take your temperature, and you need to get out of those wet clothes."

"Oh. Okay." She seemed disoriented.

She stood and wiggled out of something that looked like a snowsuit, as if she was going skiing. She was well insulated against the weather, and that appeared suspicious to him. He quickly shifted his focus—the woman needed help now.

He poked the thermometer in her mouth. "That suit protected you," he commented, as he waited. After removing the thermometer, he added, "Your temperature is ninety-five. We have to get you warm. Sit in the chair and I'll get blankets."

"My clothes beneath aren't wet," she called after him as she folded the suit and laid it neatly beside the chair with her boots and gloves. Rascal sniffed at the items and then went back to his bed.

In a minute he was back with blankets. "First, I need to check your hands and feet to make sure you don't have frostbite."

She held out her hands. Her fingers were long and her nails were bitten almost to the quick. But the color was good, and her nails were clear. Stephanie always had polished nails. It was a luxury she would never do without.

He squatted in front of the woman to check her feet and waited for her to remove her socks. She had on three pairs, and once again he wondered about her clothing. Her toes were good. No frostbite.

"Are you hurting anywhere?"

Her hand touched her head. "I bumped my head when the car hit the tree."

He stood and looked at the bruise that was slowly turning blue. "It looks superficial, but it's gonna hurt tomorrow." He reached into the medical kit. "I need to check your eyes."

Her pupils were clear. No concussion. One thing caught his attention—her eyes were dark. Very dark. They reminded him of the time he and his friend Bo had unearthed an old well on Bo's grandfather's property.

Looking into the long, deep hole, all he could see was pitch-black darkness, very similar to the woman's eyes. Lying on their bellies staring in the hole, Cole and Bo wondered what was at the bottom. They fantasized that it might be money that someone had stolen and had stored there. They came up with all kinds of crazy ideas like teenagers do. One thing they agreed on was the well held a lot of secrets.

What secrets was this woman holding?

GRACE CURLED UP in the chair with a blanket and quilt the man had given her. The fire was so warm, and her body began to relax and the shivering eased. She had no idea where she was, but Zoe was safe and warm.

She looked around at the house. It was a nice older home with a big den, dining room, kitchen and breakfast room, kind of an open floor plan. The photos on the wall drew her attention. They all seemed to be of the same person from the day he was born until adulthood. They were everywhere and they weren't of the take-charge guy, but there was a resemblance.

He'd called the old man Grandpa, so they must be grandfather and grandson. She kept waiting for a woman to come out of one of the rooms but then realized she was alone with two men in a strange house. Oddly, that didn't make her nervous. It just made her leery. The take-charge guy had helped her, and she would always be grateful for that. But she had to find a way out of here.

"What happened to you?" the old man asked. His voice was rough and teetered on the edge of grouchiness.

"I was driving slow and my car started to skid and I couldn't stop it."

"You shouldn't have been out in this weather," he growled from deep within his chest. His voice no longer teetered on the edge of grouchiness. It was full-blown and right smack-dab in her face. She remained calm, though.

"I was going to Dallas to spend Thanksgiving with my aunt. I thought I could make it before the weather broke." That was the biggest lie she'd ever told, but she was getting good at lying. "I'm just glad Zoe's okay."

"No divine intervention at all," the take-charge guy said as he brought in her suitcases.

"You don't know that," the older man snapped at his grandson.

"Yes, I do."

"Ah, you don't believe nothin'."

What were they talking about? Divine intervention?

Before she could unscramble her thoughts, the old man pounced again. "What kind of name is Zoe?"

"Grandpa!"

"Well, I've never heard of such a name."

"You haven't heard of a lot of things."

"Don't be disrespectful. Your grandma is watching."

Grace looked around, but she didn't see Grandma, and for a moment she thought she'd been dropped into the twilight zone.

"I'm gonna give her a better name," the old man went on.

"Grandpa…"

"I'm gonna call her Grace."

Goose bumps popped up on her skin. How did he know her name? She sank farther into the blankets. "Her name is Zoe Grace."

The two men stared at each other, and the silence stretched all the way to Dallas. Finally, take-charge guy said, "What did you say?"

"Her name is Zoe Grace. My name is Grace. Grace Bennett." The words left her mouth before she could stop them. She'd given her real name, and she hadn't meant to do that. But she would be gone from here just as soon as she could.

"Told you," the old man said with a touch of glee in his voice.

She had no idea what he was so happy about.

Take-charge guy shook his head. "I'm Cole Chisholm, and this is my grandpa Walter Chisholm. You're welcome to stay here for the night, and tomorrow you can call someone to come get you. Just be prepared for a little insanity to be mixed in with reality."

"Thank you." There was only one person she could call—her friend Frannie—and she would do that just as quickly as she could. But Frannie didn't drive. And Grace wasn't going back to Austin. Her nerves tangled up like a knotted rope. She had the night to think about a plan, and by morning she would have one.

Zoe woke up and looked around. At the unfamiliar place, tears welled in her eyes and she stuck out her bottom lip. Grace was immediately on her feet. "I'm here. I'm here."

She scooped up the baby and sat back in the recliner. "It's okay." She rocked her gently so she wouldn't be afraid. But deep down,

Grace was more afraid than she'd ever been in her whole life. How was she going to get out of this mess?

"COLE, WHAT ARE you cooking for supper?"

Cole brought the rest of the woman's things into the house, and supper was the last thing on his mind. But Grandpa was one of those right-now kind of guys. Patience was a foreign attribute.

He placed a baby swing against the wall. "I was thinking sandwiches."

"Sandwiches? Your grandma never fixed sandwiches for supper."

Cole straightened—tiredness pulled at every joint in his body, and a cranky old man was revving up the pain. "What are you talking about? She made sandwiches all the time."

"But she made it seem like a meal."

"Well, think of it as a meal."

"Ah, you don't know how to cook."

Grace stood with the baby in her arms, the blankets falling to the floor. "I'll fix something."

"You've been in an accident, and you need to rest," Cole told her.

"I'm fine, really." She grabbed the baby

swing from the wall and opened it up. "Zoe loves to swing, and I'll fix supper."

"Bring her over here," Grandpa instructed, and Grace put the baby in the swing in front of him. "I'll talk to her."

Cole shrugged. "He's…"

"I know," she said as if she could read his thoughts. "I'll see what you have that I can fix quickly."

He followed her into the kitchen. "With this wind and the freezing temperature, the lights are probably going to go out."

"Where are we?" she asked, opening the refrigerator.

"Horseshoe, Texas."

"I've never heard of it."

"It's a small community of farming and ranching families."

"Oh."

His phone buzzed, and he pulled it out of his pocket. Stephanie. "I have to take this."

"Sure. You have ham and cheese, so I'll just make hot sandwiches."

"Good."

"Do you have any potatoes?"

He pointed to the pantry and walked to the end of the living room to talk. Grandpa was cooing at the baby. "What's up, Steph?"

"Nothing. I just forgot to remind you about Thanksgiving. Is that a baby I hear?"

"Yeah. There was a wreck on the highway, and I rescued a woman and her baby and brought them to Grandpa's house." He didn't want to explain any more about the baby. He was confused enough about that.

"What are they doing there?"

"The wreck happened close to the house, and the weather was too bad to do anything else. I'm sure relatives will pick her up tomorrow."

There was a long pause. "What does the woman look like? Is she young or old?"

"What difference does it make?"

"Cole…"

He gritted his teeth. "Probably in her late twenties."

"What does she look like?"

"Steph, what's up with the questions? I deal with women every day, and there's no reason…"

"Cole…"

"I haven't looked that good at her. I had other things on my mind, like saving her life."

"Well, look."

He had two options: he could click off or answer her question. He and Stephanie got along great and enjoyed being together. Lately, though, he'd been feeling a little tension between them, and he chalked that up to his grandmother's death and his loyalty to his grandfather. He wanted her to know that she didn't have to worry about other women. He wasn't like that.

Against his better judgment, he looked at Grace in the kitchen. She was standing at the stove and turned to get something out of the refrigerator. "She has dark eyes and hair and is an average-looking woman." *And fills out a pair of jeans like a Corvette fills out a showroom.* Oh, man! Where did the thought come from? He had no interest in Grace.

"That makes me feel better."

Why did you make me look? He would never understand women.

"I've got to go."

"Remember you're coming to my parents' for Thanksgiving. You promised."

He closed his eyes as if he was in pain. "I'm not sure, Steph. Depends on my grandfather. I can't leave him alone."

"You said his neighbor brings him food. Maybe she can sit with him. I really want you to meet my parents."

The obvious solution was for Stephanie to

invite his grandfather, but the offer wasn't forthcoming.

"Cole, please. This is important for us."

"Thanksgiving is almost a week away. I'll talk to you about it later." He clicked off before she could say another word. He took a moment to regain his composure. Since his grandmother's death, he felt like a wishbone between his grandfather and Stephanie. They both were pulling at him, and the urge to get out from between them and run was strong, as it had been so many times in his life. But he was older now, and running wasn't an option. He had to make a stand for what he wanted. He just didn't know what that was.

"Supper," Grace called as if she'd been cooking for them for years.

Grandpa played with Zoe; she flailed her arms at him. Baby giggles erupted, and Grandpa laughed at her antics. Cole hadn't heard his grandpa laugh in a long time, at least not around Cole's grandmother. Grandma never laughed. He'd learned that a long time ago. After Cole's father's death, there was no happiness in the Chisholm household.

Grace made to pick up the swing.

"I'll get that." Cole grabbed the baby swing and carried Zoe into the kitchen.

"Don't dump her out," Grandpa called.

"I won't."

Grace had the table set, and they took their seats. There was a hot toasted sandwich, homemade French fries and cut-up oranges and apples and grapes on each of the plates. Grandpa looked down at his, and Cole held his breath.

"See, Cole, now that's a meal—a gooey ham-and-cheese sandwich. You know how to cook, young lady."

"Thank you."

There were two baby food jars on the table, and Grace started to feed Zoe. The baby would clap her hands when Grace fed her from one jar. When she gave her a spoonful from the other jar, Zoe would frown until tears ran out of her eyes. He and Grandpa were frozen in place watching her.

"Whatever you're feeding Zoe Grace, she doesn't like it," Grandpa said. "You're making her cry."

"It's meat and peas, and I want her to eat it for the protein."

"That's child abuse. Cole could arrest you," Grandpa told her.

Grace dropped the spoon she was holding, and it clattered to the floor. "Oh, my goodness. I'm clumsy." She got up to retrieve it and put it in the sink and got another one.

"Grandpa." Cole lifted an eyebrow at him.

"Okay, I was kidding. But a child shouldn't have to eat like that."

"I didn't like spinach or broccoli, and you made me eat them."

"Yeah, I did because it was good for you." Grandpa took a bite of his sandwich and they resumed supper. And, of course, Grandpa couldn't stop talking. "Cole is a cop, though. He's a detective sergeant in Austin, but now he's home because he thinks he needs to take care of me."

"Do you need to be taken care of, Mr. Chisholm?"

"Nah. Been taking care of myself for seventy-eight years, and I don't need my grandson to stop his life for me. He's made detective now, and he has a girlfriend. He needs to go back to his life." Grandpa shook his head. "He's not like his father. Our Jamie was a gentle soul, but Cole's been rough and rowdy since the day he was born. He gets that from those other people."

"Other people?"

"My mother's side of the family," Cole answered. "Otherwise known as the aliens to the Chisholm side of the family." Every time he got in trouble in his teens, he heard that phrase. Everything bad in Cole was because of those other people. Because Jamie wasn't like that.

"Oh." Grace looked toward the pictures in the den. "Is that Jamie?"

"Yep, that's our boy. My Cora loved him more than anything on this earth. She never got over his death."

Cole's grandpa had never said a truer fact. His grandma stopped living the day James Walter Chisholm and his wife, Beth, died. But they had Cole, Jamie's son, and she'd tried to turn Cole into Jamie. His grandmother called him Jamie at least twice a day, even though he told her over and over, "I'm not Jamie." But she persisted. She had to keep her son alive. That's why there were so many photos everywhere. Cole grew up in the shadow of his father. When Cole reached eighteen, he'd bolted for freedom. He couldn't live in the shadow any longer.

But in bolting, he had hurt his grandmother deeply, and he would probably regret that for the rest of his life. Maybe that's why he really was home. He wanted to salvage something from all the years he'd been called Jamie.

Before his thoughts could take him into the pits of Jamie's legacy, the electricity went out.

CHAPTER THREE

"Sit still," Cole ordered. "I'll get the flashlights."

Zoe let out a wail, and Grace took her out of the swing and wiped her mouth. "It's okay. I'm here." Zoe wanted her bottle, and Grace was glad she'd warmed it before the lights went out. She reached for it on the counter and put the nipple in Zoe's mouth. She calmed down, sucking away.

"How old is she?" Grandpa asked.

"Nine months."

Cole came back. "I put flashlights in both bathrooms, and I'm going to put one in the kitchen and one in the den. Since the electricity is probably going to be out for a while, we better bed down in the den, because the bedrooms will get cold. The fire will keep us warm all night."

He's a cop. The words kept running through Grace's mind. Of all the places in the world, she had to land in a cop's house.

He didn't know anything about her, and she had to keep it that way if she wanted to stay out of jail.

They were busy for the next few minutes. The old man went to the bathroom and then brought back more blankets and quilts. Grace changed Zoe and put her in the Pack 'n Play for the night, making sure she had lots of cover to stay warm. Cole was on the phone talking to someone, and she could hear his side of the conversation.

"Yeah, the power's out here, too. I was going to call you a little later. There was a wreck on 77, and the woman who was driving is here with her baby. It's the safest place for her right now. Tomorrow maybe Bubba could pull her car to his shop."

He had to be talking to someone in law enforcement. She didn't know who Bubba was, but she was hoping he could fix her car and she could be on her way. That was her prayer.

When Cole went outside to get firewood to last the night, Grace fished her phone out of her purse and went in the kitchen to call Frannie. She didn't want Cole to hear.

Frannie had been her best friend for years. She was sixty-six years old and the only person Grace could count on. She lived next door and had been a godsend, helping with school work and making sure they had enough food. Grace's mother had been a free spirit and was rarely home. Grace took care of her younger sister while her mother was away. At one of the many parties her mother went to, she dived into a swimming pool and broke her neck. She'd been paralyzed from the waist down. Grace took care of her until the day she died. Frannie was always there to give her breaks so she could get out of the house. They'd formed a strong bond. That was two years ago, and life had been pretty uneventful until her younger sister got involved with an unsavory character.

"Sweetie, where are you?" Frannie's anxious voice penetrated her thoughts.

"In a little country town I've never heard of. I crashed my car." She tried to keep the desperation out of her voice, but she knew she'd failed.

"Oh, no, sweetie. Are you okay? Is Zoe okay?"

"We're okay. But it's the strangest thing. I slid off the icy road and hit a tree. I could see a light through the woods and I knew it had to be a house, so I bundled us up with the winter clothes I'd bought. There was a small hill, and going up it I slipped on the icy grass and fell. I had Zoe clutched tight in my right arm. But when the man found me, Zoe wasn't there."

"Gracie!"

"Don't worry. Someone had already brought her to this house. Cole Chisholm is the one who found me, and he said I brought her and then went back for the stuff in my car, but I didn't. I would remember that. I don't know how Zoe got to the house."

"That's really strange, but I'm glad you're both okay."

"This whole place is kind of strange."

"What do you mean?"

"Cole's grandfather Walter lives here. Walter's son died. I don't know how long ago, but I'm guessing a long time. His name was Jamie, and there are pictures of him all over the walls. I mean, like wallpaper. And not one of Cole. It's eerie. The grandfather is always talking about the grandmother, and at times I feel like she's here. And to make matters worse, Cole is a cop."

"What!"

"Yes. A cop. Can you believe that? I have the worst luck in the world."

"Sweetie, just get the car fixed and get out of there."

"That's what I plan to do."

"What's Cole like?"

Grace glanced to where he was stacking wood on the hearth. "He's tall with sandy-brown hair. Strong, prominent features that look as if they've been chiseled by the hand of God." *Where did that thought come from?* Her eyes stayed on him as he stacked the wood. "Broad shoulders and muscled. If I close my eyes and picture a fantasy guy in my head, which I would never do, he would probably look just like this guy."

"Don't close your eyes."

Grace suppressed a laugh. She had no interest in take-charge guy. She had no interest in any guy right now. Her senses were just overreacting. She brought her mind back to what was important.

"Has he been to the house?"

"Oh, yes, sweetie. He's been here twice this morning and once this afternoon. He told me to tell you if you don't bring Zoe back, you'll regret it."

Goose bumps popped up on her skin, and it had nothing to do with the weather.

"But don't you worry. I'll take care of him. You just keep Zoe safe."

"I don't know if I'm doing the right thing,

Frannie. But in my heart I feel I am. I get so confused sometimes, but my conscience won't let me abandon Zoe."

"You know, sweetie, you might try confiding in the cop guy. He might be able to help you."

Grace glanced toward Cole, who went out the French doors to get more wood. He seemed like a straight-arrow kind of guy who would never break the law.

"I better go, Frannie. I'll call again later."

"You know I'm here for you."

"Yeah, I don't know what I'd do if I didn't have you to confide in."

"I'm not going anywhere, sweetie. Take care of yourself and that baby, and I hope you come home soon. It's rather lonely around here."

Grace dropped her phone into her purse and wondered if she could trust Cole Chisholm. Would he help her?

"Were you talking to your aunt?" Cole startled her with the question. She hadn't heard him come back into the house.

"Y-yes. I told her what happened, but she can't help me because she doesn't drive. I'll figure something out tomorrow."

"You can stay here and help me," Grandpa

said out of the blue, and Cole sent him a cold stare. "That way Cole can go back to Austin."

"Grandpa, she's not looking for work." He glanced at her. "Are you?"

"Huh…no…I…I took some time off to spend with Zoe." She stammered and stuttered like a guilty person. But the offer was exactly what she needed. She could hide out in this hick town, and Joel Briggs would never find her.

COLE HAD BEEN a cop long enough to know that Grace Bennett was hiding something. He would find out one way or the other.

They settled in for the night, and Cole's grandfather started snoring right away. Grace was in Grandma's chair, Grandpa was in his and Cole took the sofa. He turned off the flashlight and the darkness covered them as warmly as the blankets, the fire the only light in the room.

"What's that noise?" she asked.

"There are actually three noises. A tree limb is rubbing against the house, and the wind is howling through the trees and is also turning the vents on top of the house."

"It reminds me of a horror movie I saw in

my teens. I haven't liked the howling wind since."

"There's nothing scary here but the weather." He twisted and turned on the sofa. It was too short, and his feet hung over the arm. "Where are you from?"

She didn't answer at first, and he knew she was gauging her response. Finally, she said, "Austin."

"I work in Austin, and I have a friend who is a member of the SWAT team there. We've been friends all our lives. We joined the Army together and did two tours in Afghanistan and then decided it was time to come home. We joined the police academy together, and Bo was offered a job in SWAT. He's a sharpshooter."

"What's your talent?"

"I can read people."

"Oh."

He let that sink in for a minute.

When she didn't say anything else, he said, "My grandfather likes you and the baby."

"I know."

"Are you interested in staying here for a while? I've been looking for someone so I can go back to work, but he doesn't like too many people. He just wants Grandma back."

"I can stay until my car gets fixed. How long do you think that will take?"

"Bubba, who owns a tow truck and gas station, will pull it over to Lamar Jones's shop. He works on cars."

"How long do you think it will take to fix it?"

"Depends on what's wrong with it. The right headlight and fender are smashed, and he'll have to order those parts and fix whatever else is wrong with the car. It's going to take two weeks or more, I'm sure. And, remember, it's Thanksgiving week."

"Do you mind if I stay here until then?"

Cole pushed into a sitting position and pulled the heavy quilt around him. "Depends on your answer."

"What answer?"

"What are you running from, Ms. Bennett?"

Silence met his question.

"I've been a cop so long that I know when someone is nervous. I know when someone is scared. I know when someone is lying, and I know when someone is hiding something. And, Ms. Bennett, you're hiding something."

His words were followed by a lengthy pause, and he didn't think she was going to respond until he heard her say in a low voice, "You're a cop. I can't talk to you."

"When I'm here at my grandpa's house, I'm not a cop. I'm just Jamie's son."

"It's weird there are so many pictures of your father in this room."

Cole didn't need to see the photos to know they were there. He was always aware of their presence.

"And there's not one photo of you."

Thanks for pointing that out. He didn't say the words out loud, but every time he walked into the den, he wanted to shout those words. It was as if his existence had been forgotten, and he'd felt that all through his growing-up years. He shook his head, trying to clear the painful memories.

"Yeah. I grew up tough because my grandparents made me that way. My only thought as I turned eighteen was I had to leave this place. I had to go somewhere where there were no pictures of Jamie."

"That's why you joined the Army?"

"Yeah. They wanted me to go to Texas A&M and drive back and forth like my father, but I bucked that every step of the way. It broke my grandmother's heart. She screamed and cried and begged, and I still enlisted. I didn't need her permission. I just needed to go. She didn't understand it, but I had to do it for my own sanity."

He stopped himself. What was he doing? Pouring out his guts to a woman he barely knew. He never did that, not even with Stephanie. It had something to do with the darkness— darkness hiding secrets. He quickly shifted back to the person in control.

"Where's your husband, Ms. Bennett?"

"I don't have one."

"The baby's father?"

"I don't know where he is."

"Ms. Bennett…"

"Could we please not talk about this tonight? My head is hurting, and I really just want to get some rest."

Cole got up to put two more logs on the fire, which sparkled, popped and hissed, bathing the room in a warm glow. Grandpa snored away.

"Please let me stay here," she said in a voice so quiet he barely caught it. But the sincerity in her voice swayed him.

"Where did you work before you took time off to take care of Zoe?"

"Golden Years Retirement Villas. I'm the

social director, so I'm qualified to take care of elderly people."

"You haven't taken care of anyone like Grandpa. He will push you to the limit, and you have a kid to think about."

"Trust me, I can handle him. He's just hurting...like you are."

"I'm not hurting." He went back to the sofa. How dare she try to analyze him. She didn't know anything about him. He yanked the big quilt and blanket over his body and lay down. "We'll talk about this tomorrow, and you're going to be completely honest."

"I feel like I should salute or something. You have a commanding voice."

He smiled to himself. Maybe he did. But Ms. Bennett wasn't going to get around him.

COLE WOKE UP a couple of times to put more logs on the fire. It kept the room warm, but the coldness was creeping in from the other rooms and from the outside.

The next time he woke up, the baby was standing up peeping over the top of the baby crib. She stared at him with the bow that had been in her hair in her mouth. She was chewing on it.

"Hey, hey, I don't think you're supposed

to do that." He grabbed the bow out of her mouth, and she smiled at him with big brown eyes. She was cute as a room full of puppies, as Grandpa would say. Then he caught the smell. Where was it coming from? He leaned in toward the baby. Oh, yeah.

Grace woke up and scrambled out of her chair. "I didn't realize she was awake. Oh—" she pulled back and then picked up the baby "—she has a dirty diaper."

"That's pretty obvious."

Grandpa woke up with a frown. "What's that smell?"

"It's the baby, Grandpa."

"What are you feeding that kid?"

"She's a baby, for heaven's sake. I'll clean her up."

Cole clicked on the flashlight so she could see and watched in amazement as she changed the baby's diaper in record time. As she stuffed the dirty diaper into a bag, she glanced at Cole.

"She's going to want her bottle, and I have no way to warm it."

"I bought Grandpa a barbecue pit for his birthday years ago and he's never used it. The burners run on propane. I'll put some water in a pot and take it outside. Where's her bottle?"

Grace hurried to get a bottle out of a small ice chest.

"What do I need something like that for when I got a stove," Grandpa grumbled. "Cora did all the cooking."

"That's very rude, Mr. Chisholm," Grace said, and Cole stopped in his tracks.

"What do you mean rude? I'm not rude. I'm just being honest."

Grace stared at his grandfather. "You're being rude, and your grandson deserves better than that. He went out of his way to buy you something special, and you should be grateful that he cares that much about you. I know many elderly people whose children just forget about them."

"I don't know how to work it," Grandpa muttered, and Cole blinked at his grandfather. He wanted to kick himself for not showing Grandpa how to use the barbecue pit. It was something new—of course he wouldn't know. Cole had gotten his feelings hurt over something silly. What had he been thinking?

Cole shook his head, grabbed a pot and poured bottled water into it. He shrugged into his big coat and boots and hurried outside. There were two burners on the grill, and they came on instantly. He wanted to cheer. He placed the pot on the burner and went back inside. Grace had a bottle waiting for him, and in minutes he had it ready for Zoe.

Grace was bouncing her up and down in her arms, but Zoe wasn't having any of that. The moment she saw the bottle, she reached out for it.

"Bring her to me," Grandpa instructed. "I'll feed her."

Grace handed her over without question.

"Now you can fix breakfast," Grandpa said.

"Grandpa!"

"Well, we have to eat something, and that pit works so we need to use it."

"You're one in a million, Mr. Chisholm."

"Call me Walt. Everybody calls me Walt."

"Okay, Mr. Walt."

As they were getting things ready for breakfast, the sun poked its way through the trees like a lazy person not wanting to wake up. It would come out and then hide behind clouds. Finally, it kind of hung in the sky for a second and then brightened the cold, dreary day.

"What's the temperature outside?" Grace asked.

Cole checked his phone. "Nineteen degrees."

"It hasn't been that cold since Jamie was five years old," Grandpa said from the den. "We bundled him up and he slept between us. Well, he slept with us all the time. Probably until he was twelve years old. He was a mama's boy, for sure."

"Is that true?" Grace broke eggs into a bowl.

Cole shrugged. "I don't know. I wasn't there, but my guess is that it is."

It was blistering cold as they went outside to make breakfast. "We have to do this fast," Cole said, rubbing his hands together.

The wind had died down, so that made it easier up to a point, but they still had to work quickly. They had a frying pan on each burner, one with eggs and one with sausage. When the eggs were ready, Grace hurried into the house, and Cole followed with the sausages. But Rascal got in the way, wanting food. Cole tried to step over him, and it didn't work. Rascal turned and Cole almost tripped with the pan in his hand. Grace stood at the door laughing.

"Is that a new dance?"

Cole laughed, too, and realized he hadn't

made that sound in a long time. At least not at this house. "I'll show you."

She squealed and ran into the house.

"What's going on?" Grandpa asked.

"Cole's dancing," Grace replied.

"Dancing? What's wrong with that boy?"

"Nothing, Grandpa. Just trying to get around Rascal."

"That dog is always in the way."

Cole didn't glance at Grace. Things were getting a little too comfy. Instead he put the dishes from the night before in the sink. Grace went back outside to make toast. Then they finally sat down to eat breakfast.

"Where's the coffee?" Grandpa asked.

"There's no way to make coffee," Cole told him.

"You can't eat breakfast without coffee."

Grace said something under her breath and then went in the kitchen. She got a pot, bottled water and the coffee canister and went outside. She came back and poured the mixture of coffee and water through a sifter and filled three cups. "Here's your coffee," she said to Grandpa.

"Now my food is cold."

"Eat it," Grace said in a tone that made even him sit up a little straighter.

Cole was beginning to think Grace could handle Grandpa. He gave new meaning to the word *cranky*, but obviously she'd dealt with that before.

As they finished eating, the lights came on. Grace clapped. "Yay!"

She was holding Zoe, and the baby started clapping, too, making happy noises. Grandpa clapped, too, and the more he clapped, the more noises Zoe made. He was really getting attached to the baby. Cole had never thought of his grandpa as liking babies. It was an eye-opener.

He got to his feet. "I'll check the heating unit to make sure it's working."

"I'll do dishes," Grace said.

"I'll play with Zoe," Grandpa offered.

When Cole came back, Grace was outside, probably getting the dishes they had left out there. Her phone pinged. It was lying on the counter in front of him. From instinct, he glanced at it. It was from a Joel Briggs. Part of the text was showing and he read it: You better bring my kid…

He could finish that sentence in his head, but he wouldn't invade her privacy. He would give her a chance. He really liked her and her sincerity, and now…

She came back in with a bowl and a spoon in her hand. He pushed the phone toward her. "You have a text."

She looked at it and then at him. "Did you read it?"

"Just the part that's on the screen. It was right in front of me."

He nudged the phone closer. "Open it."

"I don't have to."

"You're living in my grandpa's house, and I was thinking of letting you stay here. I'm a cop. I can have access to all your information in minutes."

She hung her head, probably weighing her options.

He took the bowl and spoon out of her hand and laid them on the counter. "I'm giving you a chance to be open and honest with me. I can guess what the text is about."

Her head shot up. "No, you can't."

"Ms. Bennett, tell me who you really are and who that baby belongs to. And I want the truth this time."

CHAPTER FOUR

AT THE SERIOUS look in his intense blue eyes, all thoughts of lying vanished. Grace only had one option: the truth. But would he believe her? Among all that intensity she glimpsed a gleam of hope that she had a very good explanation. Could she trust him? Could she *not* trust him?

"Who's Zoe's mother?" he asked in an authoritative voice.

She swallowed the last of her pride. "My sister."

"Where is she?"

Grace bit her lip. It took every ounce of courage she had to say the words, "She died ten days ago."

"I'm sorry," he said, his tone softening instantly.

"What's going on in here?" Mr. Walt stomped into the kitchen. "I heard raised voices."

Grace turned to him. "Where's Zoe?"

"She's asleep, and I put her in that box thing."

"It's a Pack 'n Play."

"Whatever." The old man looked from Grace to Cole. "What's going on?"

"I got it, Grandpa."

The old man's eyes narrowed. "You got what?"

Cole sighed. "I'm talking to Ms. Bennett. Could you give us a few minutes?"

"You're talking to her in your cop voice, so something's wrong." He pulled a chair out from the table and sat down.

There was a tense moment with the two of them glaring at each other. Cole folded first. "Okay. If you want to listen, you can. But you can't interrupt. Just listen."

Cole swung his gaze back to her. "Why do you have the baby and who wants her back? I'm guessing the husband."

"It's complicated and a little unbelievable." She sat beside Mr. Walt. Her hands were clammy, and a fear that she was about to lose everything she loved washed over her.

"I have all day."

"My dad died when I was five and Brooke—that's my sister—was a baby. We had to move in with my grandmother because my mom couldn't keep up the payments on our house. My grandmother and mom argued constantly. You see, my mom started going out and staying out late and not taking care of us. It was a constant battle, and then my grandmother got sick and my mom had to stay home to take care of her. I was twelve when my grandmother died. My mother started going out again, and sometimes she wouldn't come home. She left us alone and…"

Mr. Walt patted her hand. "That's okay, take your time."

"I don't know what we would've done if it hadn't been for our next-door neighbor, Frances Dupree. We call her Frannie. She's a widow, and she noticed our mother was leaving us alone at night. She had a big argument with my mother, who told her to stay out of her business. But when my mother would leave, Frannie would come over and stay with us. I was so afraid then. Frannie being there made me feel better."

It always hurt to relive those feelings of being alone and not knowing where to turn. All her life she dreamed of being part of a big family, a big happy family without arguments and anger. She'd lost so many people she loved, and it had taken a part of her soul.

She feared she was destined to always lose the people she loved. It still wasn't real that her sister was gone. All she had now was Zoe, and she would fight tooth and nail to keep her. At times she still felt like that five-year-old little girl looking for her daddy. He never came home. And she never forgot that deep hurt.

She swallowed. "I took care of Brooke. I made sure she did her homework, made her lunch and helped her with her clothes. We caught the bus together to go school. Somehow we got through those years. I received a scholarship to go to a junior college and earned a two-year degree in health care and went to work. I pushed Brooke to graduate, and then she got a two-year nursing degree and went to work, also. Our mother was somewhere in la-la land. It all came to a head one night while she was at a party. It was summer, and she dived off a diving board and broke her neck. She was paralyzed from the neck down."

Grace twisted her hands in her lap, feeling once again the burden of responsibility of taking care of her family. It was squarely on her shoulders, and without Frannie she would've never gotten through it. Her mother took all of her frustrations out on Grace, yelling and screaming at her that Grace never did anything right.

"I quit my job to take care of her. She died two years ago. She had mortgaged my grandmother's house to the hilt, and the bank gave us two weeks to get out. We had nowhere to go, and thoughts of a homeless shelter really scared me. But Frannie went with me to the bank, and they agreed to work out a payment schedule. Frannie wanted us to move in with her, but I didn't want to take advantage of her generosity. I just made sure I never missed a payment."

She clenched and unclenched her fists, trying to steady her hands. "Life settled down until Brooke met Joel Briggs. He's an ex-NFL football player who one night came into the ER, where Brooke worked, with a wrist injured in a bar fight. Brooke was crazy about him, and before I knew it, she moved in with him. I didn't like him, and she knew that. I wish I had been more..." She wiped away a tear and forced herself to continue.

"Three months later, she came home with bruises on her face and arms. I told her she needed to call the police, but she wouldn't. She said she was through with him. She started seeing an intern at the hospital, and I thought she was over Joel. Then three months later, she informed me she was going back to him. She really loved him, and he had apologized and said he would never hit her again. She got pregnant and was excited that they were going to have a life together."

She took a deep breath, trying not to let the memories derail her. "She was four months pregnant when she came home with bruises. That time I called the police, and they said there was nothing they could do. They gave him a warning and that was it. When she went into labor, she called him, but he didn't come to the hospital. Zoe was two months old when he came to see her and apologized. He said he was seeing a therapist and wanted her to come back so they could raise their kid together. She wouldn't listen to me and moved back in with him. One week later she brought Zoe to me and said to keep her because she was afraid Joel would hurt her. I told her to call the police, and she wouldn't. She said she and Joel were trying to work things out. I tried to let her make her own decisions, but I failed her badly."

"What happened next?" Cole asked. Grace

hadn't noticed that at some point he'd taken a seat at the table.

"I got a call she was in the ER. She was still alive when I got there. She said Joel hit her and she fell down the stairs outside the apartment. They had a big argument because Joel wanted to sell Zoe. He had a couple who would give him a hundred thousand dollars for her."

"Excuse me?" Cole's eyebrows knotted together in disbelief.

"She could barely talk, but that's what she said. I know it's hard to believe..."

"Was anyone else in the room?"

"There were nurses all around working with her, but I don't think anyone was listening. Brooke held my hand and told me not to let Joel have Zoe. I've been Zoe's primary caregiver since Brooke brought her to me when she was a little over two months old. She wanted me to continue to raise her. The last word she said was *Zoe*. Her hand went limp in mine, and I knew she was gone." Her voice choked on the last word.

Zoe gave a little cry, and Grace jumped up and went to get her. Gathering Zoe into her arms, she held her close. She curled up in the recliner with Zoe and wrapped a blanket around her. She held her tight, gently rocking her. But there was nothing gentle about the emotions inside her. She had this deep fear she was about to lose the last person she loved. And the look in Cole Chisholm's blue eyes made it as real as the goose bumps on her arms.

COLE STOOD IN the kitchen watching her. In his line of work, he'd heard a lot of unbelievable, far-fetched stories. This one was just like a lot of the others. The sincerity in her voice got him, though. He believed her—yet he never believed anything one hundred percent until he checked the facts.

Grace sat with her legs curled beneath her, a blanket wrapped around them. Zoe rested on her shoulder, and every now and then she'd kiss Zoe's cheek. Her left hand went to her mouth occasionally as she bit her nails. She was nervous. Scared. And had no one to turn to.

"What are you gonna do?" Grandpa asked.

He looked at his grandfather. "Check the facts."

"You say that like you don't have any feelings."

I don't have any because you and Grandma

never showed me any. The words were right there on the edge of his tongue, but he didn't say them. It wasn't that he was weak. He just didn't want to hurt his grandfather, and dredging up the past would do that. He'd left that behind years ago.

Instead of answering the question, he said, "I'm going to take a shower and change."

Grandpa followed him. "You better make sure they don't take that baby from her."

Cole stopped at the door to the bathroom. "Grandpa, I'll look into it. The bottom line is that baby belongs to someone else. And it's going to take a miracle for Ms. Bennett to keep her."

"Don't you worry. Your grandma has it covered."

Cole sighed. *Here we go again.* The moment those words crossed his mind, he knew he hadn't left the past behind. He just liked to think that he had. It was there every time he had to deal with his grandpa. He felt like that little boy trying to get his grandmother's attention, trying to make her believe that he wasn't Jamie. Some days he had this feeling that he and Jamie were one and the same and he was never going to find out who Cole really was because he was the shadow of Jamie.

He took a cold shower to give his senses a jolt. He lived in the present, not the past. And he refused to let the past control him.

Fifteen minutes later he was clean shaven, dressed in jeans, a blue shirt and boots, ready to face whatever this day brought. And he just might uncover the secrets in the dark, dark well of Grace Bennett.

Ms. Bennett was still in the chair; Grandpa bounced Zoe up and down on his lap. A scene from a normal family life, but normal never lived in this house.

"I'm going to go check on your car and make sure that Bubba has towed it to his shop," he said to her. "We don't want to leave it out there too long, or it will get stripped."

"Oh, okay." She seemed surprised.

"And I'll make sure he pulls it over to Lamar's body shop and I'll check in there to see how long it will take him to fix it. He's going to want proof of insurance. You might want to call your insurance company."

"Sure." She got up and riffled through her purse and handed him a card.

"I'll be back later." He glanced toward his grandpa. "Do you think you can take care of things here?"

"I don't see a problem," she said.

"Don't go outside. It's still icy everywhere."

"Okay."

He turned to leave, but she stopped him. "Do you believe me?"

"I try not to make snap judgments or go on emotions. I'll check the facts and get back with you." He looked into those dark eyes. "But if you have anything else to say, you better tell me now. If you lie to me, I'll be less inclined to help you."

"I haven't lied to you. Joel accused me of harassing him. That's what he told the police— that I was always meddling in my sister's affairs, which wasn't true. I let her make her own decisions. I didn't like him, but I never interfered except that one time I called the police after he hit her. I called a lot of times after she died. I wanted him arrested. He didn't even spend one night in jail. I can't even bury my sister because the coroner still has the body. The police are waiting on the autopsy to see how she died. I just want to bury my…"

He hardened himself against the anguish in her voice. "I'll check into that, too." He said he wasn't swayed by emotions, but he could feel himself being pulled into her life, her problems, and he had enough of his own.

"I'll be back around lunch." He walked toward the back door thinking of the number-one rule a cop learns—never get emotionally involved. It was a problem he'd never had. His emotions werc all locked up tight inside him, and it would take an extortionist, a priest and an exorcist to free him. And a dark-eyed beauty wasn't going to change that.

GRACE MULLED OVER Cole's words for a moment, knowing he was a straight-arrow kind of cop and he wasn't going to be swayed by her story. She knew that before she told him what had happened. Now she had to deal with the results. But somewhere deep inside, she knew Cole had a heart—or he wouldn't be here trying to take care of his grandfather.

She tidied the house and noticed there was a lot of laundry to do. "Mr. Walt, do you mind if I do a couple loads of laundry?"

"No. Somebody has to do it." He got to his feet and put Zoe in the Pack 'n Play. "I'm gonna take a shower."

"Okay."

"What are we having for lunch?"

"I honestly haven't thought about it."

"I want fried chicken, mashed potatoes with gravy, green beans and homemade biscuits, and maybe coconut pie."

Grace's eyes opened wide. "I didn't realize this was a diner."

He frowned at her. "Are you one of those women who's gonna tell me I'm a male pig something?"

She couldn't help but smile. The old man was lonely and missing his wife, and she would pamper him for this day. Everybody needed a little pampering. "Where would I find the chicken?"

"In the freezer in the utility room."

"Is it cut up?"

"No. You have to do that."

"I don't know how to cut up a chicken." Nor did she know how to fry one. She'd never fried a chicken in her whole life.

"I'll show you."

"Well, then, I guess I better thaw it out."

"I know you're a woman who can tell a man how a cow ate the cabbage, but you're also kind and gentle. My Jamie was like that. Cole, he's different."

She had no idea what he was talking about, but the last part caught her attention. It was none of her business, but she had to ask, "Why do you always do that?"

"What?" He was genuinely puzzled.

"Compare Cole to Jamie."

"I don't do that."

"Yes, you do. You've done it several times since I've been here."

"I did not. You're talking nonsense. I'm going to take a shower." He walked toward the hall.

Grace shook her head. He was never going to admit he'd done anything wrong. He probably saw it as nothing, but when Mr. Walt had mentioned it last night, she'd noticed the look on Cole's face. It was something to him. She glanced at all the photos of Jamie on the walls and found not one of Cole. She'd bet Cole noticed that, too.

COLE CHECKED IN with Wyatt and filled out an accident report. Bubba had already hauled the car to Lamar's garage, so Cole drove there. It wasn't far from town. Lamar's ancestors had bought the land cheap after the Civil War, and they were still there. Lamar loved to talk and tell stories about his family.

Ms. Bennett's car was parked in his driveway, and Cole pulled up behind it. The garage was to the right of Lamar's house. Dori, Lamar's wife, taught school, and Cole knew them both well.

Lamar, a tall black man, came out of the

house. He wore overalls and a Carhartt jacket. A baseball cap rested on his gray hair.

"Mornin', Cole."

"Morning, Lamar." They shook hands. "I see Bubba brought the car."

"Yeah, early this morning. There's a stroller and baby things he took out of the car, and you might want to get that car seat out."

Lamar helped him move everything into Cole's truck.

"Let's go to my office. It's cold out here." Lamar shoved his hands into the pockets of his jacket.

They went into a side door of the garage. It was a small space with a desk and all kinds of auto parts stacked on shelves. The desk was littered with papers and manuals. The linoleum floor was covered in muddy footprints.

Cole pulled up a metal chair, and Lamar sat at the desk.

"Has Miss Dori seen this place?"

"My wife's not allowed in here. This is my space and my business, and she's not bringing all her cleaning stuff and messing it up. I'd never be able to find anything."

Cole chuckled to himself. Miss Dori's house was spotless. At least it had been all the times he'd been there as a teenager. Cole had been good friends with their daughter, Jasmine.

"How long will it take you to fix the car? The lady is stuck at Grandpa's house until you do."

"Depends on how long it'll take to get parts."

"Soon, Lamar. Soon."

Lamar put on his wire-rimmed glasses and pulled a manual toward him. Then he looked up. "You know what. I get parts from a junkyard over in Temple. The car is a 2018 Camry. They probably have that fender over there. If they do, I can get it fixed quickly."

"Good deal." Cole reached into his pocket and placed the insurance card on the desk. Lamar made a copy and gave it back to him. Cole hadn't seen the computer or the printer. They were behind a tall stack of manuals.

"I'll take care of it," Lamar said.

"Thanks."

"Have you been watching LJ play?"

LJ was Lamar's son, who played in the NFL. "Every chance I get."

Lamar got to his feet and walked Cole to his truck. "I guess you know he got married."

"Yeah, Miss Dori told me after the funeral."

"Married a white girl. Broke his mama's heart."

When Cole had talked to Miss Dori, she didn't seem all that upset about it. So that meant Lamar was upset about it.

"Thought he'd come back here and live on this land that his ancestors bought for mere pennies. But I don't see that happening now. She's a city girl."

"Give her a chance, Lamar. She might surprise you."

"That's what Dori says," Lamar mumbled almost to himself.

Cole patted him on the back. "See you later."

Family relationships were never easy. Cole saw it in his work and in his own life. Was there such a thing as happiness? Or was it just a dream, like clouds floating across the sky—beautiful one minute and dark and dangerous the next. Was anything real? Or forever?

MR. WALT CUT up the chicken. Grace figured if he knew how, he could do it. She fixed everything Mr. Walt wanted according to his directions, even the coconut pie. She wasn't exactly a cook and had never made a pie. Mr. Walt got his wife's recipes down, and she followed them to the letter. She had more flour on her and the counter than she did in the pie crust. But it turned out, to her surprise.

She searched for green beans and couldn't find any in the pantry. "Mr. Walt, there aren't any green beans."

He came into the kitchen with Zoe in his arms. He had shaved his scraggly beard and was in clean jeans and a flannel shirt. "Sure there is. You just have to look."

"I've looked everywhere."

"They're in the cabinets in the utility room above the washer and dryer."

Grace opened the doors and found a treasure trove of canned vegetables, from green beans, peas, corn, carrots and squash to pickles and peaches.

"Cora cans vegetables from the garden every year."

Grace grabbed a pint of green beans.

"Don't put anything in them. They just need heat."

Zoe became fussy, and Grace took her. "I wish I had her high chair. She'll sit in it and play."

"There's one in the attic. I'll get it down."

"No." She stopped him before he could

move. "You will not climb into the attic. I'll do it."

"Suit yourself. The ladder's in the hallway. It has a string and you have to pull it down."

"I know, Mr. Walt." She handed him Zoe. She had no problem pulling the ladder down.

"There's a light switch to the right, and the chair should be on the left." Mr. Walt continued to give instructions.

Grace flipped on the light and paused at the sight before her. Everything was covered in plastic, and Jamie's name was written in big black letters on every box. Everything that Jamie had ever touched or owned was up here. It was like a shrine.

She removed the plastic from the high chair and just stared. It was a dark oak, and carved on the inside at the back was Jamie's name, surrounded by painted butterflies and tiny flowers.

Oh, good heavens! This was hallowed ground—she couldn't use this chair. She could almost hear the music from *The Twilight Zone* playing in her head. There was a lot in this house that was unnatural.

And then she realized the Chisholms cherished all of Jamie's things in a way to keep him alive. But Jamie had left the most important part of him behind—his son. And he wasn't covered in plastic with years of dust clinging to him. Yet, the Chisholms never saw that. Maybe it was time someone pointed out this fact.

Of course, it was none of her business, but something about this place and the two men tore at her heart. One clung to the past and the other was desperate to escape it.

She grabbed the high chair and carted it down the steps. Time for a little reality.

CHAPTER FIVE

Cole's phone buzzed, and he stopped at the cattle guard to answer it. Stephanie.

"Cole, are you coming to Austin tonight?"

"I wasn't planning on it."

"I was hoping you could come to the city and we could do something."

He took a long breath. Stephanie never seemed to hear what he said. She only heard what she wanted to. "I'm still dealing with my grandpa. I told you I won't be back until the Monday after Thanksgiving."

"But you're coming to my parents' for Thanksgiving, aren't you?"

"I'll try." That's the best he could do. He really didn't want to deal with this. He had so much other stuff on his mind.

"Cole." He was beginning to dislike her whiny voice.

"Go out with your girlfriends. Y'all always have a good time. I just can't come to Austin right now."

"I have so much more fun with you."

"I have to go, Steph. I'll let you know about Thanksgiving and how things are here." She never once asked about his grandfather, and that bothered him.

Stephanie's father was a defense attorney, and Stephanie wanted to follow in his footsteps. She was working at another firm but soon would transfer to her father's. Cole disliked defense attorneys. They always got criminals off, and that didn't sit well with him. But he'd liked Stephanie, and the relationship had worked well up to this point. Now he was second-guessing himself. Maybe he just needed to get back to Austin, to his own life. He was grumpy right now with everything that had fallen onto his plate.

He glanced out at the dreary day. The temperature was now in the thirties, and the sun's breath was melting ice everywhere. It was a welcome relief that the sun would continue to warm the day.

But truly, only one thing occupied his mind: Grace Bennett. She'd had an awful childhood, just like he had. Yet she was a strong woman, and he admired her courage in trying to keep Zoe safe. But she might have to fold on this one. He worked with cops and lawyers, and when it came to custody situations, parents had the upper hand. Unless everything Ms. Bennett had told him was true. The only way to find that out was to investigate. He had a feeling it had already been investigated.

He wasn't a knight in shining armor, and he didn't rescue damsels in distress. That wasn't his thing. But Ms. Bennett needed someone. And to live with a clear conscience, he would try to help her.

He picked up his phone and called his best friend, Beauregard Goodnight. He couldn't have gotten through his childhood without Bo. They both had dysfunctional families. Bo had a terrible relationship with his dad and it probably would never change. His dad had cheated on his mom several times with other women. Even after the divorce his mom continued to take the man back when he was down on his luck. Every time that happened, it revved up Bo's blood pressure.

The two of them had leaned on each other during those hard times. They spent many a night in Cole's grandpa's barn because Bo didn't want to go home if his dad was there. Sometimes Grandpa would come looking for Cole. He would tell him he was keeping Bo company and would be inside later. He would say okay, but his grandmother never seemed to know he wasn't in the house. She never seemed to know he existed.

"Hey, what's up?" Bo's strong, familiar voice sounded in his ear. It reminded him of all the plans they'd made as teenagers. The number-one plan was to join the Army and leave Horseshoe, Texas, and their families as soon as they turned eighteen. They would make their own lives. Their own decisions. They would find happiness somewhere in that big old world. The plan sounded great in their young minds, but heartache was heartache everywhere you took it.

"Hey, Cole, are you there?"

Bo's voice jarred him back to reality, and he told him about Grace Bennett. "I feel I should help her." After they'd left the service, they'd both joined the police academy, starting out as beat cops and slowly moving up the ranks. They both made sergeant about the same time. Cole chose detective work, while Bo was a member of an elite SWAT team.

"I've heard about the case. Colin Parker is the lead detective. Ralph Tenney's his partner, and I talk to him a lot. He's trying to get into SWAT. He says the Joel Briggs situation is an open-and-shut case. They're just waiting on the autopsy to close it."

"I know. Grace Bennett is very sincere and I tend to believe her, but I will check facts first. I'm trying to follow protocol and not step on anyone's toes."

"Parker's pretty sensitive. He doesn't like anyone messing in his cases. He's been on the force thirty-plus years, and he thinks his word is the end of it. Do you have something concrete to dispute his decision?"

"Just Grace Bennett's word."

"Going all in for the lady, are you?"

"A nine-month-old baby is involved, and she deserves the very best. We had lousy childhoods, but this kid has a chance at a good life. And I don't believe it's with Joel Briggs."

"I can't help you, but since I work with SWAT, I can rescue you when all this hits the fan, so to speak. If you confront Parker, there will be fireworks."

"I don't plan on confronting anyone. I plan to talk detective to detective."

"Let me know how that goes."

"Are you saying my negotiating skills are weak?"

"Remember that time we were in Kunar,

Afghanistan, at a small bar taking a break? The barmaid wanted to marry one of us so she could come to Texas. Remember what you told her?"

"Bo…"

"You told her that she didn't want to go to Texas and she asked why. You stole one of Grandpa's sayings. It went something like this—a famous general once said if he owned Texas and hell, he'd rent out Texas and live in hell. She said she didn't know what that meant, and you told her that Texas was hotter than hell. She frowned and wouldn't serve us any more drinks. The good ol' days, Cole."

"There were never any good ol' days."

"Yep, you're probably right. How's Grandpa?" Bo had always called Cole's grandfather Grandpa. It just seemed natural.

"You're not gonna believe it. He's taken a shine to Ms. Bennett and the baby. He says Grandma sent them."

"It's always been crazy at your house, and I mean haunted house and *Looney Tunes* crazy."

"Like your family is sane," Cole shot back.

Bo laughed again. "My family was just highly dysfunctional. Yours had a ghost-and-hereafter feel to it."

Cole laughed this time. "Yeah, and those ghosts come out regularly." Cole glanced at the time on his dashboard. "I gotta go. I told Ms. Bennett I'd be back by noon."

"Good luck."

Cole laid his phone in the console and drove to the house. As he entered through the back door, he heard Grace and Grandpa talking. He didn't know why he didn't walk in. Something held him back.

"When are we going to eat?" Grandpa asked.

"Cole said he'd be back by noon, so we're waiting," Grace told him.

"Ah, you can't go by Cole. He might not come back until this afternoon."

"I sense that Cole is a man of his word."

"But I'm hungry."

"A few minutes, that's all."

"You're letting Zoe Grace eat."

"Because she's a baby, and she's used to eating at this time. You're not a baby, are you?"

Grandpa didn't answer, and Cole started to walk in until Grandpa spoke.

"I told you the high chair would work. She likes it."

"Yes, but I'm afraid she's going to scratch it or something."

What high chair? It couldn't be Jamie's high chair.

"I'll fix it. I had to fix it after Cole grew out of it. He had it all bunged up. Jamie hardly got a scratch on it, but Cole was…"

"Mr. Walt, please don't say that again."

"Now what are you on about?"

"You were fixing to compare Cole to Jamie again."

"I was not."

"Mr. Walt…"

"Oh, all right. I'm just used to doing that."

What had happened while he'd been gone?

"You need to stop. How do you think Cole feels when you do that?"

"I don't know. He never says nothin'."

"Mr. Walt…"

"You're making my head hurt. I need to eat."

"May I ask you a question?"

"No. I don't like your questions."

"Why are there no pictures of Cole on the walls? There have to be at least a hundred pictures in here and not one of Cole, your grandson."

"What? Sure there is. There's one right there."

"Mr. Walt, that's a picture of Jamie holding Cole when he was a baby. You can barely see Cole. He's wrapped in a blanket. It must've been when Cole was born."

"Yeah. Jamie was so proud of his boy."

"Then why are there no photos of Cole?"

"Ah, that was Cora's doing. That's how she dealt with Jamie's death. Every day she'd find a picture and up it went on the wall. She spent a fortune on frames. I couldn't stop her. She wouldn't listen. It was her way of grieving."

"There are no photos of Cole's mother, either."

"Cora got rid of all those. She blamed Beth for Jamie's death, for taking Jamie away from us. It wasn't right, but Cora was out of her mind with grief."

"Cole has no pictures of his mother?"

"I saved some before Cora could rip them up. I have them put away for Cole."

Cole had been told at an early age not to mention his mother, that it would upset his grandmother. So Cole never asked questions, but he'd wondered so many times. And now Grandpa was saying he had saved some pictures. Cole had never seen them.

"That's nice."

"Yeah, I'm not heartless, you know."

"Mr. Walt, I never said you were. I think you've been grieving all these years, too. But you and your wife forgot one important thing."

"What?"

"That attic is like a shrine to Jamie. All his things are up there. It's all saved and wrapped in plastic so it will last a lifetime. But Jamie left something much more valuable for you and your wife. He left a part of himself—his son. Cole is alive and breathing and needs much more attention than those relics in the attic."

Cole thought he should just walk in, but again he didn't. He seemed depleted of energy. No one had questioned his grandparents about Cole's upbringing. They knew it was unusual, but no one intervened, except Miss Bertie. But no one listened to Miss Bertie. She was an eccentric character everyone dismissed.

Now this stranger was poking her nose into Chisholm business, into the Chisholm family. He didn't need her to fight his battles. He was capable of doing that on his own. But a small part of him was cheering. Someone had noticed, and someone spoke up. But how much did it matter now? He was a grown man.

"Mr. Walt, are you crying?"

Cole stood up straight. He'd never seen his grandfather cry. He'd been a baby when Jamie had died, and his grandfather was good at keeping his emotions in check even when Grandma had passed on. Why was he crying now?

"I'm just hungry."

"Mr. Walt…"

"Okay. We failed Cole. We really did. I tried to get Cora to see what we were doing was wrong. We needed to make a life for Cole, but she was fixated on Jamie and nothing got through to her. All she wanted was Jamie back, and there was nothing I could do about that. I was grieving, too. Cole—he just got left out. But he's a strong man now, and I'm proud of him. And…"

"And what?"

"It wasn't Cora. It was Jamie."

"What was Jamie?"

"I thought Cora sent you and Zoe Grace, but it wasn't Cora. It was Jamie. He doesn't want me grieving. I should've figured that out. It was Jamie."

"Mr. Walt, you're not making any sense."

Cole had heard enough. He slammed the door. "Grandpa, I'm home."

"Cole, Cole, come here." His grandfather met him in the doorway to the kitchen. "It wasn't your grandmother. It was Jamie, your father."

He glanced over Grandpa's head to Ms. Bennett. Her dark eyes looked as confused as he was. But he knew what his grandpa was talking about.

He slipped out of his coat and hat and hung them in the utility room like he usually did, giving himself time before answering Grandpa.

"Did you hear me?"

"Yes, Grandpa. I heard you."

"I had it all mixed up."

"You get a lot of things mixed up, but once again, neither Jamie nor Grandma sent Zoe from heaven."

"Of course not. But he had something to do with Grace coming this way and running off the road near our house. And you can't explain how Zoe Grace got on our front porch, either. I know how, and soon you'll know, too." Grandpa sat at the table with a smug expression.

"What's Mr. Walt talking about?" Grace was still confused.

Cole took a long breath. "Grandpa's under

the impression that Grandma somehow brought Zoe to the house when you fell on the ice last night. Well, now he thinks it was Jamie. Divine intervention from above."

She ran her hands up her arms. "That's spooky."

"I'm hungry. Let's eat." Grandpa spoke up.

Cole went to wash his hands, and Grace put the food on the table. He stared at the table covered with food. He pulled out his chair. "Are we celebrating something? This looks like a special meal."

"Mr. Walt ordered it and told me how to make each thing. He wanted it like his wife makes."

For the last three months, Grandpa hadn't had much of an appetite. People brought food, and he ate a little and then put it in the refrigerator. Cole had to throw it out. Now he was hungry. What was up with the old man?

Zoe grew restless, waving her arms and whimpering. Grace got up and fixed her a bottle, and then she took her out of the high chair. "I'm going to put her down for a nap."

"After I finish this coconut pie, I'm taking a nap, too."

Grandpa was shoveling food in like it was his last meal. Maybe he'd just made the turn from grieving back to his old self. Cole really hoped that was the case. He'd also shaved and put on clean clothes. Cole had been trying to get him to do that for two days.

Grandpa got up and went into the den and turned on the TV. Loud.

Grace bounced Zoe up and down in her arms. "I don't think Zoe can go to sleep with the TV that loud. Can I put her in one of the bedrooms?"

Cole walked into the den. Grandpa was already asleep. He picked up the remote control and turned down the volume. Grace settled Zoe in the playpen, and she went to sleep.

"Thank you."

Cole got a cup of coffee and sat at the table, needing to talk to Ms. Bennett.

"Could we talk for a minute?" he asked as she came into the kitchen.

"Can we talk while I do the dishes?"

Cole helped her. "You know you don't have to cook everything he asks for."

"He's lonely and grieving, and I couldn't resist. After all, you've been very kind to me and so has Mr. Walt."

Cole leaned against the counter. "You're very good with him."

She closed the dishwasher and set it. "I'm

used to the elderly. I work with them every day. Sometimes the grumpiness is a way to deal with life." She turned to face him. "I don't get the part about Grandma or Jamie bringing Zoe to the house. But then again, I can't explain how she got here. I had her in my right arm when I fell before I blacked out."

"I guess we'll never know, but she's safe however she got here." He poured another cup of coffee and sat at the table. "Lamar is going to work on your car as soon as he gets the parts. It will depend on how soon he can get them. He took your insurance information, and he'll let us know."

"Thank you."

"I'll look into your sister's case. But it's a touchy situation, because detectives don't react well to other detectives looking into their work."

She sat facing him, her dark eyes huge in her face. The bruise on her forehead was already healing. She had a young look about her, but he knew her inner strength was much older and wiser.

"I really appreciate it. Maybe Mr. Walt's ramblings are true. Maybe I slid off the road near your house for a reason."

"Don't go there, Ms. Bennett. Soon you'll

be back in Austin dealing with Joel Briggs and a custody battle. And, yes, you will have to go back and face him. You have to do this the legal way. For Zoe. And for yourself."

"But a judge will give Zoe to her father. You know that and I know that."

"Ms. Bennett, you have to prepare yourself for that fact."

She jumped to her feet, anger flashing in her eyes.

"Sit down, Ms. Bennett."

"Stop calling me Ms. Bennett."

"Do you have another name?"

"Yes. Grace."

He leaned back in his chair, watching her eyes blast him with more fire than he'd ever seen. "Okay. Grace."

She sank into her chair. "You're such… such a lawman."

"That's my job—to bring criminals to justice."

"I'm not a criminal. I'm trying to save my niece."

He leaned forward. "Then, first thing tomorrow you need to go into Horseshoe and see Gabe Garrison. He's an attorney, and he will help you file a petition for custody of Zoe. That's the first step. He's a good attorney, and he'll tell you exactly what you need to do. In the meantime I will do everything I can to find out what happened between your sister and Joel Briggs."

She picked up a napkin from the table and squeezed it. "Thank you."

"You're welcome, and please, try to think sensibly about this. If Joel Briggs is guilty, he's going down. You just have to be patient."

"He's a charmer. He knows how to work people, and the detective who worked the case was a big fan of his. I don't see anything changing."

"Do you know what the word *patience* means?"

She frowned at him, and he'd never seen anyone frown that pretty.

When she didn't say anything, he added, "And another thing. When I came in, I could hear you and Grandpa talking."

One dark eyebrow shot up. "You eavesdropped?"

"Yes," he said without guilt. "I just want to make it clear that you are not to interfere in my life. I do not need a savior. I can take care of my own problems. I've been doing it since I was a child."

She glanced at the photos on the walls. "So you're okay with all of this?"

"I've learned to ignore it. My grandmother was not herself after she lost my father. It was the only way she could cope."

"She's not here anymore. Why not take them down?"

"The photos don't bother me."

"You're lying." She stared him straight in the eye, and he found it hard not to flinch. How could she get under his skin so easily? He was an expert at showing no emotions.

"This doesn't concern you." His phone pinged, and he reached for it in his pocket. "This is over. Do you understand?"

"Should I salute?"

They stared at each other in tense silence, and he swung away to answer his phone. The woman was getting under his skin like no one ever had. He'd dealt with hardened criminals, high-ranking officers in the military and on the police force, but one petite woman was about to make him break every rule he'd ever made.

CHAPTER SIX

GRACE GRITTED HER TEETH, walked into the den and sat on the sofa. Slowly, she counted to ten. That was her deal. If she took time to count to ten, she could calm down and not react out of anger. Not that she was angry. She was just...

What was she doing? Meddling in other people's lives wasn't like her. Yet, that's what she did on a daily basis—keeping peace between elderly people and their children. It was a daily battle. This was different, though. She wasn't at the retirement villa, and she wasn't being paid to be here.

She drew a deep breath. She should go home and face her uncertain future—yet she couldn't help but feel her chances of keeping Zoe were better if she worked with Cole. She had enough sense to recognize that.

"Don't let him get to you."

"Mr. Walt, I didn't know you were awake."

"I'd have to be six feet under not to hear you two."

Grace didn't think they were that loud, but then, she wasn't paying attention to the volume of her voice, just the aggravation that Cole instilled in her.

"I'm sorry we woke you."

"You didn't wake me. When Cole turned down the TV, I woke up. The noise helps me sleep."

"I'll turn it back up," she offered.

"No, then you'll wake Zoe Grace. I don't sleep much anyway."

There was silence for a moment as Grace dealt with her thoughts. "I'm sorry I interfered in your life, Mr. Walt. I had no right."

"Don't worry your pretty head about that. I'm old, and I've got life's track marks all over my old body. There ain't much you can throw at me that I can't handle. You didn't say anything that I didn't need to hear. For years everyone walked on eggshells around me and Cora, afraid they were going to say something that would upset us. You said exactly what everyone else should have said."

"Mr. Walt…"

"No," he interrupted her. "Don't apologize. You're right. Jamie gave us Cole, and we fed and clothed him and sent him to school, but we didn't give him any emotional support. We weren't there for him and…I…"

Grace didn't interrupt, because Mr. Walt had to deal with his own emotions. "Cole grew up strong and tough, and I'm proud of everything he's done with his life. Like my granddaddy used to say, he's so tough he can pick his teeth with barbed wire. My Cole has a backbone of steel and ribs of iron. You're never going to get anything past him, but you got his attention."

"Mr. Walt, I don't understand half the things you say, but that's tough if you can pick your teeth with barbed wire. And I sincerely hope that underneath the steel and iron there is a heart."

"You can bet your bloomers on it."

Grace wasn't betting her underwear on anything. In a few minutes Mr. Walt was sound asleep, snoring, blowing bubbles through his mouth. She stared at Zoe sleeping peacefully. Her face was turned sideways with a slight smile and her butt was stuck in the air. That's the way she always slept. She was so precious, the only thing Grace had left of her sister.

What did the future hold? Heartache? Pain?

She had no answers, just a heavy feeling in her chest. And her options were limited. Actually, she had only one option. In that moment she knew she would bet her bloomers on Cole Chisholm any day.

COLE WENT TO his room, sat at his desk and opened his laptop. Within minutes he was on the Austin Police Department database searching for the Bennett-Briggs case. He downloaded pictures to his phone and reread Parker's notes. After going through everything thoroughly, one thing became clear: Grace Bennett had lied to him.

"Damn!"

He didn't want to make rash judgments because the case had a lot of holes in it and a lot of unanswered questions. The Brooke Bennett described in the case was not the person Grace had described.

His cell buzzed, and he reached for it on the desk.

"Hey, Cole. I finished my shift and ran into Tenney as he was leaving. He asked about SWAT, and I asked if there was any new evidence on the Bennett case. He said no and Parker didn't see any need to investigate further."

"Why not?"

"Parker's confident with the preliminary autopsy of accidental death. But he's going to wait until after Thanksgiving, when the full autopsy should be available."

"Parker is a fan of Briggs's and he's buying in to his story without much resistance," Cole said. "Briggs played football in Austin and made it big in the NFL—hometown hero and all."

"Tenney was just venting about the case, and I just happened to be there. I don't know anything else."

"Grace Bennett lied to me." From the time he had been with her he had her pegged as little Miss Sunshine, bringing joy to all, a do-gooder from her heart. There didn't appear to be a dishonest bone in her body. Guess he was wrong.

"Don't they all?"

"Not every woman is like Becky." Every time Cole and Bo talked about women, Bo would inevitably bring up Becky's name. She was Bo's high school sweetheart, but she'd married someone else and Bo had never gotten over it.

"I didn't say she was," Bo said in a voice

Cole knew well. He was getting irritated. "What's Ms. Bennett like?"

Cole took a moment. He kept very little from his best friend. They'd shared many heartaches over the years, but something in him was holding back. "She's nice."

Bo laughed, and then asked, "Did you tell her that?"

"No, I didn't tell her. I didn't tell her much of anything."

"So what she's like?"

Cole knew Bo wasn't going to stop. "She… she has Grandpa eating out of her hand. She ignores his grumpiness and deals with him like I've never seen anyone deal with him. She even has him talking about the past." Cole told him about what he'd heard at lunch.

"She brought up the pictures?"

"Yes, and he even let her use Jamie's high chair."

"Wow. She has some amazing powers."

That rolled around in Cole's head. That's who she was—amazing Grace. He shook the thought away. "I tore a strip off her for interfering in my life. I've adjusted to the pictures being everywhere, and I don't need her to stand up for me."

"I think she's getting under your skin."

"I gotta go," Cole said. He didn't want to talk about Grace anymore.

"What are you going to do about the case?"

"Talk to Ms. Bennett and see if she can explain what's in the file."

"Parker won't do anything until after Thanksgiving, so you have some time if you feel so inclined."

"Yeah. Stephanie wants me to meet her parents on Thanksgiving."

"Whoa, where did that come from?"

"She's been pushing me a lot lately for the big C, and I'm not sure I'm ready. I really like her…"

"If there's a question in your mind, then you're not ready."

"There's so much going on in my head with Grandma dying and Grandpa's crankiness. I don't need anyone else making demands on my time. I need space more than anything."

"Remember the pact we made when we were about, what? Eighteen?"

"Yeah, when Becky said if you leave and join the Army, you could kiss her goodbye because she wasn't waiting for you."

"Did you have to bring that up?"

"She meant it."

There was a long pause on the line. "Yep.

I think we need to reinstate the pact—stay bachelors for the rest of our lives."

"I'm clicking off on that."

"Let me know how this turns out."

Cole laid his phone on the desk, mulling over everything he'd learned. Now he had to confront Grace once again, and it wasn't something he was looking forward to. Bo was right. She was getting under his skin.

GRACE FELL ASLEEP on the couch. She hadn't intended to and was startled when she woke up and didn't see Zoe in the playpen. Glancing around, she saw she was in Mr. Walt's lap, waving her hands and smiling at the old man. Grace relaxed and wondered where Cole was. Turning her head, she saw him in the kitchen at the table eating coconut pie and drinking coffee.

What must he think of her taking a nap? She never took naps. Maybe it was cooking all that rich food and then eating it. She got up and walked into the kitchen.

"Would you like another cup of coffee?"

He glanced up. "Grace, you're not the maid around here. And I'm capable of getting my own food."

"Yes, sir."

"And don't be smart."

She wanted to make a face, but he was staring right at her with his steely blues. She wondered if they ever warmed up.

"I brought the rest of your things from your car." Cole pushed to his feet. "I'll bring them in."

"Oh. Thanks." She was always startled by his brusqueness. It was like someone slapping you and then kissing your cheek. She was never sure where she stood with him.

Cole brought the stroller into the house as Grandpa came into the kitchen with Zoe in his arms. Zoe seemed to recognize the stroller, waving her arms and blowing bubbles with her lips.

"She wants to get in it," Grandpa said. "Let's take her outside for a while. I have to check on the animals."

Grace was eager to go outside and away from the house. The pictures on the walls were depressing the daylights out of her. She couldn't imagine what it was like for Cole. But then, he'd said he'd learned to live with them. Maybe he had. Maybe she was blowing it out of proportion.

They all bundled up, and she pushed the stroller out the back door. Cole was bringing firewood in for the night, and they left him behind. The temperature was in the forties, and it was nice to breathe in the fresh, cool air mixed with an earthy scent. Huge live oak trees surrounded the house, and shrubs grew against the farmhouse along with wintry-stiff rosebushes. The flower beds were clean and manicured. White and red chickens pecked in the dirt. A red barn with a rusty tin roof wasn't far away. The sun glistened off it. An old wood corral was attached. It was a rustic country scene with the feel of olden days.

A red rooster rushed out of the barn and cock-a-doodle-dooed his head off. Rascal barked at him.

"That stupid rooster," Grandpa grumbled. "He's so old he can't remember when morning is, so he just crows anytime he wants."

The rooster flapped his wings and seemed upset.

"He won't hurt Zoe, will he?"

"Nah. He's just a lot of hot air."

"Does he have a name?"

"Otis."

The rooster excited Zoe. She tried to stand up in the stroller, and Grace had to hold it so she wouldn't flip it over. It was good to see Brooke's baby so happy.

Mr. Walt went into the barn, and Grace pushed the stroller closer to the corral. There were three animals inside: a potbelly pig, a mule and a ram goat with big horns. Mr. Walt dumped feed into a trough, and the animals ambled toward it. *What a hodgepodge of creatures!*

"Where did you get these animals, Mr. Walt?" she asked, hanging on to the fence.

"One by one they wandered here. We fed them and they stayed. They fight sometimes, but mostly they get along. They're old, too, and I guess nobody wanted them."

"Did you name them?"

"Yep. The pig is Goober, the donkey is Gomer and the ram is Barney."

"Wait a minute. Those are names from an old sitcom I used to watch with my grandmother."

"It sure is, *Andy Griffith*. Cora and I watched it all the time, and it's still on. We watch it every night after supper. She's gone now and I…"

"I'm sorry, Mr. Walt."

"Mmm…mmm…mmm." Zoe waved her arms to the animals and wanted to get closer.

Grace leaned down to her level. "You want to pet the animals?"

Zoe bounced up and down.

Rascal barked and stuck his nose close to Zoe. She slapped at his face, and Rascal didn't move. He was enjoying the attention. Zoe giggled, and the sound floated across the lovely afternoon. Grace felt as if she was in paradise, a place where no one could hurt her—where no one could take Zoe away.

Zoe was beside herself with excitement, pointing to Mr. Walt. She wanted the old man to take her.

"Yes. That's Mr. Walt. He's busy right now."

"She calls me Grandpa," Mr. Walt stated.

Grace looked up. "She doesn't talk."

"You just can't hear her."

"Mr...."

"Figure that one out," Cole said from behind her. She hadn't even heard him walk up. "Or don't try to figure it out, because you never will. My grandfather is in another time zone. His own."

The trio of animals came out of the corral and gathered around Zoe, as if to get a close-up look at the tiny human. She turned her neck this way and that way, trying to look at all of them. But they were a little too close for Zoe's comfort zone. She stuck out her lip and started to cry.

Grace patted her back. "It's okay. They won't hurt you."

Zoe blinked back tears and watched as the animals moseyed away.

"Where are they going?" Grace asked.

"To the pond," Cole told her. "They like the water there, but they'll be back and go into the barn for the night."

"What are we having for supper, Grace?" Mr. Walt asked.

"Leftovers" was her immediate response.

"I don't like leftovers."

"Then I guess you won't eat."

Mr. Walt frowned. "Are you going to be like that?"

"Yes. We have a lot of food left over, and we're going to eat it. Everyone is. Clear?"

"Ah, I can't get nothin' past you."

Mr. Walt took the handle of the stroller and pushed Zoe toward the house. She and Cole walked behind. As she walked she had a sense of being part of a family here on this farm. It was ridiculous and she didn't know where it had come from. She wasn't a part of the Chisholm family. She was only a guest.

AFTER SUPPER, COLE was biding his time, waiting for a moment to talk to Grace alone.

Grandpa was asleep in his recliner with the TV on. Grace was putting the playpen in a bedroom for Zoe so she could put her down for the night. He sat nursing a cup of coffee, waiting.

Finally, Grace came into the kitchen. Her shirtsleeves were rolled up to her elbows, and water had splattered the front of the shirt. She tucked her hair behind her ears. "She's finally asleep. She's usually easy to put down for the night, but she was so excited about seeing the animals. That was a real treat for her."

"Can we talk for a minute?" he interrupted, thinking she might just go on and on and on.

"Sure." She sat facing him. "I know Mr. Walt's getting attached to Zoe, but…"

"That's not what I want to talk about."

"Oh." She was genuinely confused.

"I want to talk about your sister."

"I told you everything I know."

He scooted forward, his hands on the table. "You lied to me."

"What?" Her eyes were huge, and he realized not for the first time just how beautiful they were. He was mesmerized by them for a brief second. "I didn't lie to you."

The only way to deal with this was to ask

questions. "How often did your sister see Zoe?"

"She stopped by every day after work."

"What hours did she work?"

"She worked from seven in the morning until seven at night. Those were long, hard days and she was exhausted by the end of them, but she always stopped by to see Zoe."

"How long did she stay?"

"An hour or so."

"Then she'd go home to Briggs's?"

"Yes." Her voice was getting clipped and angry, but he had to keep pushing.

"So I'm guessing with Austin traffic and all that she probably arrived at his place before 9:00 p.m."

"I suppose."

"What did she do on her days off?"

"Usually she'd come and get Zoe and spend some time with her, like taking her to the park or something."

"All day?"

"No. She…huh…she wanted to spend some time with Joel."

"Did she ever take Zoe to see her father?"

Grace fidgeted in her chair, but she didn't hesitate in answering. "No. Not that I'm aware of."

"Doesn't that seem a little strange to you?"

"I told you," she shot back. "Joel was abusive, and she didn't want Zoe around him."

"Why? Joel is the father, and if your sister was there to watch him, why wouldn't she want Joel to spend time with his daughter? Why wouldn't she want him to see her? That's a reasonable question, isn't it?"

Grace bent her head, her dark hair falling forward. She looked down at the table as she dealt with the question. "I can't answer that. I don't know what was going on in Brooke's head. I kept telling her if she and Joel were trying to work things out, Zoe needed to be a part of their lives. She told me to stay out of her business. So I let her live her life the way she wanted. As long as Zoe was safe, I was okay with that. I couldn't change Brooke's thinking."

As Cole listened to Grace, he knew without a doubt that she was a patsy in all of this. Her sister used her as a babysitter to get what she wanted. What that was Cole wasn't sure about just yet, but he had to tell Grace the truth if there was any chance of her keeping Zoe. And Cole felt the chances were very slim.

CHAPTER SEVEN

"YOU'RE NOT SAYING ANYTHING," Grace prompted when Cole sat there staring at his hands on the table.

He raised his head, and she saw a flicker of light in his eyes. "This case is complicated and there's something you need..."

"What?"

"I don't believe you lied to me."

"Why would I? You're trying to help me."

"You didn't know your sister all that well."

"Of course I did!" she snapped. "I've known her all my life, and I know everything about her."

His eyes captured hers, like a trap captures a criminal. "Did you know she worked as a cocktail waitress?"

Her mouth fell open, and she immediately closed it. Fury gripped her, and she had to take a deep breath. "W-what?"

He pulled out his phone, pushed some buttons and slid it across the table. A young girl with long dark hair wearing a skimpy skirt and a halter top was in the photo. Her eyes were dark and sultry. Grace hardly recognized her. She shook her head. "That's not my sister."

"Take a closer look." His finger moved the screen to more photos of the same girl.

She put her hands over her face. "Stop it."

"You didn't know she had a second job?"

Grace removed her hands, gulped in a deep breath and forced herself to admit that the girl was Brooke. Her sister. Zoe's mother. It didn't make any sense, and she didn't know how to explain it.

"No."

He gave her a moment and then said, "There's more."

She tucked her hair behind her ears, as if somehow that would give her strength. "Like what?"

"The place is a high-class gentlemen's club, and the men are known to touch. We get calls there regularly. The detective on the case said that's what they were fighting about that morning. Briggs's friend had gone into the club, and he called Briggs the next morning and told him about Brooke. He confronted her, and they had a big argument. He told her she had to stop, and she refused. He admits he slapped her, but according to him, she slapped him back several times. She ran from the apartment and slipped on the stairs. The detective believes Briggs."

"He's lying."

"They don't have any evidence to prove otherwise." The words were aimed at her with as much force as possible.

She had no response. Thoughts ran helter-skelter through her head, and she couldn't make sense of any of it.

"Think about it," Cole said. "Did Brooke need money?"

"I don't know." She buried her face in her hands again. "She had a good job. I don't see why she would need more money."

"Usually it's drugs," he slipped in like the seasoned detective he was.

"Huh…" Grace thought back to the last few weeks of Brooke's life. She always seemed to be in a hurry and not to have any money. And she hadn't been able to pay her half of the mortgage lately. She didn't think anything of it at the time, but now… "She asked if I could buy Zoe's diapers and things—she said that she was behind on her car payments and she would pay me back."

That's when righteous indignation or whatever people called it exploded in her. She wasn't going to sit here and listen to him making her sister a druggie. Brooke wasn't like that. And she would prove it. She got up and grabbed her purse from the den and marched back to the table.

She pulled out her phone and quickly found pictures and placed it in front of him. "This is the Brooke I know." There were photos of Brooke and Zoe and several of her and Brooke. Two sisters, side by side, looking very much alike. Then she showed him more pictures— Brooke with bruises on her face and on her arms.

"He hit her. See the bruises? That's when I called the cops. They gave him a warning. That should be on record. He wasn't this nice football player that everyone loves. He was dangerous and violent, and I didn't want Zoe near him. I didn't force Brooke or push her to take Zoe to him. I didn't think it was a good idea. Brooke is not this person they're portraying."

Grace ran her hands up her face, a new kind of pain cozying up to her heart. "It was easy for her to let Frannie and me take care of Zoe until she got her life straightened out."

"You said Zoe was nine months old. Brooke had a long time to figure out that the relationship with Briggs wasn't working. I don't get what was keeping her from raising her child."

Grace gritted her teeth, not able to hear one more bad word about her sister. "Brooke wasn't like you're thinking. She loved Zoe. She wouldn't do that. I know it. He must've forced her."

"How could he force her? All she had to do was walk out and go home to you."

"I don't know." But then what did she know? It seemed as if she barely knew her sister. "I don't know. I don't know." She choked out the last word and forced herself not to cry.

Cole got up and came around the table. She took a step backward. "Tomorrow I'm going into Austin to dig a little deeper, and you have to be prepared for whatever I find. But the bottom line is if they close the case, Joel Briggs will get his kid."

"Cole, please don't let them do that. He hasn't wanted her in all this time. I don't understand why he wants her now. You can't let them take her. Cole, please." The tears she'd been fighting slipped from her eyes, and she quickly brushed them away. She was stronger than this, but the fear inside her was a powerful thing that held her in its grip.

"Hey, hey." Cole held her at the elbows, and his touch instilled in her a strength she hadn't expected. His touch was light and gentle. "You can't fall apart now. This is just starting."

"It's…"

"I know. Tomorrow you'll go see the attorney, and I will go into Austin and do what I can. And then we'll go from there."

She lifted her head to look at him. "You believe me, then?"

"It's kind of hard not to. You have a very sincere voice."

"Oh…" She was flabbergasted. He'd complimented her. She almost swooned. There was a lot of softness in Cole Chisholm, but it was buried so deep that it would take more than sincerity to break through it.

As if realizing he was standing too close to her, he took a step backward. "Okay. Tomorrow the weather should be better, and you probably should see the lawyer early."

"Yes…um… I don't have a vehicle."

"You'll have to drive Grandpa's truck."

"I've never driven a truck."

He sighed. "I'll give you a driving lesson

first thing in the morning. It's easy. It's just like a car, and Horseshoe is small, so you shouldn't have a problem."

Without thinking, she stepped forward and rested her head on his chest. He stiffened, but she didn't draw away. He was solid steel, just like Grandpa had said. But beyond the steel, inner warmth radiated, and that's what attracted her. Cole would help her, and maybe somewhere along the way she could help him.

ON MONDAY MORNING Grace was up early and took a shower, hoping not to wake Zoe. Wrapped in a bathrobe, she hurried back to her room and stopped in her tracks. Cole, fully dressed, was holding Zoe. Or trying to hold Zoe. He had his arms under her armpits and held her out as if she was contaminated or something.

"She's not a bomb about to go off," Grace said.

"I've never held a baby," he said in a hoarse voice. "She was whimpering, so I thought I'd pick her up. She weighs nothing."

Grace took Zoe around the waist and placed her on Cole's shoulder. "Pat her back and she'll go to sleep on your shoulder."

Cole had a paralyzed look on his face, and Grace wanted to laugh.

"Grace, it's time for breakfast," Mr. Walt hollered from the kitchen. Rascal barked in response.

Cole quickly handed off Zoe. Their arms and hands got all tangled up. "Wait," Grace said, unable to stop laughing. "This should be easier. Just let me take her from you." That worked, and Zoe thought it was a game. She gurgled happily.

Cole held up his hands. "I'm free."

"Have you really not ever held a baby?"

"Do you need more evidence?"

How sad! She made a decision in a split second. "Why don't you take Zoe to Mr. Walt while I change clothes."

One eyebrow shot up. "Are you kidding? I don't think I can hold her and walk at the same time."

"Oh, for heaven's sake." She placed Zoe on his shoulder again. "Keep your arm under her bottom and your hand on her back. She's pretty flexible. For a big ol' detective like you, it should be a piece of cake."

"Huh…" Before Cole could voice his concerns, his arms immediately went into position.

"Now walk." She didn't laugh, but it was

hard not to as he slowly made his way down the hall to the kitchen as if he was holding a bomb.

"There's my girl," Grandpa said, and Grace let out a long breath. Mission accomplished. Cole made it to the kitchen without incident. That set the tone for the day.

After breakfast, Cole and Grace went to the barn for a driving lesson. Grandpa's old truck was parked in the barn and about as old as dirt, she figured.

"Don't you want to drive it out of the barn first?" Grace asked, looking at the vehicle as if it might be something out of a museum.

Cole shook his head. "No. Backing it out will be your first lesson."

"Oh, gee, thanks."

She got into the driver's seat, and Cole slipped in on the passenger side. It was a small truck and clearly not made for a man Cole's size. The seat went all way across, and there was also a very small back seat. No bucket seats for this vehicle. And hardly any room. The truck smelled faintly of hay, sweat and Old Spice.

"That's the gearshift right back of the steering wheel. It's an automatic, so it should be easy to use."

"Yeah, right. Didn't I see a car in the garage?"

"That's Grandma's car, and Grandpa doesn't let anyone touch it."

"Why not? She's not here anymore. Is she? Sometimes I'm not real sure with Mr. Walt talking to her."

A grin split his face, and it was a wonderful thing to see. "I'm not sure, either. Things have always been a little strange around here."

"How do you mean?"

"My birthday is December eleventh, and my parents died on December twelfth. After that my grandmother was different, they said. She never celebrated Christmas, nor did she celebrate my birthday. It was too painful, Grandpa said. It reminded her of Jamie's death."

"You've never had a birthday party?"

He shook his head. "No. I think she wiped it from her mind. Grandpa was right there for me, though. He'd order two big cupcakes from the bakery in town and buy some soft drinks, and we'd sit right here in the barn and eat cupcakes and celebrate my birthday. He'd give me a gift, and if Grandma saw it, she would ask where I got it. I'd say Grandpa, and she'd just nod."

"Oh, that is so sad."

"Christmases were the worst. All the other kids had trees in their homes, but we never did."

"Cole, that is too depressing to even think about. Please tell me your grandpa did something for the holidays."

"Yeah. A few days before Christmas, we'd go to the woods and cut down a cedar tree and put it up in the corner of the barn. There's no electricity there, so we couldn't have lights. Grandpa found some sparkly plastic ones that looked like lights, and we put them on the tree with some tinsel and some ornaments I made in school."

"This is going to make me cry."

He glanced at her. "Do women cry about everything?"

"When it's this sad," she said with a spark of defiance.

"It's not sad. It was the way life was back then, because my grandma was grieving herself to death and we didn't want to upset her."

"Heaven forbid! She needed to see a doctor."

"Grandpa took her, but she wouldn't go back. And that was the end of that."

They were about sixteen inches apart on

the seat. His knees were up to the dashboard, and his left hand rested on the seat.
He clenched and unclenched it as he talked,
and she knew the past still bothered him. But
he was talking to her, and that was good. She
wanted to know more.

"So you'd spend Christmas in the barn?"

"On Christmas morning I would get up and
put my house shoes on and run to the barn.
Grandpa would be there sitting on a bale of
hay with milk and cookies, and there would
be presents under the tree. I was so excited I
could barely eat. I just wanted to tear into the
presents. Grandpa always seemed to know
what I wanted—a fishing rod, a bike, a horse,
a BB gun, a knife, boots, a cowboy hat. And
there was always candy and fruit."

"And your grandma never noticed this?"

"My grandmother lived in her own little
world, but like I said, sometimes she would
ask me where I got such and such and I'd say
Grandpa, and she would just nod like it was
nothing."

Grace had no words. She didn't tell him
it was sad or that she wanted to cry. It was
his life, and she couldn't change a thing. No
one could.

"I thought my upbringing was unusual, but yours takes the prize."

He glanced at her, his eyes twinkling. "I didn't know it was a competition."

"It isn't," she replied, feeling breathless from the light in his eyes.

"My grandmother just wanted her son back, and when that didn't happen she tried to make me into Jamie."

"What do you mcan?"

"She called me Jamie. Every time I'd come through the back door, she would yell, 'Jamie, is that you?' and I would reply, 'No, Grandma. It's Cole.' She would say 'Oh' in a disappointed voice, and every time I felt as if I failed her."

"You know that you didn't, right?"

"Yeah." The light in his eyes disappeared as he dealt with memories from his childhood.

"You know what you need, Cole Chisholm?"

He glanced at her again. "No, but I'm afraid you're going to tell me."

"You need a hug. I mean a big ol' hug, a squeeze-the-daylights-out-of-you hug. One that would make all those bad memories go poof, right out of your mind."

His eyes caught hers. "Are you volunteering?"

"I could, but Mr. Walt said you have a girl-friend and I…"

"For your information, Ms. Bennett, I do not need a hug. Now, would you start this damn truck? We're wasting half the morning in here gabbing."

Unable to resist, she saluted.

He frowned. "Stop it."

She turned the key, and the truck roared to life. Really roared. Loud. Chickens flew out from under it, and the rooster landed on the hood and crowed.

Cole rolled down the window and shouted at the rooster. "Get off of there, Otis." The rooster flapped to a bale of hay.

"This truck is too loud!" she said above the roar. "What's wrong with it?"

"It has a hole in the tailpipe. I thought Grandpa had it fixed."

"I guess you were wrong." She turned off the key. "I can't drive this. It's too loud. It would scare Zoe."

"It's all we have right now."

She glared at him. "There's the car."

"You can't drive Bertha. It would upset Grandpa."

She chuckled. "You named the car?"

"Grandma did, or Grandpa, I'm not sure. The car's over thirty years old."

"Is there anything new around here?"

"No. I'll take you into town and go to Austin later. That's the only solution."

She shook her head. "No. I'm going to talk to Mr. Walt." She opened the door and got out and had to sidestep chickens to make it to the barn door.

Cole got out, too, and tripped over a chicken. The hen was not happy, squawking at his feet. "Grace, come back here."

She kept the laughter inside. "Your grandmother and Jamie are gone. They're resting in peace in heaven, and that car sitting in the garage is not helping anyone."

"Grace…"

She ran toward the house. Bertha was getting an outing. And somehow, some way, the Chisholm family was moving into the twenty-first century. Ghosts and all.

CHAPTER EIGHT

COLE FOLLOWED MORE SLOWLY. She was the most infuriating, irritating, interfering and nosiest woman he'd ever met. As if the world's problems could be solved with a hug and a kiss. Why couldn't she understand this was his life and he didn't expect it to change? He knew by the time he was five that his grandmother was sick. He'd accepted that. Some days it was hard when she called him Jamie over and over. He'd just go to his room and read comic books and dream of saving the world like a superhero.

He paused at the back door and took a deep breath. There was no way he would allow her to hurt his grandpa. He'd walk through fire before he would let that happen.

Grace knelt by Grandpa's chair, and Cole stood in the kitchen listening to her weave that magic she seemed to have. The baby was on a quilt on the floor, sitting up and chewing on a doll.

"Mr. Walt, I can't drive that truck."

"Why not? It's old, but it still runs good."

"It's loud and it would scare Zoe."

"Ah, yeah, I was supposed to get that fixed. It slipped my mind." Grandpa looked at Cole. He'd reminded his grandpa three times about the truck, and he now realized he would have to do it himself, just like paying Grandpa's bills. About a year ago, he got a call from his grandpa that the electricity had been turned off and he didn't know why. It turned out he hadn't paid his bill. From then on he'd been taking care of all the bills for his grandparents. Grandpa couldn't remember what he'd paid and what he hadn't.

"It's okay, Grandpa. We'll take it in one day this week and see if Lamar can fix it."

"I need a car today, Mr. Walt."

"Well, Cole can take you to see Gabe."

"He has to go to Austin to check on my sister's death. He really needs to do that, so I can have a good chance of keeping Zoe."

"Then you'll have to use the truck."

"There's a car in the garage," Grace slipped in smoothly.

"Oh, no, no!" Grandpa sat up straight in his chair. "That's Cora's car, and nobody drives it."

"Why?"

Grandpa shrugged. "I don't know. That's just the way it is."

"So you're going to let it sit in the garage forever as a tribute to your wife?"

"If I want to."

Grace touched Grandpa's hand gripping the chair. "I'm sorry, Mr. Walt. I'll drive the truck. I don't want to upset you."

"We bought that car when Cole was little. Cora didn't want him riding the bus by himself. I took him to school every morning in that car, and some days Cora would pick him up. Bertha has a lot of special memories. Like one time when Cole was about four, we went into town to buy groceries. On the way back, Cole said he felt sick. He had been stuffing his face with candy that I'd bought him. Cora was yelling stop and I pulled over and yanked Cole out of the seat. I held him around the waist, and he puked all over my boots. We laughed about that. One of the rare times Cora laughed." Grandpa looked at Cole. "Remember that?"

"Yeah," he replied. But he didn't. He'd been too young. A warm feeling touched his heart. So many times he wanted to deny that his grandparents cared anything about him, but when he listened to his grandpa he knew they did. It was just different, like he had tried to explain to Grace.

Those times when he would get ready for school with his backpack, Grandma would kiss the top of his head and say, "Be good in school, Jamie." He would reply, "Grandma, I'm Cole." Then she would add, "You be good, too."

That's when he started feeling like two people. Was he Jamie? Or was he Cole? In his mind he knew who he was, but he could never convince his grandmother otherwise.

Grace got to her feet. "I guess I'll go fire up the truck again and drive it around the barn or something. I might need a helmet and earplugs."

She was taking this with a sense of humor. He liked that. She could handle Grandpa, but he knew Grandpa wasn't going to budge on the car unless…

At that moment Zoe rolled to her stomach and scooted over to Grandpa. She grabbed onto his jeans and pulled herself up, reaching out her hands for him to take her. He lifted her to his lap. In a short amount of time, those two were forming a strong bond. He made a decision in a second.

"Grandpa, don't you think it would do the

car good to drive it? It's been sitting there for so long. And Grace really needs a safe vehicle to drive Zoe to see the lawyer so she can file for custody."

Grandpa glanced at him briefly while rocking Zoe. "You think so? I just…you know…"

"Grandma is in heaven with Jamie, and I know she's happy. She's finally with him again, and I don't think she'd mind at all if Grace used the car. Grandma wanted all cars to be safe, especially for children. Remember?"

"Yeah. She didn't want to haul you around in that old vehicle we had. She said we needed something safe and new. And we took Bo home many a time because she didn't want him walking home alone. She was a good woman, but she just couldn't deal with the loss of our son. She…"

"It's okay, Grandpa. We'll just leave the car alone." He wasn't letting anyone touch the car unless Grandpa was okay with it. One hundred percent okay.

"No." Grandpa shook his head. "It's time to dust the ashes off the car and get some use from it. Grace needs a car, and I know Cora would want this little one—" he bounced Zoe up and down "—to have a safe home. Grace needs to do that as soon as possible."

"Are you sure?"

Grandpa looked at Grace. "Are you a good driver?"

"Yes, Mr. Walt. Saturday was my first wreck, and I've never gotten a ticket."

"You can't use your phone while you're driving."

"No, sir. I wouldn't do that with Zoe in the car."

"Then you can use Bertha. I'm going with you."

Grace gave a nervous smile. "Okay, deal."

Cole glanced from Grace to his grandpa. "Then I'll leave you two to it."

Grace followed him to the door. "Now I'm nervous about driving it."

He paused with his hand on the doorknob. "You're nervous? Now that I can't believe. You rush in where angels fear to tread. So good luck."

"When will you be back?"

He stared into her dark pools of worry. "Depends how my day goes. But I'll try to get home by six."

"Okay." Her anxiety coated the word.

"What? You fought to drive the car. Now drive it."

"It's just…it's just easy to forget why I'm

here. I'm just nervous about what's going to happen in Austin and that there's a real good chance I could lose Zoe."

"Just keep fighting, Grace. And if you're lucky, I just might let you hug me one day."

GRACE TRIED NOT to let Cole's parting words get to her, but at the oddest moment she would think about what it would be like to put her arms around him. And then she would push the thought from her mind. He had a girlfriend. She had to keep reminding herself of that. And she wasn't ready to get involved with anyone.

She wanted to leave early, but Mr. Walt had to feed the animals, and she couldn't go without him. When they finally got in the car, Grace was surprised to see Zoe's car seat already installed. Cole must've done it before he'd left. Cole Chisholm's heart was alive and well and hadn't been damaged by his childhood.

The car was like new, without a speck of dirt in it, or at least none she could see. It was blue on the outside and blue on the inside with bucket seats that looked barely worn. There was a slight musty smell from being closed up, but it was big and roomy.

With Mr. Walt on the passenger side, she

turned the key and the car purred to life. Her hands were steady and her mind was clear. She was ready to go.

"Listen to that motor," Mr. Walt said. "They don't make 'em like that anymore."

"I'll have to take your word for that."

The car drove great, and she expected Mr. Walt to give her driving lessons, but he didn't. He seemed okay with Bertha on the highway.

"You'll have to give me directions."

"This county road goes straight into Horseshoe."

"Got it."

Zoe made gurgling sounds in the back seat.

"She's happy," Mr. Walt said. "Cora's happy, too. I talked to her before we left."

"What did she say?" Grace asked without a second thought.

"She said I was a crazy old fool. Can you believe that? What good is a car sitting in the garage?"

"I'm glad she's okay with it," Grace replied like an insane person. But if it made Mr. Walt feel better, then she was all for it.

She made it to the small town of Horseshoe, Texas. An old limestone courthouse sat in the middle of a town square. Big oak trees surrounded it, and she was sure they'd been there for at least a hundred years. Two elderly men huddled in winter coats sat on a bench beneath the trees. People milled around the quaint country-style stores that surrounded the courthouse. This was small-town Texas, just as she'd heard about. A place some people called home. It had that feel to it, as if you'd want to return again and again.

She pulled up to Gabe Garrison's law office, which was located on the square across from the courthouse, and parked at the curb. She got the stroller out of the trunk and put Zoe in it.

"I don't see why you brought that thing," Mr. Walt complained. "I can carry her. She weighs nothing."

"She gets heavy after a while, and you can push her around while I talk to the lawyer."

The lawyer was tall with dark hair that was graying at the temples. He was quite handsome. A picture of his wife and kids took pride of place on his desk. She introduced herself, and he invited her to sit.

"I'm going to push Zoe down the street," Mr. Walt said.

"No. She doesn't know anybody, and she might get scared." She trusted Mr. Walt, but she didn't want to be too far away from Zoe.

"I'll bring her back if she gets scared." He opened the door before she could stop him.

"Where would you take her?"

"I'm going to show her off and take her down to the bakery to meet Margie and I'll stop at the cake shop to see Anamarie and then look in on Lacey, Gabe's wife, who runs the floral shop. Then we'll mosey down to Maribel's diner and wait for you. Maybe we'll eat lunch there. Yeah, we'll eat lunch there. It's good food."

"Mr. Walt…"

Her words fell on deaf ears. Mr. Walt pushed Zoe out the door, and Zoe didn't even cry for her.

"She'll be fine," Gabe told her.

For the next thirty minutes, she told Gabe her story and about what had happened to her sister. He said he would draw up the custody papers as soon as possible and he would check in with Cole to see about developments in the case. He was nice and said all the things Grace wanted to hear.

There was hope.

COLE HEADED FOR I-35, and even though it was early, the traffic was congested. Everyone was going to work. But he knew shortcuts and he made it to the station without incident. On the way he thought about the right way to go about talking to Parker. It wouldn't be easy, but Cole wanted in on the case. First thing he had to do was speak to his lieutenant and be as persuasive as possible.

As he walked toward the lieutenant's office, he thought about his and Bo's journey and where they were today. At eighteen they'd yearned for adventure and had found themselves on the front lines fighting the Taliban in Afghanistan. The experience wasn't quite what they'd envisioned. Then intelligence needed someone to infiltrate the insurgents to get information. And without a single thought to their safety, they'd volunteered and found themselves in more danger than they could've ever imagined.

Intelligence trained them and they learned how to protect themselves and how to lay it all on the line without any thought for their own lives. Bo had the gift of gab and could pretty much lie his way out of any situation. Cole always had his back. But they got valuable information that saved soldiers' lives. Their captain said they had a death wish. After that, they decided if they were going to die, they wanted to do it on American soil. After four years, they came home and joined the police academy. They knew if they wanted to move up the line, they needed a criminal justice degree. They were patrol cops and went to school at night. They were busy, which was what they wanted—to avoid their families.

BEFORE HE KNOCKED on the lieutenant's door, Cole thought he should call Grace and see how things were going at home, but she was a strong person and he trusted her. If anything happened, she would call him.

"Come in." The lieutenant's booming voice came through the door.

"Lieutenant…"

"What is it, Chisholm? Aren't you supposed to be home helping your grandfather? I mean, you took time off, so I assume that's what you're doing." The man was on his computer, and he never looked up.

"Something's come up that I'd like to talk to you about."

"Go ahead."

Cole told him about Grace and Zoe. He didn't say Grace was in hiding, which was probably the first time he'd lied to a superior officer. But because she was trying to keep Zoe safe, he figured it was okay. As that thought ran through his mind, he realized he was crossing lines for Grace. Lines he never would've crossed on his own.

Slowly, the lieutenant raised his eyes and leaned back. "Homicide handled the case, but as soon as the coroner's report comes in, Parker will close it. Do you have evidence to prove otherwise?"

"No, sir. But after talking to Ms. Bennett, my instincts say something else is going on. I'd like the opportunity to join Parker and his team."

"It doesn't work like that, Chisholm. You have to give me something before I can give you something."

Cole took out his phone and tapped it a couple of times and placed it in front of the lieutenant. "That's Brooke Bennett. She was being abused by Briggs. He denies it, but…" Cole tapped the screen and showed more pictures. "These photos tell a different story. I got them from Grace Bennett, her sister. And then there's this." He tapped the phone again. "This is nine-month-old Zoe. Ms. Bennett has raised her almost from the day she was born. Now that Brooke Bennett is dead, Briggs will get his daughter. I want to make sure it's the right home for that little girl. If he's abusive, it's not."

"What is it with you and kids?"

His gut tightened. "I can't answer that, sir."

"You know, you're in missing children because of your instincts, and I'm going to trust you on this one." The lieutenant pointed a finger at him. "But if this is about a pretty face getting you all tangled up, then you and I will have a long conversation and you'll find yourself sitting at a desk."

"Yes, sir."

"I'll talk to Parker."

"Thank you, sir."

While he waited for the call, he went to his truck and called Grace.

"How are things going there? Did the car drive okay?"

"Yes, much better than that truck. And Mr. Walt seems fine with it. I'm just leaving the lawyer's office, and I'm looking for him."

"Isn't he with you?"

"Well, he was, and then he insisted on pushing Zoe around to show her off to other people. He told me to meet him at the diner, and I have no idea where that is."

"If you're standing outside Gabe's office,

look to your right and across the street and you'll see a big sign that says The Diner."

"I see it. I'm heading there now. Cole, we really need to talk about Mr. Walt and Zoe. He's getting attached and so is Zoe, and I don't know what's going to happen when we have to go back to Austin."

"I'll talk to him and make him understand that Zoe will soon go home." The thought gave him a jolt. Grace and Zoe had just dropped in to their lives, like from heaven. They had been almost like a gift for Grandpa, to ease his grieving. It was almost a miracle.

Grace had him talking about his childhood, something he never talked about to anyone but Bo. No one had uncorked that bottle but Grace. And he was beginning to wonder if his lieutenant's words were right. Could his instincts be turned by a pretty face?

CHAPTER NINE

COLE SAT IN his truck with his brain on overload. He always did the right thing. He was known for that. He and Stephanie had a good arrangement, and now Grace filled his head with images he didn't want. That wasn't him. If Stephanie knew he was in Austin...

He picked up his phone and called her. She had a right to know he was in town.

"Cole, what a nice surprise. I wasn't expecting you to call today. Are we still on for Thanksgiving?"

"Yes. I'll be there. What time?"

"We usually eat around one, but I'd like for you to get there around ten and visit with my family."

Ask about my grandpa. Just ask about Grandpa so I can feel better about this relationship.

She didn't.

"I'll try, but it'll probably be closer to

eleven. I don't want to leave my grandpa too long on a holiday."

Invite my grandpa.

She didn't.

"Cole, really? This is getting aggravating."

"Maybe it's best if I don't come."

"Cole, please. I didn't mean it that way, but what kind of life can we have if you're constantly running back to that small town?"

He didn't have an answer for that. "Listen, Steph, I have to go. I had to come into Austin to work on a case, and I don't have much time."

"You're in Austin?"

"Yes. And I'm returning to Horseshoe just as soon as I interview someone."

"Why didn't you call me? We could've done lunch."

"Stephanie, I don't have time for lunch."

"Where's your grandfather?"

Cole's hand gripped the steering wheel. "The lady who ran off the road is still there, so I know he's okay."

"She's still at your house?"

"Yes. She's waiting on her car to be fixed."

"Couldn't she have called someone?"

"I don't know, but it helps for someone to

be there. That way I can work. Listen, I've got to go. I'll call you later."

"Okay, and Cole, I'd like for you not to wear your boots to dinner on Thanksgiving."

"What? What's wrong with my boots?"

"My mother likes for Thanksgiving to be formal, and boots would not fit in."

He took a deep breath. "I wear boots all the time, Stephanie, and if you want me to come to Thanksgiving, I will be wearing my boots. That's just who I am. I can't be someone I'm not. And if you feel that way, we need to talk about this relationship."

"I knew you were going to be this way. Sometimes boots are not appropriate."

"I'm not having this conversation. I'll talk to you later."

He sat there fuming. He thought he knew her, but evidently he didn't. When she'd told him she was a defense attorney and her father, Harlan Myers, was also a defense attorney, a very well-known one, that's when he should have questioned the relationship. But they had a good time together, and never once had she mentioned his boots. What was wrong with his boots?

His phone buzzed. The lieutenant. He had a meeting with Parker.

He went into the meeting with a little more vigor than he'd planned. He wanted to be calm and cordial and not to ruffle any feathers. But right now he felt like taking on the world.

Parker sat at his desk, not looking up, much like the lieutenant, typing information into a computer. Tenney sat at another desk next to Parker's. Cole pulled up a chair.

Parker was a veteran cop in his late fifties, and he was known for his take-no-prisoners style. He leaned back in his chair. It creaked from his weight, and it was the only sound Cole heard in a room full of detectives, computers and electronic devices. His attention was solely on Parker and the scowl on his face.

"What's your interest in this case, Chisholm?"

Cole pulled out his phone, tapped it a couple of times and placed it in front of him. "That little girl."

Parker frowned. "Who is she? I didn't realize the case was connected to a missing child."

"That's Brooke Bennett's daughter, and I would like to see her get the home she deserves."

"Where did you get this?"

"Grace Bennett."

The scowl deepened. "You talked to her? She's a nutcase. She's on and on about how she wants Joel in jail. And how he hit her sister and caused her to fall. Yet we have no evidence to prove that. She doesn't seem to understand plain English. We need evidence. No one saw Joel hit her. And no one heard Brooke Bennett say Joel hit her, except for her sister, and then she comes up with this scheme about Joel trying to sell his daughter. Again, no evidence. Joel wants his kid back, and I promised to help him get her."

That news hit Cole's stomach like a sledge-hammer, but he remained calm. He didn't miss that Parker was calling Briggs by his first name like they were old friends.

"Why?"

"Joel Briggs is a hometown boy and made it in the NFL. I talked to him several times, and I'm impressed with the young man he's become. He busted up his leg in a game and had to retire, but he spends a lot of his time in schools trying to steer kids in the right direction. The people we interviewed were impressed by him and so was I. We found no evidence that Joel abused Brooke Bennett, as her sister insisted he did."

Cole reached over and tapped his phone again. "That looks like abuse to me."

"The sister showed me those, too. But we have no evidence that proves Joel put those bruises on her. Anyone could've hit her. She worked in a gentlemen's club, for crying out loud, and Joel said she saw other men behind his back. I believed him."

"Without evidence?"

Parker stood up in a quick move. "Okay, Chisholm. Tenney and I will be out the rest of the afternoon working another case." He waved his hand across the desk. "The Bennett case is all here. Knock yourself out. If you find something that proves otherwise, I'll buy you a beer. If you don't, I'll report you for misconduct." After saying that, he charged out of the room with Tenney at his heels.

Cole took a long breath and moved around the desk to take Parker's seat. He wasn't worried about Parker writing him up because he knew somewhere in this case there were a whole lot of lies told by Briggs. Now he had to prove it.

For the next four hours, he went over everything from written notes by Parker and

Tenney to lab results to witnesses' statements and the ME's preliminary findings. The witnesses said they didn't see anything. Every statement was almost verbatim. There were no drugs in Brooke's system. He studied the ME's report. The fractured ribs, broken leg, broken arm and bruise on her head were consistent with the fall. The ME noted that the bruising around her neck and her right wrist were not. Then he saw Parker's note:

During the altercation between Briggs and Bennett, Bennett slapped Briggs and he caught her right hand to keep her from slapping him again. Then she slapped him with her left hand and he put his hand around her neck to push her away.

He mulled that over—something about it bothered him. Briggs was a defensive end and stood six feet four inches tall and weighed 275 pounds. He was a big man. If he grabbed Brooke's wrist hard enough to bruise it, Cole didn't figure she had enough strength left to slap him again. But there was no way to prove that. Brooke was dead, and Briggs was the only living participant.

Something else that bothered him was Briggs telling Parker that he had met Brooke in the ER when he'd hurt his wrist playing football with kids in the park. Grace had said he had injured his wrist in a bar fight. He believed Grace.

He read more on Parker's notes, and another one caught his attention.

Briggs stated Brooke was nice but he didn't plan on calling her. Then she started calling him and asking him out for a drink. He finally accepted and they got along well at first and then she became jealous and everything was an issue with her. He broke it off. He was tired of the drama. But then she started calling him again, and they got back together. He wasn't happy about the pregnancy but accepted it. Then she saw him looking at another woman and she took the kid to her sister's and wouldn't let him see her. Brooke always agreed with the sister.

This was all one-sided. Briggs's side. The only voice Brooke had was Grace.

At four o'clock, Parker and Tenney returned to the office. Cole stood and stretched his shoulders. He'd been sitting too long.

"Find anything?" Parker asked with a touch of a sneer.

"Not much." Cole would keep his concerns to himself for now.

Parker took his seat. "You're not going to find anything. Brooke Bennett wanted to be in Joel's life, and she did everything she could to make that happen. Chasing him and harassing him. It just ended in a bad way."

"Did y'all interview anyone at the hospital about his injured wrist?" Cole asked.

"What? What are you talking about?"

"The file says he injured his wrist playing football with kids in the park. Ms. Bennett says he hurt his wrist in a bar fight."

Parker laughed out loud. "Oh, man. That woman has you tied up in knots."

Cole let that slide. "Then you wouldn't mind if I checked it out at the hospital."

"Go ahead."

"I'd like to interview Briggs, too."

That brought a scowl to Parker's face again. "He's just going to tell you the same thing he's told us."

"Then you don't mind?"

"Knock yourself out, but you're wasting

your time, and you're wasting the department's time."

"It's my time." He reached out and touched the file. "Nowhere in here does Briggs mention a concern for his daughter, for her welfare or her safety. For a man who wants custody, in my book, he should at least know his daughter and what she looks like. And he should especially be concerned that she's being well taken care of."

This time Cole was the one who walked out.

GRACE HAD A great day until they returned home. Grandpa went to sleep in his recliner, and she put Zoe down for a nap in the living room. Mr. Walt wanted her close to him, and Grace didn't fight him on it. He'd helped her a lot today. Then she unloaded the groceries they had bought. She was busy in the kitchen when the doorbell rang.

She hurried to the front door so it wouldn't wake Zoe and found a stranger standing there. He was probably in his seventies and wearing a baseball cap. A teenager stood behind him.

"Is Walt home? I have his delivery."

Delivery? Did Mr. Walt order something?

Before she could finish that thought, Mr. Walt stomped up behind her. "Bring it on in."

"What did you order, Mr. Walt? And when? And does Cole know?"

"Ah, it ain't nothin'. And it's my money."

Grace stared in disbelief as the man and the boy brought in a baby bed. A beautiful, white baby bed. "You bought this?"

"Zoe Grace needs a place to sleep. You can't keep her in that pen all the time."

"Mr. Walt, I'm very upset with you. Zoe has a bed—it's in Austin and we will be returning there soon."

"No returns, Walt. That's my policy," the man said.

"Bring it in here," Mr. Walt told him. The man and the boy followed Mr. Walt into Grace's bedroom. She stood there transfixed, not knowing what to do, and watched as they went outside and brought in the mattress and a box of sheets. The man shook Mr. Walt's hand and left.

Grace walked into the bedroom and stared at the bed. "Where did you get this?"

"Resale shop in town."

"This is a new baby bed."

"Sometimes he gets new furniture, and

while you were with Gabe, I went and looked around. Zoe Grace liked it, so I bought it."

"What did you pay for it?"

"Twenty dollars. It was worth it."

She shook her head. "Mr. Walt, you paid more than twenty dollars for this, the mattress and sheets. I didn't want you to buy a bed, and yet you did."

"So sue me. I want Zoe Grace to have a nice bed. Now help me put the mattress on it."

She gritted her teeth. The Chisholm men were infuriating. She counted to ten and then proceeded to help him.

THE FIRST THING Cole heard as he opened the back door was "How are you going to explain this to Cole?" That was Grace's voice.

"It's my money!" his grandfather shouted.

Cole followed the voices and found them in Grace's bedroom staring at a baby bed.

Grace was the first to notice him. "Your grandfather bought a baby bed while I was at Gabe's office. And they delivered it this afternoon. I knew nothing about this, and I'm very upset with him."

He walked over to the bed. "It looks nice."

Rascal barked and interrupted the conversation.

"Zoe's awake," Grace said. "I'll get her."

"Now before you start," Grandpa warned him, "it's my money and I can spend it any way I want to."

"I wasn't going to say a thing. You're right. It's your money."

"Then I don't see what all the yammering is about."

Cole took a deep breath. "Grandpa, I'm just a little concerned."

"About what?"

"Your interest in Zoe. I think it's very nice that you like the baby, but you do realize they will be leaving soon, don't you?"

"Of course I do." His shaggy eyebrows knotted together. "I'm not senile."

Cole nodded. "Good. Then we're clear on that."

"Did you find a way to help Grace?"

Before Cole could answer, Grace brought Zoe into the room, and Grandpa immediately took her. "There's my girl." He took her over to the bed. "This is your new bed. You have a place to sleep now." He laid Zoe in it, and she rolled to her stomach as if to go to sleep.

"See." Grandpa beamed with delight. "She likes it."

The sleep didn't last long. Zoe scooted to

the rail and pulled herself up and stood there smiling at everybody. And Cole knew he'd do whatever he could to ensure Zoe had a home where someone loved her and would care for her.

COLE DIDN'T SEEM upset about the bed, and Grace relaxed. She was anxious to ask Cole about what he'd learned today, but he went to feed the animals so Mr. Walt wouldn't have to. It was chilly outside.

She put Zoe in her walker and let her go. She chased Rascal around the house. Rascal would go down the hall and back into the living room and she would follow, making little noises. She was happy. Grace never knew Zoe liked animals.

As she chopped the last bit of chicken and stirred it into mashed potatoes for Zoe, Cole walked in and stared at the mess on the counters. "What are you doing?"

"Making Zoe's supper. She can eat food from the table now. I just have to be careful what I give her. She was frowning the other night because she didn't like the organic food I had bought."

He leaned against the counter and folded his arms across his broad chest. "I honestly believe there's nothing you can't do. On Saturday when we had the ice storm, Grandpa didn't want to live anymore—he wouldn't eat lunch. He said he wasn't hungry. He's eaten very little since my grandma died. And now he's eating and he's completely captivated by Zoe. I don't know how you accomplished that."

Unable to stop herself, she smiled. "Divine intervention."

"Yeah, right." He smiled back, and the soft expression on his face took her breath away. The blue of his eyes wasn't steel anymore. They were warm and bright like the sky on a summer day.

"When's supper, Grace?" Mr. Walt called and broke the moment.

"In a minute," she shouted back, and her mind focused on what was important. "Did you find out anything today?"

"We'll talk after supper," he said. "Grandpa's not going to give us any peace until he's eaten. It seems he's making up for lost time."

Grace hurried and cooked the chicken fried steak that Grandpa had ordered. He'd helped her prepare everything. She had zero expertise on chicken fried steak, which was the reason for the big mess in the kitchen. She'd clean it up later. With the food on the table, she called Mr. Walt and put Zoe in her high chair. The meal seemed to go on forever. She was anxious to talk to Cole.

Zoe rubbed her eyes with her hands, getting food all over herself. Grace wiped her hands and her face and then gave her a bottle.

"I'm going to put her down for the night. She's had a big day."

When she made it back to the kitchen, the table was clean and the dishes were in the dishwasher. He was such a sweet guy.

THEY SAT AT the table. Cole stretched his broad shoulders. "It's tiring sitting at a desk for hours."

"Is that what you did?"

"Yes. I went over every word in that file, and you're right, Parker is a fan of Briggs's. He's promised to help him get Zoe."

The blood drained from Grace's face, and she went limp. "What?" She could barely squeak out the word.

"Don't panic," he said in a rush, and she took a long breath.

"Can he do that?"

"If he feels Briggs is the better parent, but I'm going to find something to disprove that.

It might take a while, and I have to be back to work next Monday. So I have to spend all my time investigating Briggs's story. I'd like to ask you some more questions."

She scooted forward in her chair. "Sure. Anything."

"You said Briggs injured his wrist in a bar fight. The file says he injured it playing football in the park with a bunch of kids."

"Brooke said that's what he told her at the time in the ER when she was asking him questions, but later he told her he'd only said that because he didn't want any bad press. He was really in a bar and a man said something derogatory about him and he took offense and hit him, injuring his wrist."

"Did she tell you the name of the bar?"

"No. I don't know if she knew."

Cole pulled out his phone. "Let's go over this again. After the ER visit, who made the first call?"

"He did. He came back to the ER to get her number. She was so excited that he had done that. She'd thought he wasn't interested."

"She didn't call him?"

Grace shook her head. "As far as I know, he did all the calling."

"According to Briggs, he had no interest

in Brooke, but she kept calling him and he finally gave in."

"That's a lie." Grace was appalled that Briggs would go so far to sully her sister's name.

"I'll check into that at the hospital. Who are her friends there?"

"Amber Lewis and Brooke have been friends since grade school. She works in the ER, too. Heather Wright. They used to go out together a lot."

"Let's go over the timeline again." Cole looked down at his phone. "She dated Briggs and then moved in with him. Three months later she came home with bruises."

"Yes."

"Then three months later she went back to him and became pregnant." Cole was reading from his phone, so he must've written everything down she'd told him. "She was four months pregnant when she came home again with bruises?"

"Yes. And she stayed until Zoe was about two months old. That's when Briggs apologized and asked her to come back."

"And up until that time he'd never seen Zoe?"

"That was the first time he saw her, and he

never even picked her up. Brooke put her in the carrier, and they left."

"You told me he was seeing a therapist. Do you know which one?"

"No. I'm sorry. Brooke never said."

"One week later Brooke brought Zoe back to you?"

"Yes. I begged her to stay home with Zoe, but she left anyway."

Cole leaned back in his chair. "I'm guessing that's about the time she started working at the gentlemen's club. She didn't have time to take care of Zoe at night, so she brought her to you. I just can't figure out why she would do that."

Grace shook her head. "I don't get that part. That's just not my sister."

"The name of the club is in the file, and I will check it out, too."

"Thank you, Cole, for doing this. Please don't let Joel get Zoe. He doesn't love her. I know that deep inside."

"I'll do everything I can, but like I told you, you need to start facing the fact that there's a good possibility he will get her. He's her father, and he has rights."

"Because Parker's behind him."

Cole nodded. "Partly. A cop's recommendation is going to go a long way, but I'm not through by a long shot. I'm going to leave early in the morning, and I won't come home tomorrow night. I'll sleep at my apartment. Do you think you can handle Grandpa that long?"

"Does a duck waddle?"

Cole grinned. "You've been around my grandpa too long."

"He introduced me to a lot of people today, and they were very nice. I'm known as the lady who slid off the road. Maribel, the owner of the diner, has twin boys with dark hair and dark eyes. They're not identical, but they're close. She has a Pack 'n Play set up in the corner with toys. They were supposed to stay there, but they'd climb out and run all over the diner. When they saw Zoe, they came over and stared at her and jabbered. Zoe jabbered back. I think they had their own language. Then Maribel said, 'Daddy's coming,' and they shot back to the Pack 'n Play and crawled over busying themselves with toys. A tall, nice-looking man walked in."

"That would be Elias Rebel. His family owns a big ranch right outside Horseshoe."

"The moment he opened the door, they were out of that Pack 'n Play again and flew to him, one around each leg. He kissed his wife and picked up the boys, one in each arm, and walked out. We all watched as he put the boys in car seats in a big truck. He was parked in the middle of the street."

"That's Elias. It sounds as if you had a really good time today."

"It was just…" Words tumbled around in her head as she tried to explain it. "It was the first time since my sister died that the rope around my heart loosened a little. Gabe gave me hope, and I witnessed happiness here in Horseshoe, Texas. It made me feel good."

Or maybe it was Cole. He was always telling her to be prepared for the worst, but she knew he was just trying to make her face reality. And the reality was she might lose Zoe. She also knew though, with Cole on the case, she had a chance. He gave her more hope than Gabe.

CHAPTER TEN

COLE WAS UP EARLY, intending to be in Austin before seven. He shaved and showered in Grandpa's bathroom. As he tied his bathrobe, Grandpa stomped into the room in his boxers and a T-shirt, scratching his gray head.

"What are you doing in my bathroom?"

"I thought I'd give Grace the privacy of the other bath."

"Good." Grandpa nodded his head.

"Grandpa, I'm not coming home tonight. I'll be interviewing and gathering information to help Grace."

"That's fine. Grace is here, and we're going grocery shopping."

"Grocery shopping? Didn't you do that yesterday?"

"Yeah, but now we have to get stuff for Thanksgiving. I told Grace I wanted turkey and dressing, and she said she doesn't know how to make it. What are mothers teaching their girls these days?"

"Probably that they don't need to do all the cooking. These days men know how to cook."

"That's nonsense. Women need to know how to cook, too."

Cole didn't have time to get into it with his bullheaded grandfather. He was set in his ways and would probably never change.

"I've got to run, Grandpa. Just remember I will be spending Thanksgiving at Stephanie's, so don't buy a lot of food for just you and Grace."

"I'll buy whatever I want to."

Cole sighed deeply. He could feel the weight of a cantankerous old man seeping into his bones.

"Get out of my bathroom. I have to shave and shower. Zoe Grace will be awake soon."

Cole gave up and hurried to his room to change clothes. He wore jeans and a white shirt. He pulled out his blazer because the weather was still cold. As a detective, he could now wear street clothes. As he slipped on his boots, he thought he shouldn't complain about his grandfather. At least he was shaving and showering. Amazing Grace. A smile touched his face.

He made his way down the hall and stopped. He heard a sound coming from

Grace's room. The door was open, but the light wasn't on. He glanced around the doorjamb and saw Zoe standing up in her bed. Grace must be in the bathroom. As soon as Zoe noticed him, she held out her arms.

"Mmm. Mmm. Mmm."

He had to go and Grace would be out in a minute. The problem was Zoe kept pushing against the bed and holding out her arms over the rail. He was afraid she would tumble out of it. When he stepped into the room, she got all excited, wiggling and moving around, making happy noises.

"Grace will be out in a minute." He found himself standing in the moonlight streaming in from the windows talking to a baby who didn't understand a word he was saying. When he didn't take her, she stuck out her lower lip and crocodile tears leaked from her eyes. He couldn't stand it. He gently picked her up.

He patted her back. "Is that better?"

Her happy face reappeared, and she snuggled against him, rubbing her cheek against his. He wondered if Jamie ever held him like this. Did he have that overwhelming joy and endless gratitude for holding something so precious, so unique and special in a way that it could never be replaced? In that moment he looked beyond the shadow of Jamie to the son of Jamie.

His dad must've held him every day like this and dreamed about the future and a little boy who would grow up with the love and support of his parents. The tragedy of his parents' death had changed all that. And for the first time he wanted that love back. He wanted to feel that love again.

Zoe rubbed her face against his again.

"What are you doing?" he asked in a voice he'd never heard before. He was talking baby talk. If Bo heard him, Cole would never live it down.

"She's giving you smooches," Grace said from the doorway. She was in a bathrobe with her damp hair nestled against her face.

"What?" he asked, distracted.

She walked farther into the room. "She's giving you smooches." She rubbed Zoe's back. "Are you giving Cole my smooches?"

Zoe wiggled and flailed her arms.

Grace stared at him.

"What?"

"Give her smooches back. Kiss her cheek."

"Grace—"

"Kiss her cheek."

He kissed Zoe's cheek, and as he did he sensed the heartache and sadness of the past shrinking inside him. It wasn't dominating him, controlling him like it had before, all from the soft, enduring touch of a child. But it also made him feel helpless and vulnerable in a way that frightened him. He quickly handed off Zoe to Grace.

"I've got to go." He walked out of the room as if his boots were on fire. In his truck he unlocked his glove compartment and reached for his gun and badge. He was back to being Cole Chisholm, a hard-nosed cop who didn't get his feelings all squishy from holding a baby.

Grace had her hands full with Mr. Walt. He was giving her orders left and right, and she could barely keep up.

"I'm going to feed the boys and the chickens, and then we'll fire up Bertha and go buy groceries for Thanksgiving."

"Mr. Walt, there will only be the two of us. We don't really need a turkey."

"Sure we do. Everybody has turkey on Thanksgiving."

"But I've never made turkey and dressing."

"I'll teach you. My Cora lost her mind, but

she still knew how to cook." He pointed a finger at her. "That's a lesson to be learned. If you lose your mind and know how to cook, you'll still be able to feed yourself."

She burst out laughing. "Mr. Walt, that is hilarious and chauv—"

"I know. The pig thing, but it's true, and we've had that conversation already."

Grace reached for her cell to call Frannie and share about her life in bizarro world. Though it wasn't feeling so bizarre anymore.

"Wait a minute. Why does the old man think you can cook?"

"I made sandwiches the first night, and I guess they were good."

"Does he know your middle name is *takeout*?"

Grace laughed. "Hey, you taught me to make biscuits, and I have a feeling I'm going to be making them every morning while I'm here."

"I don't know how you made fried chicken and a coconut pie."

"His wife has all her recipes in a box. I made it according to the directions, and of course he was there to instruct. He did most of it. He's really a lovable old man."

"I'm glad you're somewhere safe and comfortable."

"Me, too. I crashed at the right place."

"And I'm really happy that take-charge guy is helping you."

"Me, too. He's really very nice."

"You opened your eyes, didn't you?"

"A little."

Frannie laughed. It was good to talk to her friend. Frannie had always been her anchor, her voice of reason when she thought she would go insane from all the heartache. Grace didn't mention all the details about her sister and the gentlemen's club, and she wouldn't until Cole had gathered all his information.

"Has Joel been back?" Grace asked.

"No, I haven't seen him. Maybe that's a good thing."

"I haven't gotten another text from him, either. I don't know. It's like he's biding his time or something."

"Just be strong, Gracie."

"I'm trying."

"Robert called and wants me to spend Thanksgiving with my grandkids in Virginia. The new great-grandbaby will be there, and

I'm thinking of going now that you're tucked away safely."

"Go, Frannie. You rarely get to see your family, and I'm okay."

"Are you sure, Gracie?"

"I'm sure." But inside she felt her anchor, the one she depended on for security, shake. It seemed she was destined to always lose the ones she loved. And the more she held on, the harder it was to let go. She yearned for the one anchor that no one could ever take away from her—Zoe.

She bit on a fingernail and replied again, "I'm sure. Send me pictures."

"I will, and don't kill that old man."

Grace clicked off with a smile, but her eyes filled with tears. She had always known that one day Frannie would move to be near her son and grandchildren. Her son was a colonel in the Army, and when he retired, Frannie would join them. And then Grace would be truly alone. Without Brooke... Without Zoe...

She ran to the bathroom to get herself under control. "I hope you're happy, Cole Chisholm. I'm preparing myself for the worst." Then she dried her tears and got ready to spend the day with Mr. Walt. She knew he would certainly make her laugh. And she needed a little craziness right now.

COLE WENT TO the office and made copies of things he needed, and then he headed to the ER listed in the file. The only place to start was at the beginning. Grace and Briggs had different stories, and he had to prove which one was lying. Although he already knew. And that's when he realized he had really crossed the line. Facts didn't seem to matter anymore, and he couldn't quite explain that to himself. Or he didn't want to.

It was after seven when he reached the ER, and it was busy. Emergency personnel were coming and going. People were waiting to be treated. Others were waiting on family members. He walked around several people to get to the desk and spoke to a nurse. He pulled out his badge and introduced himself. "I'd like to speak to Dr. Kevin Colson." The doctor had treated Briggs when he'd injured his wrist.

"He's assisting a patient," she told him. "It's going to take a minute."

"I'll wait." He took a seat in a waiting area and watched gurneys being pushed in and out. He stared down at his boots, wondering when the doctor would show.

Cole stood when he saw a doctor in a white coat walking toward him. The man held out his hand and shook Cole's. "What can I help you with?" he asked.

Cole showed him the paper he held in his hand. "I'd like to talk to you about that."

The doctor looked at the wrist injury report of Joel Briggs. "Yes. I treated him. It was severely swollen, and he thought he'd broken it. After the X-ray, I determined it was only sprained. I told him what to do and gave him a pain prescription for five days and released him."

Cole pointed to the bottom where it said "cause of injury." "Is that consistent with a fall?"

"Yes."

"What else would it be consistent with?"

"What?" The doctor adjusted his stethoscope and looked away. He was nervous.

"How else could that sprain have happened?"

The doctor didn't reply, and Cole could almost see the wheels turning in his head.

"How about a punch to the face or the stomach?"

"Sure, that's possible, but Mr. Briggs said he injured his wrist in the park playing football with kids. And that's what's in the report."

Cole didn't press him. He would need more information for that.

"Look, I've got to go," the doctor said. "The report is correct, if that's what you're asking."

Cole didn't leave it at that. He went to medical records—with luck, Vera would be there. She was about fifty, with a quick tongue and a heart of gold. Cole had gotten information from her many times when he was in a hurry, and she always complied without a lot of red tape.

"Hey, Vera." He leaned into the window where she sat at a desk.

She looked at him over the rim of her tortoiseshell glasses. "Sergeant, how can I help you today?"

"I'm looking for information, and I hope you'll help me."

"And you don't have a subpoena?"

"No, ma'am, but it involves a possible homicide and a nine-month-old baby."

"What kind of information?"

"I'd like for you to check your ER database and see if there was a head, chest or shoulder injury on these days." He slid a piece of paper in front of her.

Her eyes opened wide. "Are you kidding me?"

"Now, Vera. You know I don't kid when I'm working."

"If you weren't so good-looking, I'd kick you out of here."

"But you won't?"

"When you mentioned a nine-month-old baby, you had me."

She let him into the office, and he followed her into another room with computers. She sat down at one of them and he looked over her shoulder. "What do you need again?"

He explained one more time and watched her fingers go to work.

"Here's a busted nose."

"Who is it?"

"A twelve-year-old boy."

Damn. "No, that's not it."

"Fractured ribs?"

"Who?"

"An eighty-four-year-old woman."

"No, that's not it, either."

"A dislocated shoulder? Thirty-two-year-old woman."

"No." Cole sighed, and it went it like that

for the next thirty minutes. He finally had to admit that no one had been treated in this ER for a possible punch by Joel Briggs. This wasn't the only ER, and for the next ones he would have to have a subpoena. He knew a judge he worked with a lot who was a supporter of children's rights. He called him and explained the situation. He had a subpoena within the hour and started visiting ERs across Austin.

At five o'clock, Cole was frustrated. He had two more ERs to visit, and for the first time he had to consider that Brooke hadn't told Grace the truth. Or whoever had been in the fight didn't go to the ER. For Briggs to injure his wrist that badly, there had to be a victim somewhere.

The next one was a large hospital and he knew it would take some time. A young girl of about twenty helped him. She had on fake eyelashes, and her long nails were a deep purple. The tips of her nails flew across the keyboard, and he couldn't imagine how she did that so fast. But soon she had a list for him.

He glanced at it, and something immediately jumped out at him. A fractured jaw. Bingo! He got the name, address and phone number and made an appointment to meet

Allan Hernandez. He managed a sporting goods store, and that's where they arranged to meet.

The man was medium height and probably weighed around 190 pounds. No match for Joel Briggs. They sat in his office.

"What's this about?" Allan asked.

Cole laid the medical report in front of him. "I'd like to ask about this."

The man pushed back in his chair, a neutral expression on his face. "That was a long time ago."

"Can you tell me what happened?"

"I got a sucker punch right to my jaw and had my lights put out. I woke up in the ER, and they admitted me to the hospital. My jaw was broken, and I had to have surgery. It took two pins to put it back together." He rubbed his jaw self-consciously.

"Who hit you?"

Allan shook his head. "I don't know."

"What do you mean?"

"I was in a bar talking trash, trying to get the attention of some pretty cocktail waitresses, and the next thing I know I'm in the ER."

"You have no idea who hit you?"

The man shook his head.

"What were you saying that was so insulting?"

"I don't remember. I had about four Jacks on the rocks, and all I wanted to do was flirt with a gorgeous waitress."

Cole touched the paper. "This is assault. Why didn't you file charges?"

"I don't know, man. It's all fuzzy. I opened my mouth when I shouldn't have, and I got what I deserved."

The man was lying so bad it showed all over his guilty face. Why? That's what Cole couldn't figure out.

"You deserved a broken jaw?"

"I didn't belong in that club, and I paid a price."

"Why didn't you belong?"

"I'm Mexican, and that was a rich white man's club."

"What happened, Mr. Hernandez?"

"My wife had gone to her mother's for a couple of days, and I was at loose ends. There's this club I drive by when I go home. There's always pretty women going in there, and I thought I'd just check it out. It's a fancy place with valet parking and all. Inside it's even fancier with a curved mahogany bar and a million glasses that sparkle like diamonds.

I'd never been in a place like that. I sat down at the bar and ordered Jack on the rocks. The big-screen TV was on, and a football game was playing. Those guys in suits and chinos and expensive shirts were saying, 'watch this player' or 'watch that player.' I'd had a lot of liquor by then, and I said I didn't think the play was all that great. I remember this enormous pain hit the left side of my face, and I woke up in the ER. I had to tell my wife because I was in the hospital. She was furious for a while, but she forgave me. I just want to put that night behind me."

"What was the name of the club?"

"Deuces."

Joe Penetti's gentlemen's club. The club where Brooke Bennett worked. At the very least, the club was the front for Penetti's high-stakes gambling games. He'd been arrested before, but a good defense attorney always managed to get the charges dropped. That attorney was Harlan Myers, Stephanie's father.

Cole stood and reached inside his jacket for a business card. He slid it across the desk. "When you're ready to tell me the truth, call. It's very important."

He could push it further, but for now he'd let Allan Hernandez simmer for a while.

Back in his truck, he thought about what he'd just learned. Mostly nothing. But Brooke worked in that club, and since she worked there, his guess was Joel Briggs was a frequent visitor. Briggs had said he didn't know Brooke was working at night, but again, Cole was guessing that he did. Why Brooke took the job in the first place was a still a big question mark. He intended to find out exactly what hold Joel Briggs had over Brooke.

His next stop was to visit with the man himself. Joel Briggs.

But as he drove, a thought occurred to him— if an ambulance was called to the club, the cops would have responded, too. He hurried back to the station to gather more information. He had what he needed within minutes, and then he went over to patrol to talk to Officers Gibbons and Collins, who had answered the call. He found them in the locker room at the end of their shift.

"Hey, Sarge," they said as he entered.

He handed the police report to them. "Why isn't the attacker's name on this report?"

"Sarge, that's a long time ago," Gibbons responded.

"Wait, that's Deuces," Collins said. "When we got there, the place was almost empty.

Only the bartender, the manager and a few waitresses were there, and they didn't see anything, of course. No one could identify the man who hit Hernandez. They said he ran out the door, as did the customers as soon as the ambulance was called. We checked in with Hernandez at the hospital, and he said he didn't know who hit him. The case was a brick wall, and we moved on."

"Is something wrong?" Gibbons asked.

"No. Very good police work."

"Thanks, Sarge."

It was after nine when he crawled into his truck. His lonely apartment wasn't all that appealing. He thought of going home to Horseshoe, Grandpa, Grace and Zoe, but he had to keep digging, and he had to start very early in the morning.

He had to gather every bit of information he could so Grace would have a better chance of keeping Zoe. That was his goal, and he wasn't stopping until it happened.

CHAPTER ELEVEN

GRACE HAD TO bite her lip a couple times during the day, but otherwise everything went well. She had everything she needed written down for the recipes Mr. Walt wanted to cook. She wasn't buying anything else, except for diapers and things for Zoe.

The first hitch came when Mr. Walt said Horseshoe's grocery store wasn't big enough and he wanted to go into Temple. After a seemingly endless conversation, she agreed to go. The store was much bigger and had a lot more choices. Mr. Walt disappeared for a moment and came back with a small teddy bear in his hand and gave it to Zoe. Before Grace could grab it, Zoe had a plush arm in her mouth and was slobbering away.

"Mr. Walt, you can't put this back now. Zoe has chewed on it."

"I don't want to put it back. I bought it for Zoe Grace."

"Mr. Walt, we've had this conversation, and…"

"And we're probably gonna have it again."

"Mr. Walt…"

He pushed Zoe farther down the aisle and left Grace there fuming. The Chisholm men were so infuriating. She was good at dealing with elderly people, but Mr. Walt was pushing her buttons.

The turkey was the last thing on the list. She looked through all the turkeys, trying to find a small one.

"Here's one, Grace," Mr. Walt said.

She pushed the cart to where he was standing and looked at the enormous bird. "That's a twenty-pound turkey."

"Yeah, it's just right."

"No, we do not need that big of a turkey for just two people."

"Zoe Grace will be there."

"Zoe is a baby and will not eat hardly anything. We do not need this big of a turkey."

"Yes, we do. Cora always cooked a big turkey. I want it to be like when Cora was here. I want everything to be like—" Big tears filled his eyes, and Grace's heart dropped. "I know she was out of her mind, but I miss her."

Grace put her arm around his shoulders.

"It's okay, Mr. Walt. I'll fix everything just like Cora did. My cooking may not be as good as hers, but I'll do my very best. But—"

"What?"

She stepped over to the turkeys and picked up one that weighed almost twelve pounds. "I think Cora would be happy if we cooked this turkey and we won't waste so much. What do you think?"

He wiped away a tear. "Yeah. That one is just right."

She gave him another hug and pushed the cart toward checkout. She thought of calling Cole, but everything was okay and she didn't want to worry him. Mr. Walt was just feeling sad, and she knew how that felt.

Mr. Walt insisted they eat lunch out, so they stopped at a pizza place. He got Zoe out of the car seat and carried her inside. Grace let him. For a seventy-eight year old man, he was healthy and spry. She never sensed any weakness in him, except for his sadness.

When they reached home, Mr. Walt helped her take the groceries inside and then crashed in his chair. She put Zoe down for a nap and went over the recipes she would have to cook for Thursday. She laid the cards out on the counter and realized she would have to make some of the things earlier. Everything wouldn't fit in the oven at one time. Her head began to throb, and she sat on the sofa cuddling a pillow, listening to Mr. Walt snore.

Cole hadn't called all day, and she wondered if he'd found out anything. She hoped that there was something somewhere that would indicate her sister had been murdered. In her heart, Grace knew her sister wouldn't willingly wait tables in a skimpy outfit, but the evidence proved otherwise. And there were moments she wondered if she knew her sister at all. Then their childhood would come back, and she was confident she knew Brooke better than anyone. There had to be a reason her life got all tangled with a destructive person like Joel Briggs.

She cuddled the pillow harder. She missed her sister, her smile, her laugh and her boundless energy that Grace could still feel. Tears slipped from her eyes, and she curled into the sofa and remembered a sister she would never see again.

She must have fallen asleep, because the next thing she knew, the back door opened and someone hollered, "Walt!"

She jumped up and saw someone standing in the kitchen. She thought it was a woman, but she wasn't sure. There was a worn hat on her head, and she wore a flannel shirt over baggy jeans tucked into work boots. She held a covered dish with something on top of it in her hands.

She took one look at Grace and bellowed, "Who are you?"

"Um… Grace."

Mr. Walt trailed into the kitchen. "Bertie, don't you keep up with the gossip in town? This is the woman who slid off the road in the ice storm."

"Oh. I didn't realize she was so young."

"That's because you're so old."

"You're the same age as I am," the woman came right back at Mr. Walt. "So don't talk about old unless you can chew gum and whistle 'Dixie' at the same time."

Oh, no. Not another language barrier.

Rascal barked and trotted into Grace's bedroom.

"Now, look what you did. You woke up the baby."

"What baby?"

"Bertie, really? She has a baby, and they're staying here until Lamar can fix her car."

Grace slid around them to go to Zoe. She

changed her diaper and listened to the conversation in the kitchen.

"I made a pot roast and brought some for you and Cole. There're some yeast rolls on top."

"Thanks, Bertie, but now that Grace is here, you don't have to worry about me. She's cooking."

"Oh, are you sure? She doesn't look like she can boil water."

Grace went back into the kitchen with Zoe on her hip. They were talking about her and she felt she should be present. She resented that the woman thought she couldn't cook. Maybe because it was the truth, a little voice whispered in her hand.

Mr. Walt took Zoe out of her arms. "Bertie, look at this baby. Isn't she the most beautiful thing you've ever seen?"

The woman shook her head. "No. My Annie is the most beautiful thing I've ever seen."

"Ah, you don't know what you're talking about."

The woman placed the bowl on the counter and looked at Grace. "That's my pot roast, and it's enough for y'all. I'll get the dish later. Just don't put it in the dishwasher. I don't like my dishes in the dishwasher."

"Yes, ma'am," Grace replied. "I'll take real good care of it."

The woman looked at Mr. Walt. "I'll bring Thanksgiving supper about five on Thursday."

"I told you, Bertie, Grace is cooking."

The woman's sharp gray eyes zeroed in on Grace. "Can you cook?"

Grace refused to be intimidated. "I can read a recipe."

"Yeah. I'll bring supper."

"No, please don't," Grace responded. "We went to town today and bought everything to cook Thanksgiving dinner, so please don't bring more food. It won't be needed."

"Yeah, whatever. You'll be calling me." She stomped out the back door.

Grace placed her hands on her hips. "Well, I've never met anyone so rude."

"Never mind Bertie. She's missing a knocker or two."

"Mr. Walt, that doesn't make sense."

"Neither does Bertie. She lost a son and she's never been the same, just like Cora. We all hurt and grieve in different ways. I've known Bertie all my life, and she's a good neighbor and a good friend. Life has made her a little rough around the edges, though."

"I didn't know." Grace felt bad about talking back to the woman. In this small town, there was heartache and sadness just like everywhere else, but here they took care of each other—it was nice to see. Next time she would be more patient with Miss Bertie.

She thought about Mr. Walt's words. Life had a way of changing people like Miss Cora and Miss Bertie. Would it do the same to her? Would she become a bitter woman, not caring about people's feelings and just going through the motions of living?

Death touched everyone, and how they dealt with it was what mattered. She would embrace her sister's passing with sadness and love and remember all the good times. And she would make sure Zoe remembered her, too. That was, if she got to keep Zoe. That still was a big if. She would stand strong and deal with life as her grandmother had told her. Her grandmother would say, "You're not like your mother. You're strong and you'll make better choices." Her choice to run had been a bad one, but it had brought her to the Chisholm home, and now Cole was her only hope for a life where she could adjust and heal.

COLE PICKED UP something to eat and went to his apartment. After supper, he took a shower and crawled into bed with his phone. He called Grace, and her soft voice lifted his spirits. He told her about his day and that he hadn't found out anything important.

"Don't panic," he told her. "Tomorrow I'll do a little more pressing. It's a slow go right now, but soon something will pop up. How was your day?"

She told him about Grandpa and the turkey. He sat up straight. "He cried in the grocery store?"

"Yes, but he's okay now. It was just an emotional moment. He wants everything to be just like when your grandmother was alive, and I told him I would do my best to make it that way."

"Are you sure he's okay? Do I need to come home?" Grandpa didn't ever cry, and that worried Cole.

"No. He's fine. But I did meet your neighbor Miss Bertie, which was an unusual experience."

"Yeah. She's eccentric, but she has a good heart and she's helped me a lot with Grandpa."

"That's what Mr. Walt said. The next time I'll be better prepared."

That's what he liked about Grace. She adjusted and moved on. She had more strength than he had ever seen in a woman—and he just might be getting in over his head.

"I'll be home tomorrow night. Call me if anything comes up. I don't want my grandpa to be upset."

"He's not upset. He's planning Thanksgiving and is all excited about it. I just hope I don't let him down."

"You won't." If he knew anything, he knew that.

He sat with his phone in his hand wondering how he'd gotten so emotionally involved in just a few days. Usually he was detached from people, but the sound of Grace's voice took him places he wasn't ready to go. How had this happened?

THE NEXT MORNING Cole met with Heather Wright, Brooke's friend. She was in her early twenties with brown hair and blue eyes. They sat in the same ER chairs as he had with Dr. Colson.

"How long have you known Brooke?"

"We went to nursing school together."

"So you know her pretty well?"

"Yes. We used to go out after work, but after she met Joel, I didn't see her much."

"When Briggs came in here for treatment, were you in the room?"

"No. Dr. Colson and Brooke were in the room."

"How did Brooke and Briggs hook up?"

"Brooke was gaga over him, and I told her he's a jerk. All he does is brag, and I pointed that out to her, but she said that didn't bother her. She thought he was great."

"So they made a date that night in the ER?"

Heather shook her head. "No. Joel came back the next day and asked for her number, and they made arrangements to meet that night. I told her to watch her step. I just didn't like him from the start, but I trusted her judgment and let it go."

"Did you see bruises on her?"

"Yes, we had a big falling-out about it. I told her to get out now, and she said that it had been her fault. I couldn't believe it. After that, we didn't talk much. I was just glad Grace was there for Zoe."

"Do you know why she took Zoe to Grace?"

"I asked her one time why she wasn't staying with her baby, and again she told me it was none of my business, so I let it go. It was her life, but I worried about her relationship with Joel."

"Do you know if she worked outside the hospital?"

Heather frowned. "No. She couldn't even keep up with this job. She was late so many times, the head nurse was about to give her her walking papers."

"Do you know why she was late?"

"She was out at night in clubs with Joel. That's what he liked to do...party."

"Do you know the name of the clubs?"

She shook her head. "Like I said, we didn't talk much. You need to talk to Amber. They grew up together and were close."

"Do you know how I can reach her? I tried her cell, and she didn't answer. I left a message, but she hasn't responded."

"Amber was very upset about Brooke's death. She had to get away. She and her boyfriend went camping without phones. Quiet time was all that she wanted. She's not expected back to work until Friday morning."

Cole thanked her and tried to put the pieces together in his head. Briggs was lying once again. He'd initiated the relationship, not Brooke. It bothered Cole that nothing was making sense—by now it should be. Why had Brooke taken the job at Deuces? The only person who could answer that was Joel

Briggs, even though he said he wasn't aware that she was working there. Cole planned to rattle his cage a little bit. He hadn't made it there last night, but this morning his next stop was Briggs's apartment.

He lived in an exclusive, gated apartment complex with a pool, gym and tennis courts. A pass code was needed to get in. When a car went through the gate, he followed through before it could close.

There were about thirty-two apartments in the complex. Briggs's was in the first set of eight that faced the street. The staircases caught his attention. They didn't go directly up to the apartment. They were slanted, and were actually two staircases going up to the apartments. It looked like two big Xs, with the centers not touching, on eight apartments. It had to be some sort of architectural design.

Brooke had to fall down one set to a landing and then get up and fall the rest of the way to the ground. That would be a lot of hits to her body and head. Maybe the ME wouldn't find anything else. But what had made her run headlong to her death?

He made his way up the first set of stairs and noticed a dark spot on the landing. Brooke's blood—that stain would be there forever or until the stairs were destroyed. He wondered how Briggs felt when he went by it every day.

Cole made his way to the large stained glass front door and rang the bell.

Joel Briggs answered it himself. He narrowed his eyes. "Can I help you?"

Cole pulled out his badge and introduced himself.

"I don't understand what you're doing here. Parker said the case was closed."

"I'm just double-checking the facts. That's what we do before we close a case." He nodded his head toward the apartment. "Do you mind if I come in?"

Briggs stepped back, and Cole realized for the first time just how big the man was. Broad shoulders, muscled neck, solid arms, legs and chest. He couldn't have gotten that big without steroids.

He glanced around the large apartment. Posters of Briggs in his football uniform were everywhere, some when he was a kid, some when he was in high school, others when he was in college and in the NFL. Awards, memorabilia and footballs signed by famous players were in a large glass case. The place was like a museum of Briggs's life.

"Do you like football?" Briggs asked.

"Yeah, who doesn't?"

"I started playing when I was about eight, and I never wanted to do anything else. I'm one of the best defensive ends ever to play the game, and I have the stats to back it up. I've sacked many a great quarterback. I have film in the game room. Would you like to watch?"

He was like a little boy wanting to show off his trophies. "Thanks, man, maybe another time. I'm working." He wanted to get Briggs on his side, and to do that he had to play nice.

"Sure, sure. What do you need to know?"

Cole sat on the white leather sofa, and Briggs took the red leather chair across from him. A glass and stainless steel coffee table was between them. Briggs started talking about a football game where he made spectacular plays and went on and on and on.

"Man, I could listen to you all day, but I'm here to check facts." Cole pulled out his notebook from his jacket. "According to you, Brooke Bennett contacted you after your visit to the ER and continued to call you and harass you until you went out with her."

"Yeah, girls do that all the time and I try to ignore them, but she was beautiful and I finally gave in. We went out to eat, and after that I really liked her. She moved into my apartment, and we got along for a while, then she started getting jealous over little things. Women look at me and women like me. I can't stop that, but she'd get so jealous and go into childish tirades. I told her to get out."

"Yes, I read all of that in the file, but you see, I have a little problem."

Briggs frowned. "What?"

"I spoke with nurses at the ER, and they said you came back the next day and asked for Brooke's number." He didn't want to implicate Heather, so he played it cool.

"I came back the next day to tell Brooke to stop calling me. She called me at all hours of the night and wouldn't let me sleep."

Briggs was full of excuses. And Cole knew it wouldn't do him any good to go further. Briggs would only lie. But Cole had an ace up his sleeve.

"Do you know Allan Hernandez?"

Nothing showed on Briggs's face. He was probably a good poker player. "No. I've never heard the name. Is he a fan? I'll autograph a football for him."

"No, he's not a fan. He's a victim. His jaw was broken at Deuces Gentlemen's Club. Have you heard of it?"

Briggs stood in one easy movement, his muscles tense. "No, and I'd like for you to leave."

Cole slowly stood. "I have a lot more questions, Mr. Briggs, especially about your daughter."

Briggs pointed a finger at him. "My daughter is none of your business."

"You're wrong about that. You plan to take her from the only person who loves her. Why do you want your daughter now?"

Briggs pulled out his cell phone, the veins in his neck bulging out. "I'm calling Parker, and he'll have your badge for harassing me."

Cole slid the notebook back into his pocket. "He doesn't have the authority to do that. This case isn't over, Mr. Briggs. It's a long way from over." He walked toward the front door and then went down the stairs.

When he got in his truck, his cell buzzed. Parker.

"What the hell do you think you're doing?"

"My job. Checking facts, and the facts don't match what's in your file."

"What are you talking about?"

"When I get it all together, I'll put it on your desk with a big bow."

"Chisholm—"

"Briggs is guilty as sin, and if you don't want to go down with him, you better start listening to me. He's lying. Every word that comes out of his mouth is a lie."

"You don't know that."

"You let his fame get to you, and you never looked beyond it. There's a whole lot of ugly behind Joel Briggs. I'll catch you later."

"Chisholm—"

Cole slipped his phone into his pocket and drove to Deuces. It wasn't open this time of day, but maybe the staff could give him some answers, some details that would tie Briggs to the club. He parked in the empty parking lot and walked in. The club was just as Hernandez had explained it, expensive and shiny. A Mexican boy about eighteen was cleaning tables and glanced at him curiously. A man behind the bar wiped glasses and didn't seem to notice Cole. He walked over to him.

The man looked up with a scowl. "How did you get in here? We're not open. José!" he shouted to the boy. "Lock that damn door!" And then the man trained his eyes on Cole. "And you can leave before he locks it."

Cole pulled out his badge and introduced himself.

"What do you want?"

"Answers." Cole placed his badge back into his pocket.

"Fresh out of those."

Cole looked around at the empty club. "I could come back with a team of cops to search this place, or we can make it simple. Your choice."

"What do you want to know?" The man wasn't taking any chances on cops searching the club.

"Do you know Joel Briggs?"

"You mean the football player? Yeah, I know who he is."

"Does he come in here?"

The man shook his head. "I've never seen him in here."

"Are you sure?"

"A lot of men come in here. I can't be positive, but I think if Joel Briggs came in, I would notice him."

Another dead end. Or the man could be lying. Cole wasn't giving up.

"Do you know Allan Hernandez?"

"No, I've never heard of him."

"Think a little harder."

The man shook his head. "No, sorry, never heard of the man."

Cole leaned on the bar. "You know, if you're

lying to me, I will be back, and I won't be alone." He strolled toward the door.

"Mr., Mr...." The Mexican boy ran toward him as the man at the bar disappeared into a back room.

Cole stopped and stared at the boy.

"Is Allan in trouble?"

"Why do you ask?"

"You're a cop, and you're looking for him. He's a good guy. He wouldn't do nothing wrong."

"You know Allan?"

"Yeah, he got me this job."

The break he was looking for—just a tiny detail. "Allan is a customer here?"

"Yes. He just comes in to drink and look at the pretty girls. He doesn't do nothing wrong."

"I see. How often does he come in?"

The boy shrugged. "Couple times a week."

Another lie. He thanked the boy and assured him Allan wasn't in any trouble. Not yet. Not until Cole got his hands on him.

CHAPTER TWELVE

It took Cole less than ten minutes to drive to the sporting goods store. He retrieved a big pad and pen from his briefcase and marched inside. He walked through the store to Allan's office in the back. The door was partially open, and when he kicked it with his foot, it banged against the wall.

Allan jumped in his seat and carefully laid the cell he was holding on his desk. Obviously José had called.

Cole placed the pad in front of him. "I want the truth this time."

Allan got to his feet. "I had to lie. If my wife found out, she would leave me."

Cole poked the pad. "Write down what happened the night someone broke your jaw. Every detail."

"Will my wife find out?"

"If you don't tell me the truth in writing, I will personally pay her a visit." He was bluffing, but Allan didn't know that.

Allan sat down and began to write. Cole patiently waited. It was a tiny break, but it was a good one. It proved Briggs was violent and had a temper, which would help in a custody hearing. But it didn't prove Briggs had done anything to Brooke. This was just the tip of the iceberg, though—a tiny piece of a big puzzle that he had to put together. The more he investigated, the clearer the picture became. He had to keep poking to get to the truth.

When Allan finished writing, he ripped off the page and handed it to Cole.

"So that was your first night at the bar?"

"Yes, that happened just like I told you. The bouncers weren't at the door, and I just walked in. Joel was bragging how he was a better player than the ones on the TV screen, and after too many drinks I said, 'I've seen you play, and you're not that great.' That's when he hit me. I woke up in the ER and he was there."

"Briggs was in the ER being treated?"

"No. He came to see me and he apologized. He said he was sorry he lost his temper, and he asked that I not mention his name. He gets TV commercials and stuff like that, and his income would suffer."

"And you agreed?"

"Yeah. He's a celebrity, and I should have kept my mouth shut."

"He assaulted you. That's a crime, and he should be punished for that."

Allan shook his head. "I'm done, and I'm not bringing charges against anyone. Besides, he kind of made up for that by buying stuff from the store, and he got me into Deuces. After my jaw healed, he cleared it with the manager and I can come in any time I want."

"So Briggs has power at Deuces?"

Allen shrugged. "I guess."

"Did you ever see Brooke Bennett in the club?"

"Yeah. She's a waitress, and everyone knows she's Joel's girlfriend. She's beautiful and the guys like her. They're always giving her big tips."

"Had she worked there for long?"

"No, at first she just came in with Briggs to get a drink and visit with people and leave. I guess it was about six months later I noticed her waiting tables. I didn't understand that. If she was Joel's girlfriend, why would she have to work at that job? But I didn't ask."

Another piece to the puzzle.

"Briggs was okay with other guys touching her?"

"I don't know. He never stayed around that long."

"What do you mean?"

"They'd come in, and he would sit at the bar while she got into her outfit and went to work. It would get busy. I'd look around, and he was gone. I never knew where he went."

"But Brooke was still there?"

"Yeah."

Another piece fit perfectly into the picture. Briggs was in the back room gambling while Brooke was working. That had to be the answer. Briggs was a gambler. He probably was addicted. Cole had to be sure, though.

Back in his truck, he went over every detail. If Briggs was violent and a gambler, Grace had a good chance of keeping Zoe. Cole had Heather and Allan's statements, but he still needed more. He didn't want to get Grace's hopes up until he was positive she could keep Zoe.

He stretched his shoulders and realized it was almost six o'clock. He had to check on his grandpa and see how things were going with Grace and Zoe. For the first time in a long time that's where he wanted to go—home.

GRACE WAS BUSY trying to keep up with a cantankerous old man. It annoyed her that he seemed to have more energy than her. All day they worked on preparing food for Thanksgiving, and Grace was exhausted. She'd never dreamed this much work went into a meal. And it was only for two people.

Zoe rolled into the kitchen in her walker mumbling. Grace squatted in front of her. "What's wrong, smooches?"

"Ah, she was playing with Rascal, and he got tired and retreated to his bed. She wants to keep playing."

"She's tired, too," Grace replied. "She's been chasing him all day."

Grace was about to take her out of the walker when she heard the back door open. It had to be Cole. Her heart skipped a beat. She couldn't believe how excited she was to see him.

Cole appeared in the doorway, and Zoe immediately rolled over to him and held up her hands. Cole lifted her and patted her back. "Are you fussy?"

Was he talking baby talk? A smile touched her face.

Mr. Walt took her from Cole. "She's just tired. I'll rock her for a little while."

"Mr. Walt, it's after supper and I don't want her to go sleep just yet."

"You can't stop a baby when she wants to sleep."

Grace sighed.

"That bad, huh?"

"I haven't killed him yet, but I've come close a couple of times."

Cole grinned, and she knew he didn't do that often. He looked around at the kitchen. "Looks like y'all been busy."

She followed his glance to all the pots and pans and dishes in the sink and along the counter. It was a mess. "I will get everything cleaned up for tomorrow, but it takes a lot to get everything ready to cook. The bird is in the refrigerator. I've never stuffed so much butter up a bird's butt and under its skin in my whole life. Mr. Walt says we have to take it out early so it's room temperature when we put it in the oven. That's on my checklist."

"Grandma always worked for days to get ready for Thanksgiving."

"Tell me about it. I sliced and diced and deboned until I was dizzy. Mr. Walt says there have to be chicken pieces in the dressing and gravy. Never heard of that. Giblets, too. *Really* never heard that. And hard-boiled

eggs in the dressing and gravy. Seriously."
She took a long breath. "I really don't know
what I'm doing. I think Mr. Walt is pulling
my leg most of the time."

He smiled that smile again, and it made her
light-headed, which she was sure had nothing to do with tiredness. "That's the way my
grandmother made it."

"The corn and green beans are easy because your grandmother canned them and I'll
have to just heat them, but I really don't get
the sweet potatoes recipe. I peeled them like
Mr. Walt told me, and then I cut them in half
and then again. I lightly boiled them and put
them on a plate, and they're in the refrigerator. Tomorrow Mr. Walt wants me to roll them
in sugar and fry them. Truly have never heard
of this. I told him he's the one who's going to
do the frying."

"I'm sure he will."

She leaned against the counter for a moment, forgetting what was upmost in her
mind. "Please tell me after this long day that
you have good news."

She listened as he told her about the bar, a
man named Hernandez and Briggs. "So you
have more proof he's violent?"

"Yes. He broke a man's jaw, but Briggs got

him to lie. I sent the information to Gabe, and he'll try to get a hearing just as soon as he can. It's information that will help you, but we really need something else. I'm waiting to hear from Amber, but I don't think we'll ever be able to prove that Briggs pushed Brooke down the stairs. I'm hoping, at least, that we can get enough information to secure Zoe's future."

Unable to resist, she hugged him around the waist. She expected him to be stiff, unyielding, but he actually returned the hug. Stepping back, she looked into his beautiful blue eyes, feeling warm all over. "Thank you."

His hand reached out toward her face. "You have flour in your hair."

"Oh." She brushed at her hair. "I just finished the pies. I'm sure I have flour all over myself."

He glanced at the pies cooling on a rack. "Grandma always did them in advance, too. Did you use her recipes?"

"I sure did."

"Her pies were the best I've ever eaten. I don't know what she put in them, but they're just good. Grandpa probably wouldn't eat the pie if you didn't make it by her recipe."

"Oh, yes, he pointed that out." She picked up the index card with "Cora's Pumpkin Pie" on it. It had food stains from years of use. She then reached for the pumpkin can on the counter. "It's the same as the recipe on the can."

His eyes narrowed. "No—"

"Compare them, Detective."

He took them from her hands and glanced from one to the other, disbelief etched on his face. "This can't be right." He looked up. "It must be in the crust, then. Did you use her pie crust recipe? It's flaky and out of this world. I never tasted pie crust like it before."

She picked up the card with "Cora's Pie Crust" and handed it to him. Then she picked up the Crisco can. "It's the same as the one on the Crisco can."

He shook his head. "Something's wrong. Did you tell my grandpa this?"

"No, but I figured you were strong enough to take it."

He frowned. If she had known it would upset him, she would never have said anything. She just thought it was amusing. She should've kept the amusing part to herself.

"Do you know what you're feeling when

you eat your grandmother's cooking, her pies?"

"No, but I'm sure you're going to tell me."

"It's the love she put into everything she cooked for you. That's what you feel."

His frown eased into a blank stare, and then he shook his head again. "You're making my head hurt." He turned on his heel and walked out of the kitchen.

She checked to make sure Mr. Walt and Zoe were okay and then followed Cole to his bedroom. The hall light was on, but his room was in darkness. She could see him sitting on the side of the bed. She sat down beside him.

"I didn't mean to upset you."

"As a child I waited and waited for a sign that my grandmother loved me, that she actually knew I was alive and not Jamie. And all the time... Looking back, I can see I was fixated on the bad stuff, but there really were some good times. Before Thanksgiving she would make this big chocolate cake. I love chocolate cake. I thought she made it from scratch, but who knows—it probably was from a box. It didn't matter. She made it for me, and it was delicious. She would say, 'Eat all you want, Cole. It's your birthday.' Even though I knew it wasn't my birthday, I soaked up all those good vibes. She'd call me by my name. Then she would kiss the top of my head. I'd forgotten that."

"She loved you the only way she could in her grief," Grace said.

"When Bo and I decided to join the Army, Grandpa said I had to tell her. She threw a fit and screamed, saying I couldn't go, that I would get killed and she would never see me again. She begged me not to leave, but I went anyway. That is something I will always regret." He took a long breath and ran his hands up his face. "Every time I came home on leave, she would have a chocolate cake waiting, and I had to take chocolate chip cookies with me when I left. That was my grandma. She cooked. Even though they weren't her own recipes, she cooked them better than anyone."

"Yes, she did," Grace replied, linking her arm through his. "Feel better?"

"Yes." He gazed at her through the darkness, and she could feel the warmth of his eyes. "I think I'm going to have to start calling you Amazing Grace."

"You do and I'll smack you."

"Have you ever smacked anyone?"

"No, but there's always a first time."

"I don't think so."

"Cole?"

"Hmm?"

"I really like you."

"I like you, too."

"But you have a girlfriend."

"Yeah. There's that."

The silence hung between them like a curtain that needed to be pushed aside, but he made no effort to do so. And she wasn't sure she wanted him to.

Rascal barked in the living room, and Grace got to her feet. "Zoe's awake, and I have to give her a bath and put her to bed." She walked out of the room, feeling something she couldn't explain.

She was getting too close. She cared too much about him, and she didn't want to upend his life, so she had to back away from her feelings. Besides, she had too much on her plate to get involved with anyone. He'd been too nice to her for her to do otherwise.

COLE WOKE UP at five and could hear voices in the kitchen. Grace was already up. She and Grandpa were getting an early start. He went to the bathroom, shaved and took a shower.

In his bedroom he put on jeans and a T-shirt and headed for the kitchen.

At Grace's door, he stopped. Zoe was in her bed, sitting up and playing with something. She wasn't crying. Unable to walk away, he stepped into the room. Zoe crawled to the rails and pulled herself up. She smiled at him, and he could see her two bottom teeth.

"Do you want out of there?" He had to stop talking baby talk. Jeez, that was annoying.

She held up her arms, and he lifted her out of the bed. He patted her back and then made his way to the kitchen.

Grandpa was at the stove, and Grace had her hands in some dough. Flour stained her blouse, and there was a smudge on her face and in her hair.

She glared at him. "Did you wake her up?"

"Nope."

"You have to feed her," she told him. "I'm busy making yeast rolls."

Feed her? Was Grace serious?

Grace nodded toward the counter. "Her cereal is there. Mix it with milk and zap it in the microwave." He followed the instructions and had to go around Grandpa to put it in the microwave, but soon he had the bowl in front of Zoe with a cup of coffee for himself. It was easy-peasy for a thirty-four-year-old man. She opened her mouth every time for a spoonful. Afterward, he took her into the living room to give her a bottle, mainly to get away from the two cooking fiends in the kitchen.

He sat in his grandmother's chair for the first time in years. He could almost feel her kissing the top of his head and saying, "You be good, Jamie." And he would say, "I'm not Jamie, Grandma." She would reply, "You be good, too, Cole."

Memories, the tearstains on his heart. But the thought didn't hurt like it used to. He glanced toward Grace in the kitchen, where she was punching down dough with her fist. Amazing Grace. She'd opened his heart. His mind. And now he was able to see a grieving old woman for who she really was—his grandmother, who'd loved him the best way she could.

Zoe fell asleep on his shoulder, and he put her back in her bed. Grace said she'd sleep about an hour. He went back to the kitchen to try to help before he had to leave for Austin, but soon realized he was more in the way than helping.

It was time to get ready for Thanksgiving dinner with Stephanie's parents. He changed into slacks and a long-sleeved white shirt. He sat on the bed and paused, looking down at his boots. What was wrong with boots? He wore them everywhere. Staying true to himself, he slipped them on.

In the kitchen he pulled Grace aside. "You really don't have to do all of this."

She glanced to Grandpa at the stove. "Oh, I think I do. It's helping him to deal with his grief."

Cole could see that. Grandpa was energized and seemed happy.

"Grace, we have to watch this turkey," Grandpa called.

"Okay," she called back.

He stared at her and wondered how someone could be filled with so much good. She didn't have any bad habits, except for biting her nails.

"What?" She caught him staring. "Flour in my hair?"

"Highlights," he said and tried not to smile. "Grandpa, I'm going."

Grandpa waved a hand. "Go. Grace and I are fine."

"Have a good time," Grace told him.

He thought about that as he got into his truck. Visiting with Harlan Myers was not his idea of a good time. He'd agreed to do it, and he tried to never break his word. But he and Stephanie would soon have to talk about their relationship.

The Myers family lived in Westlake, a very expensive neighborhood. There was a wrought iron fence around the big two-story home. He drove through the gate and parked at the front of the house. Several cars were near the garages. He glanced at the well-manicured lawn and walked to the front door. A maid in a black uniform and white apron answered the door.

"Cole Chisholm," he said.

She opened the door wider, and he stepped in.

"Cole!" Stephanie shouted and ran into his arms; the scent of perfume drifted to his nostrils. He held her for a moment, and she drew back and looked down at his feet. "You wore your boots." She fingered his jacket. "And a sport jacket."

He held out his arms. "This is me."

She patted his chest. "It doesn't matter. Come meet my family. They're in the den."

The house was glittery—that was the only word he could think of to describe it. Like a photo from a magazine, everything was in its place and everything looked expensive, from the polished floors to the paintings on the walls to the chandeliers. The den was much the same, with comfy chairs and sofas and a large area rug. Everyone held a wineglass, and they stood as he entered the room. Stephanie introduced him. He shook hands with the brother and his wife and the sister and her husband and Harlan and his wife, Kay. Four children sat on a small sofa, two boys and two girls. The boys wore white shirts with bow ties and slacks, and the girls wore frilly dresses with bows in their hair. They didn't move or show any reaction, and he thought they looked like mannequins sitting there. Usually kids were running and playing.

Harlan poured him a glass of wine. The man was of medium height, and there wasn't a speck of gray showing in his dark brown hair.

Cole took the glass and sat on a love seat with Stephanie. They talked about Thanksgiving and sports, and then Harlan leaned forward in his chair and said, "I've heard a lot of good things about you, Cole."

"Thank you."

"I've never had a case where you were involved on the other side."

"No." Cole didn't understand why the man was turning the conversation to him, but he could play it cool.

"I have a new client, and I think you know him."

"Who?"

Harlan swirled his wine for a second and then replied, "Joel Briggs."

Nothing showed on Cole's face. He made sure of that. "Yes. I met him yesterday, as I'm sure you know."

"He's getting a rough deal from the police department and asked for my help."

"The police have treated him very fairly. I'm not sure what his beef is."

"He wants his daughter, and I've been hired to make sure he gets her."

Without skipping a beat, Cole said, "I thought you were a criminal defense attorney."

"I wear many hats."

"For Joel Briggs to get his daughter, he first has to be cleared in Brooke Bennett's death."

"I'll see to that, too."

Cole carefully set his wineglass on the coffee table. "Mr. Myers, you and I have nothing else to say to each other." He stood and turned his gaze to Kay Myers. "Thank you for the invitation, but I really must go."

"Daddy, you promised," Stephanie accused.

"Harlan, how could you! You've ruined Thanksgiving."

Their voices trailed away as Cole headed for the front door and his truck.

"Cole!" Stephanie called, but he kept walking.

She caught him as he opened the door of his truck. "Cole, wait."

"Whatever you and I had, Stephanie, is over."

"Because of my dad?"

"Did he pressure you to invite me?"

"I invited you weeks ago."

"But the last couple of days he's pressured you, right?"

"Yes, but that has nothing to do with—"

"You're right, it has nothing to do with us." He waved his hand from her to him. "You and I don't jell. I like my boots, and I love my grandpa. I'm never putting him in a home, even if I have to quit my job to take care of him."

As he crawled into his truck, he realized the love he thought he'd never gotten as a child he'd gotten tenfold. He just hadn't recognized it.

"When you cool off, we'll talk."

"Don't call me ever again."

As he drove away, one thought ran through his mind—with Myers as Briggs's attorney, he would turn the custody battle into a power play. He'd confuse and intimidate the judge until Briggs would be granted full custody of Zoe.

Cole planned to combat that power. He drove to his office to do more digging. He had to find out more about Joel Briggs, even if it was Thanksgiving.

CHAPTER THIRTEEN

EVERYTHING WAS COMING together for Thanksgiving dinner. Grace thought the dressing was a little dry, so Mr. Walt added more broth. She had no idea how it was going to taste—Mr. Walt was the chef, and he was guiding her hands on everything.

The dinner was just about ready, and they were waiting on the rolls in the oven.

"Oh, no, Grace, we forgot the flowers. Cora always bought flowers for the table on Thanksgiving."

She patted him on the shoulder. "No worry, Mr. Walt. I'll figure out something for decoration."

She went to her room and searched around and came back with a red wool cap of Zoe's that had a white fuzzy ball on the top. She fitted it over the napkin holder. "How's that? It looks like a flower with a white bloom."

"Yes, it does. But what will we use for napkins?"

She reached into the cabinet and pulled out more napkins. "These."

"Okay, we're just about ready."

"While waiting on the rolls, I'm going to change. Keep an eye on Zoe, please."

From cooking in the kitchen, sweat clung to her body. She took a quick shower and changed into skinny jeans and a white turtleneck sweater. After brushing her hair and putting on lipstick, she slipped on her boots. Now, she was spruced up and ready for the holiday.

When Mr. Walt saw her, he said, "My, you're as pretty as a speckled pup in a red wagon on Christmas morning."

"Huh…thank you."

"Watch those rolls. I'm going to change, too. I'm all sweaty."

When he came back, he had on a clean shirt that wasn't flannel. He'd combed his hair, and she caught a whiff of Old Spice. She hugged him around the shoulders. "Happy Thanksgiving, Mr. Walt."

Mr. Walt carved the turkey, and they ate. The food was better than she had expected, and she really liked the sweet potatoes. Grace was nervous about the pumpkin pie, but Mr. Walt loved it and so did Zoe. Mr. Walt finally pushed back from the table.

"That was just like Cora cooked. Thank you, Grace."

"You're welcome, Mr. Walt."

"Now I'm going to take a nap."

Grace cleaned up Zoe and put her down for a nap. Then she cleaned the kitchen and crashed on the sofa. Rascal's barking woke her. She glanced at the old clock on the wall and saw it was almost three o'clock. Good heavens! She jumped up and went to get Zoe.

She played with the baby for a while until she noticed an old record player and records in a corner. "Mr. Walt, are those some old albums?"

"You betcha. Seventy-eights. Cora and I used to go dancing every Saturday night at the VFW hall. Bertie and her husband would be there, too. We always had a good time. As we got older, it wasn't quite so often, but we still went dancing, until…"

The words hung in the air. Grace didn't mention Jamie. Suddenly Mr. Walt got up and went to the record player and pulled out an album. "Do you like to dance?"

"I used to, but after my mom's injury, I didn't have time."

"You ever heard of Ernest Tubb, Ray Price or Bob Wills?"

"No."

"Well, young lady, you're going to learn something." He reached for an album and put it on the record player. Grace was surprised that it worked. Chords of "Waltz Across Texas" filled the room.

"Let's move this coffee table and roll back the rug."

"What?"

Before she could blink, Mr. Walt had pushed the coffee table toward the patio doors. She helped him roll the rug toward the sofa. He hurriedly started the record again, and she found herself waltzing around the living room with Mr. Walt. Then he put on an Elvis Presley record and "Jailhouse Rock" came on. She jitterbugged until she giggled like a teenager, as Mr. Walt danced the sadness away with memories of olden times.

It was a moment out of time for her, too. She hadn't thought about Brooke and her death all morning. But the future was waiting just beyond the Chisholm home.

How she wished Cole was here.

COLE WAS ELBOW-DEEP in Parker's files, and he hadn't found anything out of sync. It was frustrating. The squad room was almost empty since it was a holiday, so he went to the internet to see if he could find out anything about Joel Briggs. He learned that Briggs's parents moved to Austin when he was twelve. He didn't attend a Texas college, nor did he play for a Texas NFL team. He only came back to Texas after he retired.

His parents had moved into the Westlake area a few years ago. They probably were friends with Myers and his family. The connection fit. He wondered, though, why Briggs's parents didn't want to see their grandchild. He had no clue about that one. Unless they didn't know about Zoe.

He sat back in his chair, trying to figure out how he could get personal information about Briggs. Cole found lots of information about his football career and his statistics, but very little personal information, even on Facebook and Instagram.

He snapped his fingers. He had it. He pulled his cell out of his pocket and called Lamar. It was Thanksgiving, but he would only keep him a minute. The man answered immediately, and there was a lot of noise and chatter in the background.

"Hey, Lamar, happy Thanksgiving."

"You, too, Cole. Wait a minute." There was

a long pause. "Dori wants to know if you need Thanksgiving dinner."

"No, thank you. That's been taken care of."

Lamar shouted to Dori, and it was a moment before he came back.

"I won't keep you, but I was hoping I could get LJ's number from you."

"You can talk to him yourself. He's right here."

A little luck for a change.

"Hey, Cole, what's up?"

"Happy Thanksgiving, man. I'm glad you made it home for the holiday."

"I flew in early this morning and fly out early this afternoon, but I wanted my wife to see where I come from. I wanted her to see my roots."

"That's great, LJ."

"Why do you want to talk to me?"

"I wanted to see if you knew Joel Briggs. He's involved in a case I'm working on, and I have very little personal information."

"Before he retired, we played against his team a few times. He's a bruiser. He'll hurt you if he can. He's put the hurt on a lot of quarterbacks."

"Yeah, I know all that. I was hoping for something more personal."

"Well, his wife used to attend the games."

Cole sat up straight in his chair. "He's married."

"I think he's divorced. When we played them, she was in the stands. I guess someone alerted the camera people, and the camera was on her a lot. She's a model, a gorgeous blonde."

"Do you know her name?"

"Oh, man, I can't remember. It something short like Kati or Jilli or…Niki… I think that's it. I know the name ended in an *i*."

"Thanks, LJ, this helps a lot. Enjoy Thanksgiving."

"I wish I had time to bring my wife to meet you."

"Maybe next time."

"You got it."

Cole went back to the internet, searching for models with the name Niki. It didn't take long before he found her: Niki Reed. He sent her a message on Facebook telling her who he was and saying he needed to talk to her as soon as possible. He gave her his cell number. Since it was Thanksgiving, he probably wouldn't hear back from her until tomorrow. Or she might not answer at all. She must get thousands of messages. But she might give him something to go on, something about the breakup of her marriage. But he had a sinking feeling he was running out of time.

He stretched his shoulders and realized he was hungry. He hadn't eaten all day, and it was past four in the afternoon. He wanted Thanksgiving dinner, and he knew where to find it.

On his way to Horseshoe, his cell buzzed. He fished it out of his pocket and glanced at the caller ID: Niki Reed. He hadn't expected her to call so quickly. He pulled over to the side of the road.

"Ms. Reed, I'm glad to hear from you so quickly."

"Why did you leave me a message? Is something wrong? The girl who takes care of my social media said the cops were looking for me."

"I'd like to ask you some questions about Joel Briggs."

"Joel? For heaven's sake, I haven't seen him in years. I'm on a shoot in France, and I don't have time to talk about Joel. As a matter of fact, I'd rather not talk about him at all."

He told her about Brooke and Briggs and what had happened. "I don't want to invade your privacy, but could you tell me a little bit about what happened in your marriage?"

"I didn't enjoy being hit. The first time, he said he was sorry and he didn't mean it and I let it go. The second time, he said he was sorry and would get counseling. I believed him. He didn't, and I packed my bags and left."

"That's the same story Brooke Bennett told."

"Then she's telling the truth. He doesn't like it when things don't go his way. My face is my living, and I wasn't letting him screw that up. He's good at lying. He lied to me so many times. I thought one day we would have children, but then I found out he had a vasectomy before we even met."

"What? Wait a minute. He had a vasectomy?"

"Yes. He told me there was no use for birth control because he had a vasectomy to keep from having unwanted babies. He doesn't want children, and he forgot to mention that little fact when we were dating."

Cole told her about Zoe.

"Well, I guess he could've had it reversed, but I'd be very skeptical about that. He was adamant about not having children back then."

"Thank you, Ms. Reed, for taking the time to call me back. This is going to help a great deal."

After she clicked off, Cole sat there thinking. This was the missing piece that would make everything fit together. Make everything make sense. But it didn't. If Joel wasn't the father, then who was? It might explain why Zoe didn't live with Brooke and Briggs. If she'd cheated on him, why did he let her stay? The question bugged him, because he couldn't figure it out.

It occupied his mind all the way to his grandpa's house. He had to ask Grace more questions to see if he'd missed something. As he opened the back door to tell Grandpa he was home as he always did, he heard music. Music?

He walked toward the living room and stopped in his tracks. Grandpa and Grace were dancing, and the music was turned up loud. Zoe sat in the Pack 'n Play clapping. How did this happen? How long had he been gone?

His grandpa noticed him. "Oh, Cole, come dance with Grace. I have to sit down and catch my breath."

A slow Ray Price song came on, and Grace drifted into his arms. Without a second thought, they moved to the beat and sailed across the living room floor. It seemed as if he'd danced with her all his life. Bo's mom had taught Bo and Cole how to dance, and they'd stepped on her toes many a time. But today he wasn't stepping on Grace's toes.

The music stopped, and they swayed together as one.

"The song ended," she said.

"I know. This is nice."

"Yes," she replied in a soft voice.

"Hey, the record stopped. Fix that, Cole."

Sometimes his grandpa was really annoying.

He closed the record player, rolled the rug back into place and pushed the coffee table to the center of the room. "Now I'm ready to eat Thanksgiving dinner. I hope there's some left."

"Oh, yes. We have plenty left." Grace hurried to the kitchen.

Zoe stretched her arms over the Pack 'n Play. Cole lifted her out and patted her back. It was quite easy now to hold her. It was natural.

"Bring her to me," Grandpa said, and Cole placed Zoe in his lap.

"Don't let her go to sleep, Mr. Walt."

"Oh, she's always harping about that."

Cole walked into the kitchen and watched as Grace put things into the oven.

"Did you eat lunch?" Grace asked.

"No." He told her what had happened at the Myerses' home.

Grace wiped her hands on a dish towel. "He's representing Joel?"

"Yes. And that's not good. He's an expert at twisting the truth, and I'm not going to whitewash this for you. If the custody case goes to court, Myers will mangle the truth and you'll lose Zoe."

"Oh, Cole, no." Sadness clouded her eyes, and he could feel it all away to his heart. In that moment, he knew that he'd never had these overpowering emotions for Stephanie like he had for Grace. And he'd only known her for a few days. He wanted to protect her, be there for her to make all her problems go away. He wanted to love her...

As the word resounded in his head, he thought he would never get to that point where he could actually feel love. But it was right there...

"I don't plan to let that happen," he told her. "Did you know Briggs was married before?"

She brushed back her dark hair, and he noticed the bruise on her forehead was almost healed. It was only slightly red now. "Married? No. Brooke never mentioned that."

"I talked to his ex this afternoon, and she told me something interesting."

"What?"

"That Briggs had a vasectomy."

Her eyes opened wide. "That can't be true. There's Zoe." He gave her a moment for that to sink in.

"Briggs told Parker that Brooke cheated on him numerous times. Do you know who else she was seeing?"

Fire lit up her eyes. "Brooke wasn't like that. She was crazy about Joel, and the only person she saw other than Joel was the intern."

"What was his name?"

"She never said, because it wasn't serious. It was just a platonic relationship. He was separated from a wife he loved and needed someone to talk to. She was separated from Joel and needed someone to talk to. They were just good friends."

He didn't push it because Grace was upset. DNA would prove paternity. He could get the intern's name at the hospital.

Grace turned toward the stove. "You should've eaten lunch with your girlfriend. She must've been very upset."

"We broke up."

She turned from the stove. "What? Why?"

"She didn't like my cowboy boots." He reached out and touched the tip of her nose with his forefinger and left her to figure that out.

GRACE RUSHED TO put supper on the table. She didn't quite understand what Cole meant about his boots and his girlfriend, and she wanted to question him more. As they made to sit down, Miss Bertie walked in.

"Hey, Bertie," Mr. Walt called. "Have a seat."

"I just came to see if you starved to death."

"Nope," Mr. Walt told her, waving a hand toward Grace. "This young lady cooked a fine meal. Sit down and have some."

"I'm stuffed, but I'll sit and visit for a while." She took a seat on the other side of Mr. Walt.

Grace placed a plate and utensils in front of her. "Just in case you change your mind."

Cole poured the tea, and before they could sit down, the door opened again.

"Hey, anyone home?"

"Come on in here, Bo," Grandpa called.

A tall dark-haired, dark-eyed man stood in the doorway. At first glance, Grace sensed he was a man who lived life to the fullest. He had a strong jaw with a five o'clock shadow that ramped up his handsomeness. There seemed to be a permanent grin on his face, but she noticed the sadness that rimmed his eyes.

Mr. Walt pointed to her and Zoe. "That's Grace and Zoe Grace. Take a seat." The other man shook Mr. Walt's hand and sat next to Miss Bertie near Zoe.

"I just came by to have a beer with Mr. Walt. I always do that on a holiday."

"And I have beer," Mr. Walt said.

Bo glanced at Zoe in her high chair. "Hey, kiddo."

Zoe pulled away from him, scared of the beard. Her little face wrinkled into a frown.

"You're scaring the baby with all that hair," Miss Bertie said.

"Hey, little one, I'm not that scary."

Zoe pulled farther away and looked for Grace. "It's okay," Grace told her. "It's Bo. Cole's friend."

Bo stared at Grace. "You know, Cole, you never mentioned Grace was beautiful."

"Ah, he doesn't notice things like that," Mr. Walt said.

"Have you lost all your marbles, Walt?" Miss Bertie jumped in. "All men notice things like that, even you."

"Cora would say knockers," Mr. Walt said in a faraway voice.

"Yeah," Miss Bertie agreed. "She was one of a kind."

A moment of sadness lingered in the room.

"Could we just eat?" Cole asked.

They finally started the meal, and Grace listened avidly as Mr. Walt and Miss Bertie told stories about Cole and Bo. They laughed and teased, and at times Cole laughed out loud. It was a joy to hear.

"Bertie, remember that time they tried to make beer?"

"You know, they scared poor Cora to death, not to mention the chickens and the cows."

"You see, Grace, these two—" Mr. Walt pointed to Cole and Bo "—decided to make their own beer because no one would sell it to them. They were sixteen years old. They ordered the bottles out of some magazine, which I knew nothing about. They were in such a hurry, they forgot to let it ferment. They poured it into the bottles and set them up on shelves in the barn. The concoction started to ferment, swelling inside the bottles, and eventually the bottle caps popped off. It sounded like gunshots. I ran outside to see what was going on. I walked into the barn and saw that mess, and Cole was right behind me. He looked at the bottles and liquid on the floor and said, 'That didn't work.'"

Everyone laughed, and then Mr. Walt said, "Jamie—"

"Don't say it, Mr. Walt," Grace said. The words came out before she could stop them. She knew he was going to compare Jamie to Cole again.

"I wasn't."

"Yes, you were."

"All right, I was, but not in a bad way."

"What are you two going on about?" Miss Bertie asked.

"Ah, she's always on me about comparing Jamie to Cole."

"Well, you shouldn't."

It didn't escape Grace that Cole and Bo shared glances.

"I was going to say that Jamie wasn't adventurous or didn't have spunk like Cole. That's not bad, is it?" Mr. Walt shook his head at Grace, and she tried hard not to smile.

"Jamie was a mama's boy," Miss Bertie remarked.

"Yep, he sure was," Mr. Walt agreed. "After losing two stillborn babies, Cora clung to Jamie, and she never wanted to let him go. Whoever thought it would end so badly."

There was silence in the room as the sadness returned. Cole sat by Grace, and she reached out and touched his hand on his thigh. He curled his fingers around hers and spared her a slight smile. From the warmth in his eyes, she could see that talk of his father didn't bother him like it had before.

This was what family was about—sharing, loving, laughing and dealing with the pain when it came. This was what it was like to be part of a family, knowing someone was always there for you. That all-consuming feeling was something she wanted to hold to her chest, this moment in time that she would never forget.

CHAPTER FOURTEEN

THE NEXT MORNING Cole was up early. He showered and changed clothes and went straight to Grace's room. He heard a little voice that drew him like a magnet.

"Hey, smooches," he said to Zoe as she leaned over the crib.

He lifted her out, and she rubbed her sleepy face against his. He kissed her cheek. "Are you sleepy?"

"After all the visiting last night, it was late when I put her to bed," Grace said from the doorway. She was wearing a bathrobe, her hair was wet from the shower and he stared a moment longer than he should have.

"Do you want me to put her back in bed?"

"No. I'll feed her breakfast and then she'll take a nap."

"I'll take her to the kitchen and put her in her chair," he offered.

Grace followed and watched as he poured a cup of coffee.

"Are you leaving early?"

"Yeah. I'm hoping to talk to Amber this morning. I'm also hoping for good news."

"Cole." Her shoulders sagged, and she bit on a fingernail. "I couldn't sleep last night thinking that this high-powered lawyer can just take Zoe."

"Hey." He pulled her hand from her mouth. "I'm on the case, and we're not done yet. There are still a lot of questions to be answered. And the autopsy still hasn't come in. Just keep the faith."

"I just want to bury my sister." Her voice cracked, and Cole gathered her into his arms.

"Try to think positive thoughts. We'll get through this."

"We?" she murmured.

"Yeah. I started this with you, and I'm not going to stop until it's finished. If I don't get much from Amber, I'll have to make another visit to Deuces."

"Why?"

"I still need a reason why Brooke took the waitress job, and I have a feeling it has to do with Briggs's gambling habit. Of course, I have to prove that."

She leaned back, and he kissed her lips lightly. "Take care of my grandpa."

"He's not up yet. He's tired after yesterday."

"I checked in on him, and he's snoring away. Call me if anything comes up. I'll see you later tonight."

"Cole!" she shouted as he headed for the door. She handed him his cup of coffee.

"Thanks." Just what he needed. He took one glance at her shining face and forced himself to leave.

On his way into Austin, his cell buzzed. It was Amber.

"I got your message. Where do you want to meet?"

"I'm on my way in. I'll meet you at the ER."

Fifteen minutes later he was at the hospital and found Amber. An ambulance had just brought in a patient and paramedics were standing around talking.

"Is this about Brooke?" she asked.

"Yes."

Tears filled her blue eyes and she pulled a Kleenex out of her scrubs pocket. "I warn you, I'm going to cry. I'm still not over this. I can't believe she's gone."

Cole gave her a minute. "I just want to be clear on a few things. Can you answer some questions?"

"Sure."

"After the first meeting of Brooke and Briggs here in the ER, who made the first move?"

"He did. He came in here the next day looking for her. Heather and I were at the desk, and Brooke was in a room."

"And it snowballed from there?"

"Yes. She was in love, and nothing anyone said made a difference."

"Do you know anything about their personal relationship?"

"He hit her a lot, and she continued to stay."

"Why would she do that?"

"Her answer was always the same—she loved him and he was getting help."

"This might be a difficult question, but why would she leave her child for him?"

Amber moved uncomfortably in her chair and wiped at her nose. "It was complicated."

"Uncomplicate it for me. It's very important."

"He was always on about Brooke cheating on him, and when she got pregnant with Zoe he said the baby wasn't his. Brooke was devastated and stayed with Grace. But she started talking to Joel, trying to convince him that Zoe was his, and she talked him into a trial period. So she took Zoe to his place to live as a family. That's what she wanted most. It lasted about a week before Joel told her to get the kid out of the house. He wasn't raising someone else's kid."

Briggs knew Zoe wasn't his. But that didn't explain why Brooke stayed.

"Why didn't Brooke leave then?"

Amber shrugged. "She loved him, and she thought she could change his mind. And Grace was there to take good care of Zoe. It just went so horribly wrong."

By the tone of her voice, he knew she meant something else besides Brooke's death.

"Did you know that Brooke had another job?"

"Yeah." She sniffled. "She said Joel was in a financial bind and she had to help him. When I asked how she was doing that, she wouldn't answer me. But I knew she had another job, because she was always late for work. The night before she died, she called me crying, upset."

"About what?"

"She came home early from her other job and caught Joel in bed with another woman. I think that's when she knew the dream of being a family was gone. She called me about three in the morning and came over. She was so upset. I'd never seen her that way. I tried to calm her down and started to call Grace, but she wouldn't let me. She said she could take care of this herself. At six she went back over to Joel's apartment. I tried to stop her, but again, she never listened to me. She said she was packing her things and leaving and she was done with Joel. The next thing I know, Grace calls and tells me Brooke is dead."

She dabbed at her eyes. "I should've told Grace. I should've—" She paused. "I'm getting married in March, and Brooke was going to be my maid of honor. Now she won't be there because I did nothing. I let that man abuse her, and I didn't say anything. Joel pushed her down those stairs. I know it. How am I supposed to live with that?"

"There was nothing you could've done. I see this in my work all too often. Women claim they're in love and allow the abuse to go on and try to change the man. It never happens. All you can do now is be there for Grace and Zoe." He didn't have any other answers for her. So many people had tried to help Brooke, but you can't help anyone unless they're willing to get help. That was a sad bottom line. He saw that all too often, too.

"Did you tell the detectives any of this?"

"Yes, I did, but Parker said I was lying. Joel had told him a completely different story, and he believed Joel. Grace talked to him, too, and he didn't believe her, either. It was very upsetting."

Cole hadn't seen a statement from Amber in the file. He would definitely ask Parker.

"I have one more question, and I want you to think before you answer."

"Okay."

"Did Brooke see anyone else while she was separated from Briggs?"

"Of course not. She was besotted with the man."

"You didn't think first."

"Oh."

He gave her a minute.

"I can't think of anyone. She and Kevin went out for a drink one night. He was separated from his wife and feeling down, and Brooke was, too. So they commiserated together. She told me she was home by nine. It was just a onetime thing, and they were friends. That was it."

One time was all that it took. "Kevin Colson?"

"Yes. He works here and is very nice. He's

back together with his wife now, and they're expecting another baby." She frowned. "Why are you asking the question?"

"Briggs accused her of cheating, and I'm just trying to find answers."

"Well, she wasn't. He was. Enough said."

Cole took a statement from her, and she signed it. After that he headed for the station to talk to Parker. He found Parker and Tenney at their desks.

He laid a file in front of Parker.

Parker's eyebrows nodded together. "What's this?"

"The result of my investigation."

He leaned back with a smug expression. "I don't have time to read nonsense. I told you the case was all but closed. We're just waiting on the autopsy. Stirring up controversy isn't helping."

Cole poked the folder. "This is not controversy. This is fact. And it's laid out for you in case you have a problem reading. Briggs did not hurt his wrist in the park playing football with kids. He hurt his hand and broke Allan Hernandez's jaw in a bar fight. The man had to have surgery and is still experiencing pain. Brooke did not chase Briggs. He was the one who came back to the ER to get her number.

He did the chasing. I have witnesses' statements confirming this. And why isn't there a statement from Amber Lewis?"

"Oh, she was going on and on about a bunch of nonsense. None of it made sense. She was just trying to cause trouble for Joel."

"Like Grace Bennett?"

"Well—"

"Your investigative skills are off, Parker, but that's not my concern. Right now I'm more concerned about Joel Briggs's hold over you."

"I resent that."

Cole let that slide. "I also talked to his ex-wife."

Parker sat up straight. "He's been married? He told us he'd never been married."

"He told you a pack of lies."

"I told you something was off." Tenney got to his feet and came to the desk, reading over Parker's shoulder.

"He's had a vasectomy?" Tenney asked in disbelief.

"That's what his ex-wife said. He could've had it reversed, but we don't know that."

Parker leaned back in his chair, the lines of his face drawn. "Oh, man. He played me."

"Yes, he did." Cole didn't hold back the punches. Parker deserved them.

"Are you with me or against me?" Cole asked.

Parker leaned forward. "I'm with you. Let's nail this SOB."

"First, we need to get Briggs's DNA, and second, I'm going to see if I can find a judge to get a warrant to search Deuces."

Parker stood. "Whatever for?"

"I know Briggs is a habitual gambler, and I need to prove it. The only way to do that is to talk to someone at Deuces, and they're not going to talk to me without a warrant. We know Briggs lied about the argument the morning Brooke died. She told him she was leaving, and that meant his cash cow was leaving, too. He had to stop her. I just have to prove it. We may never be able to prove he pushed her, but we have enough to put him away for a while."

"It's a holiday. I don't think you're going to find a judge." Tenney spoke up.

"I'll find one," Cole promised and headed out to do just that. He had to be careful and not be annoying, because he knew all judges were on holiday. He'd already asked for one favor from a judge and had to try another one.

He settled on Judge Bruhouser. He'd always been very accommodating, and Cole hoped he would be today.

It took time to get in touch with him and explain the situation. Cole didn't mention a lot of things, but he wanted questions answered for Grace. And those answers were at Deuces. He got the warrant for illegal gambling with reference to a minor child's safety. He also got a warrant for DNA for Briggs. After a stern lecture, reminding Cole of the holiday, he got more than he wanted.

Back at the station, they talked about strategy. Cole would go in alone to talk to the manager or Penetti. But the man had clubs in Houston, Dallas and San Antonio, and he wasn't likely to be there. Cole would take his chances with the manager. Parker and Tenney would offer backup on the outside. They also had patrol cars outside just for effect. Cole was bluffing. He might be a gambler, after all.

With everyone in place, Cole knocked on the locked door. It was three o'clock in the afternoon, and the place wasn't open. The young Mexican boy let him in.

"We no open, Mr. Cop."

"The manager, is he in?"

"He's in his office." The boy pointed to the back.

Cole walked past the bar and down the hall. He was stopped by two guards—or bouncers. He wasn't sure.

"Where do you think you're going?" one of them asked.

Cole held up the warrant in his hand and introduced himself. "I have a warrant to search this place."

The other man laughed. "You and who else?"

"The cops outside and the ones in the back. I'm just the announcement."

One of the men banged on the manager's door. "Hey, Al, there's a cop out here who has a warrant."

The door swung open, and a bald man in his forties stood there with a scowl. "What's this about?"

Cole handed him the warrant. "Cops are outside ready to go, but maybe we can settle this another way."

Al walked back to his desk, reading the warrant. "What the… This doesn't even make sense. Minor child? There are no children here."

"Brooke Bennett. She had a child."

"Well, the child's not here." He threw the warrant on the desk. "This is a bunch of bull."

Cole leaned over and read his name plate on the desk. "Mr. Carbaco, it's a legal warrant. I can have cops in here in less than a minute, and I'll turn this place upside down. You can count on not opening tonight. You can stop all that by answering a few questions."

His eyes narrowed. "What kind of questions?"

"About Brooke Bennett and Joel Briggs."

Carbaco got to his feet. "Give me a minute. I have to clear this with Penetti." He left the room.

Cole looked around. Stacks of cards wrapped in plastic were lined up on shelves. There was a seal on each one, so as to keep everyone honest, so to speak. A big ashtray full of cigarette butts was on the desk. The pungent scent irritated his senses. Expensive cigars in boxes were also stacked on a shelf. Skimpy outfits were on a rack in the corner. Short skirts and bikini tops. They were all shiny black material with lace around the edges. Brooke had been pulled into the seedier side of Briggs's life. For love. Nothing about that relationship had been about love.

Carbaco came back and plopped into his

chair, the scowl a little deeper. The fluorescent light glinted off his bald head. "Penetti said to give you what you need. Up to a point. And he is contacting his lawyer."

That would probably make Myers's day, although it might be a conflict of interest for him to be a lawyer for both Penetti and Briggs. Cole wasn't worried about that.

"How often does Briggs come in here?"

Carbaco shrugged. "I don't keep track of him."

"Mr. Carbaco, if you're not honest with me, I will go ahead with the search. I know this is a gambling establishment. I know you do illegal things here, but I'm not interested in that. All I'm interested in is Joel Briggs and Brooke Bennett."

Carbaco moved restlessly in his chair. "He comes in often, especially for the big games."

"How much was he into Penetti for?"

"You know I can't answer that."

"You will answer the question. I have no interest in Penetti's gambling. I've made that clear and if you don't cooperate—"

"About fifty thousand."

"How did Briggs plan to pay that?"

"Brooke."

"Waitressing?"

"Yes."

"She did it of her own free will?"

"Joel talked her into it. Penetti said pay or else. He didn't give her much choice. She hated it. She hated men touching her, but they liked her. She was naive and shy, and that turned them on. She made a lot of money, especially on big nights with big winners. Some would tuck hundred-dollar bills in her cleavage or skirt."

"How much of the money had she managed to pay back?"

"About twenty-five thousand." He moved restlessly again. "She called the morning she died—quit and said she wasn't coming back. And that Joel could pay his own debts."

The morning she found Joel in bed with another woman, and it had finally opened her eyes. But she hadn't been counting on Joel's vengeance.

"Has Penetti let Briggs back in?"

"Not since Brooke's death. Joel promised he would have the money in a few days. After that—" Carbaco shrugged.

Cole leaned over and laid a piece of paper from the printer on his desk in front of Carbaco. "I'll need that in writing."

Carbaco held up his hands. "No, man, I'm

not implicating Deuces. I gave you the answers as promised. I'm done."

"I'm not. Write that Briggs came in here to gamble and he owed a large sum of money. And that Brooke Bennett worked to help pay it off. And that she quit the morning she died. Simple and sweet. Sign and date it."

He got the statement and went out to tell Parker and Tenney. They agreed to meet back at the station. As they talked in the office about their next move, the fax machine came on. Cole got up to see what it was: Brooke Bennett's autopsy report. He read through it and placed it in front of Parker.

"That was quick," Parker said. "We weren't expecting it till Monday."

"Read it. We don't have to prove he pushed her."

Parker swallowed a few times, and his face turned red. "Man, this is horrible. How could I believe that slime bag?"

Tenney took the report from him and read, "'Blunt force trauma to the head, possibly by balled fist. Homicide violence.' It goes on to say that her brain was bleeding when she walked out or was pushed out the door. The hemorrhage caused extreme dizziness. The fall exacerbated the bleeding. All other injuries, besides the wrist and the neck, were consistent with the fall."

A spiral of relief rose up in Cole's chest. Grace had been right. Briggs killed Brooke.

Cole pointed a finger at Parker. "You need to apologize to Grace Bennett. She wasn't so crazy after all."

"Yeah." Parker hung his head. "I plan to do that, but first let's arrest this lowlife."

"Let's go," Cole said as they headed for the door. "It's going to be a joy to put handcuffs on him and watch him squirm."

Cole's cell buzzed, and he pulled it out of his pocket. Grace. He clicked on, and he couldn't understand her because she was crying. His heart did a nosedive. "Grace, calm down and tell me what happened."

"He took Zoe. Joel took Zoe, and he hit Mr. Walt. He took Zoe, Cole. She was crying and crying and he wouldn't let me get near her. He backhanded me."

His stomach clenched. "Are you okay? Is Grandpa okay?"

"We're just shaken up. Please find Zoe. She was screaming for me."

"How long ago did this happen?"

"Just now. There was a man and a woman with him."

"Did you see what he was driving?"

"A gold Cadillac Escalade."

"Stay calm and take care of Grandpa. I'm on this. I'll get Zoe back." He didn't have time to tell her about the autopsy. He needed to be with her when he did that. Right now his top priority was Zoe.

"Briggs kidnapped Zoe," he told the guys. "We have to find him. Grace said there was a man and a woman with him. My guess is he's found a way to pay his debts."

"What do you mean?" Parker asked.

"He has a buyer for Zoe."

CHAPTER FIFTEEN

GRACE HURRIED TO the refrigerator for ice. She wrapped several cubes into a towel and carried it to Mr. Walt. Her hands were shaky and clammy. "Put this on your face—it will help with the swelling. I'm going to call Miss Bertie and see if she will come and stay here for a little while. I'm taking Bertha and following Joel. I feel he's going back into Austin, and I'm going to try and find him."

Mr. Walt sat up straight. "You're not going anywhere without me."

She didn't need this right now. The longer she waited, the more time Joel had to get away. She had to go. "You're hurt, Mr. Walt." She touched the dark bruise on his face. "You need to rest."

He got to his feet. "I'm as tough as pork rind fried up and left out a few days."

Grace shook her head. "Mr. Walt, I don't know what that means. I have to go. Zoe needs me."

Mr. Walt headed for the door. "Let's go, then."

Grace grabbed two bottles out of the refrigerator and the diaper bag. In less than a minute, they were in Bertha and backing out of the garage. Grace handed Mr. Walt the towel with ice. "Put this on your face." When he started to object she added, "Now!"

Grace's heart pounded as she turned on to Highway 77 and raced toward I-35. She had to find Zoe. She had been crying so hard. Grace had never seen her cry like that. She knew she should just stay home and wait for Cole, but she couldn't do that. Zoe needed her.

Mr. Walt rolled down the window and threw out the towel and ice.

"Mr. Walt!"

"Well, it's cold and I don't like it."

"That's littering."

"So? Arrest me."

"I'm upset with you." She zigzagged around cars and tried to focus on the road.

"I'm upset, too. That big oaf took our baby."

She patted his shoulder. "I know, Mr. Walt. We'll get her back. Cole is trying very hard, and I trust him."

"Yep, he's a good boy."

Boy? Grace didn't see him as a boy. And

that was a whole other problem. Right now her focus was the traffic.

"Mr. Walt, let's see if Bertha can fly."

EVERYTHING HAPPENED FAST. Every officer in Austin was on alert for a gold Cadillac Escalade. It didn't take long to get a hit. The vehicle was located at a Valero gas station outside Austin. Cole and Parker headed there. The car was parked to the side. Empty.

Cole and Parker went inside to talk to the clerk. Cole took the lead. He introduced himself to the cashier. "I'd like some information on the Cadillac parked outside."

The clerk was busy waiting on customers, but he quickly turned to Cole. "The man said the engine was making a funny noise and a wrecker would pick it up later. He gave me a hundred dollars to not call the police."

Parker handed him a photo. "Was it this guy?"

The clerk nodded his head. "He said he was a football player, but I don't watch football."

"Was he alone?" Cole asked.

"No. There was another man and a woman and a baby. The baby was crying loudly. The man said she'd just woken up from a nap."

"How did they leave?"

"Uber."

"Thank you," Cole said as he and Parker walked outside.

"What do you think?" Parker asked.

"Briggs knows we're looking for his Cadillac, and he ditched it until he can get Zoe somewhere where we can't find her. I'm thinking airport." He reached for his phone. "Tenney, Briggs left his Cadillac at a Valero station." He gave him the address. "He used Uber to leave. Try to find where the driver took him. Get Nate to help you. He knows a lot about Uber."

"Got it," Tenney replied.

Next he called Austin-Bergstrom International Airport and identified himself. It took a while to get through to the proper person. He'd been through this before—the airport was always very cooperative. He had the information within ten minutes and without getting a subpoena. All he had to do was mention a child was in danger. It was the truth.

He slipped his phone back into his pocket. "Briggs is leaving at eight o'clock tonight for Las Vegas without Zoe. We have to catch him before he gets to the airport. I would rather not have a scene there."

"What do you think his plan is?" Parker asked.

"Briggs left the Cadillac here to throw us off. And the couple with him have to be the buyers for Zoe, just as Brooke had told Grace. He's taking them somewhere, maybe to their home. There's no way to verify that."

"We have officers at Briggs's apartment. I'll call and see if they've noticed anything." Parker took out his phone as Cole searched the Cadillac.

"No movement at Joel's apartment," Parker told him.

"The car's locked up, and since it's a rental, I'm sure the dealership will pick it up. The keys are lying on the dash. Briggs is not planning on coming back."

As they walked to the patrol car, Cole's phone pinged. He answered immediately. "Let's go!" he shouted to Parker. "Briggs is back at the apartment with the couple and Zoe. What a stupid move."

They blasted through traffic with the siren blaring. Cole turned off the siren as he neared the complex and put on his mic. "Stay out of sight," he said to the officers on the scene.

"They went inside and they haven't come out," Officer Collins said. "The baby was crying, and the woman was complaining that she cries too much."

Cole gritted his teeth and replied, "Stay on the alert and out of sight." He then called SWAT for backup. This could get messy, and he didn't want one thing to happen to Zoe.

The security gate had been breached. That meant SWAT was on the scene. Cole parked some distance away, and then he and Parker walked toward Briggs's apartment. He could see SWAT members already on the roof across from Briggs's apartment. They were only visible to those who knew they were there. Out of the corner of his eye, he saw a flash of blue through the gates. Oh, no! Grace and Grandpa were here.

He spoke into his mic. "There's a blue Buick coming through the gate. Stop it and don't let it get any closer. Wait for my orders."

The front door of Briggs's apartment opened, and Cole put everything else out of his mind. He had to focus. Briggs and the couple came out and started down the stairs. The woman was holding Zoe, who was crying softly.

"Wait for my orders," he said into the mic again.

The trio went to a silver Lexus parked at

the curb. Cole glanced at Parker. "You circle to the front of the car, and I'll get the back. We can trap them between the cars. Let's go." Into the mic he said, "We're going in. Back us up."

With guns drawn, he and Parker made their move. Briggs was stunned when he saw the guns pointed at him.

"What's going on here?" Briggs asked.

When Zoe saw Cole, she started to cry louder, reaching out for him.

His heart ached, but he had to stay focused. He spoke into the mic. "Let the woman in the blue Buick in to take the baby."

Running feet sounded on the pavement and echoed through the chilly day. Grace made it in record time and reached for Zoe, who was screaming at the top of her lungs now.

The woman pulled Zoe back. "No! This is my baby."

"She's not your baby," Grace told her and jerked Zoe away. Zoe sobbed on her shoulder.

"Go!" Cole shouted to Grace, and she took off running again. Zoe's sobs died away.

"I don't know what's going on," the man said. "But my wife and I paid money for that baby. The mother is dead and Mr. Briggs signed over his rights to us. The baby is ours."

"I don't know what Mr. Briggs has told you, but the baby does not belong to him."

Briggs appealed to Parker. "Hey, Parker, what are you doing? You know I'm that baby's father. You offered to help me get custody of her. Grace was keeping her from me and the only thing I knew to do was just go in and take her."

"And hit an old man," Cole said. "And you assaulted another woman."

"She wouldn't let go." Briggs took a deep breath. "Come on, Parker. You know me. You know how Grace has been after me since Brooke's death. She's crazy."

"Crazy like I was to believe every line you fed me?"

Briggs took a step backward.

"Don't move!" Cole shouted with his gun still pointed at Briggs.

Briggs appealed to Parker once again. "Come on, Parker, let's go upstairs and look at some videos and sort this out. I took my daughter. That's not a crime."

"It's a crime when she's not yours," Cole told him. "And do you know how I know that? Your ex-wife. She said you had a va-sectomy years ago."

Briggs paled, but he wasn't ready to give

up. "She lied. She's just jealous that I have a kid and she doesn't."

"You know that Zoe's not yours. That's why you wouldn't allow her to live in the apartment. You didn't want to raise someone else's kid. Isn't that correct?"

Briggs didn't respond, just looked a little dazed, as if he was measuring his options.

"But you let Brooke stay because she was your cash cow, wasn't she? Oh, yeah. I know about your gambling debts to Penetti. I have a statement from the manager and words from Penetti himself. You owe him a lot of money, and Brooke was your way of paying it back, a way for you to keep gambling. She loved you and she wanted to help, but you repaid her by sleeping with other women. She was leaving the morning she fell down the stairs. You couldn't let your cash cow leave, could you, Briggs?"

"You're talking crazy."

"But you got her, didn't you? You beat her up."

"I didn't push her down the stairs."

"You didn't have to. You hit her with your fist, and that did the trick. We got the ME's report. Cause of death is homicide—blunt force blow to the head. I'm only going to say this once. Joel Briggs, you're under arrest for the murder of Brooke Bennett. Read him his rights, Parker."

In a heartbeat, Briggs pushed Parker and knocked him against the car. Briggs bolted for the stairs. Cole was right behind him. With his gun pointed at him, he shouted, "Stop! Stop! Or I'll shoot!"

Briggs didn't stop.

He reached the first landing and paused. Cole watched his every move, his focus never wavering. With his right foot on the landing and his left foot on the step, Briggs reached down for something in his hiking boot. It was a small pistol.

"Don't shoot," Cole said into the mic. "I got it. Stand down. Bo, I got it." In his peripheral vision he could see Bo on the roof with a high-powered rifle.

Almost in slow motion, Cole saw Briggs's left foot slip from the step. He lost his balance and fell backward, his arms flailing. The pistol blasted into the sky. His head hit the bottom step with a loud thud. The pistol landed on his chest. Cole squatted to reach for the vein in his neck. Nothing. Briggs was dead. He took a long breath and holstered his gun. Officers moved in.

"Take over," he said to Parker. "I have to check on my grandfather."

"Go ahead."

He ran through the gathering crowd. Bertha was at the entrance, and he ran until he could see them. Grandpa was on the passenger side with his feet on the pavement, as if he'd sat for a moment to rest. He held Zoe. Grace knelt in front of him stroking Zoe's back. When she saw Cole, she ran into his arms. He held her in a tight grip until his heart subsided into a normal rhythm.

"I heard a gunshot and I thought—"

"Briggs is dead. He ran when we had him cornered, and he slipped on the stairs."

"Oh—"

"It's okay." He held her trembling body. "He's never going to take Zoe now. It's okay."

She was safe. Zoe was safe. But he wasn't so sure about his grandpa. He tamped down the anger inside him at his grandfather's bruised face. Once again he spoke into his mic. "Need an ambulance at the entrance gate."

"Cole, no. I don't need to go," Grace said.

"You do. And Zoe needs to be checked in case they gave her something. She was crying uncontrollably. That's different for her."

An ambulance was there in less than a minute. Grace, with Zoe in her arms, climbed inside. Cole helped his grandfather.

"It's going to be okay," he said to Grandpa.

"I know it is, and I don't need to go to a doctor. I'm fine," Walt insisted, but his words weren't gruff like they usually were.

He glanced at Grace. The paramedic tried to take Zoe, but Zoe held on tight to her aunt. "I'll meet y'all at the ER."

He took a long breath as the ambulance disappeared into traffic. For the first time, he felt weak in the knees doing his job. And he knew the reason. It involved family—his family. A woman, a baby and an old man had weaved their magic around his heart. A heart that had been cold for so many years was now beating like a drum at a rock concert.

THE PARAMEDIC COULDN'T do much with Zoe in the ambulance, so he decided to wait until they reached the ER. She was very agitated and clung to Grace. Once the paramedic stopped prodding her, she relaxed.

Grace worried about Mr. Walt. He was so pale, and the bruise was now caked with blood. She held his hand as the sirens blared through the afternoon. Once they reached the ER, Grace insisted on being with Mr. Walt.

They rolled Mr. Walt into the ER. He was very calm, which worried Grace. He wasn't usually this calm. He should be ranting and raving about being here. A nurse and doctor checked him.

"His blood pressure is very high," the nurse said.

The doctor looked at the numbers. "Okay, we have to get his blood pressure down."

Grace moved closer to the bed. "Mr. Walt, did you take your blood pressure pill this morning? I told you to take it."

"I guess I did. I don't remember."

"I gave you the bottle."

"Then I guess I took it."

The doctor shook his head and spoke to Grace. "It wouldn't be this high if he'd taken it. It's in the danger zone right now. Are you related?"

"No. His grandson is on the way."

A nurse pulled Grace to a chair and checked her injury and said it was only superficial. Then they checked Zoe and took blood from her. She cried for a moment and then laid her head on Grace's shoulder.

The doctor once again spoke to Grace. "We

started an IV for Mr. Chisholm and gave him something for his blood pressure. Once we get it down, we'll take him for some tests. We think the bruise is just superficial, but we want to be sure."

"Thank you. His grandson should be here any minute."

The doctor walked out of the room, and Grace pulled her chair closer to Mr. Walt. "How are you feeling?"

Mr. Walt blinked at her. "Where's our girl?"

Grace was holding Zoe, and she lifted her a little higher. "Right here. Can't you see her?"

"Oh, there's my girl."

Mr. Walt closed his eyes, and Grace thought he went to sleep. Suddenly, he started shouting, "Cora, how could you? How could you let that man take that baby? You're supposed to protect her."

Grace didn't know what to say. Clearly Mr. Walt was talking out of his head. So she just let him talk.

"But you always do your own thing, don't you? How many times did I tell you that you needed to pay more attention to Cole. He was Jamie's son. Just like Grace told me. Cole was the most precious thing Jamie left on this earth. You acted like he wasn't even there. How do you think that made him feel? Yeah, I'm still mad at you. I could never change your mind and make you realize that Jamie was dead and Cole was alive."

Grace got up and touched Mr. Walt's hand. He seemed to not even realize she was there. Her breath caught in her throat at the sorrowful voice, and she felt as if she could relive the past through him. She could feel the pain that Cole must've lived through.

"How is my grandpa?" Cole asked as he came into the room.

Before Grace could answer, Mr. Walt said, "Cole, is that you?"

Cole walked to the bed. "Yes, Grandpa, I'm here."

"Put some wood on the fire. It's cold in here."

Cole glanced at Grace, and she nodded and whispered, "He's a bit out of his head. They said his blood pressure is very high."

There was a blanket on the bed, and Cole reached for it. "Here's a blanket, Grandpa. That should warm you up." He spread the blanket over his grandfather with a loving hand.

"Is your grandma asleep?"

Cole gave a start. "Uh…yes."

"Don't you and Bo roughhouse in here. You'll wake your grandma."

The doctor came in and spoke to Cole for a few minutes. Then two nurses rolled Mr. Walt away for tests. Cole looked at her. "How are you?"

"Sad. He was talking to Miss Cora—he was so mad and fussing at her."

"Yeah. He does that a lot, but in real life he never did that. He always pampered her because he knew she was hurting." He cupped her face with his right hand. "That looks pretty bad."

"The doctor said it was just superficial, and I hope Mr. Walt's is, too."

Zoe, who had her head on Grace's shoulder, suddenly looked up and reached out for Cole. He took her.

"Hey, smooches, are you okay?"

Zoe rubbed her face against Cole's, and his expression changed to one of tenderness. He wasn't a cop. He was a man feeling all those warm emotions a child can induce.

Grace patted Zoe's back. "The doctor said she's fine, but they took blood to make sure there was nothing in her system." She took a quick breath. "What happened to Joel?"

"When we tried to arrest him, he ran for

the stairs. At the first landing, he reached down into his boot and pulled out a pistol. His left foot slipped and he fell backward, the gun going off in his hand. His head hit the bottom step and he died. We didn't even fire a shot."

"The same place that Brooke fell?"

"Yes. Pretty strange, isn't it?"

Grace brushed her hair back. Her stomach churned with so many emotions that it was hard to describe them. Joel Briggs was dead. He couldn't hurt Zoe anymore, and Cole was the reason for that. She raised her eyes to Cole's. "Thank you."

"There are some other things you need to know." And he told her about the ME's report and the other information he'd found out in his investigation. But one thing stood out above the rest.

"He killed her with his hand? She didn't die from falling down the stairs?"

"No. A blunt force blow to the head caused her brain to bleed. And it wasn't from the stairs."

Grace sank into a chair. Once again she felt so much guilt for not being there for her sister, for not confronting her and making her listen. She could have done so much more, but she didn't want to invade her privacy. She wanted her to live her own life. And it had turned out terribly. She'd always regret not talking more to Brooke about Joel and how bad he was. Why couldn't Brooke see how bad Joel was? She'd said she loved him, and Grace supposed when you were in love you saw everything through rose-colored glasses.

A nurse entered the room. "Sergeant Chisholm, there are some people out here that need to speak with you."

Cole handed Zoe to Grace. "Are you okay?" he asked in a gentle voice she was beginning to love. Take-charge guy was still somewhere in that broad chest, and she loved him, too.

"Yeah. My heart is bruised a little, but Zoe and I will be fine now."

Cole left the room, and Grace stepped out to see what was going on. A man in a suit, an officer and a woman in scrubs stood two doors down waiting for Cole. She could hear them clearly. What did they want?

Cole stopped when he reached the man in the suit. "What's going on, Myers?"

That was the criminal defense attorney Cole had talked about. Joel's attorney.

The man handed Cole what looked like

some legal papers. "I'm here to take custody of the minor child Zoe Briggs."

No! They couldn't do this. After all Cole had done, they were still going to take Zoe. She held Zoe a little tighter, but the urge to run was strong. This time, though, she would face whatever she had to face to keep Zoe. She would fight.

CHAPTER SIXTEEN

COLE STARED AT the papers shoved at him and reluctantly took them. He read through the document. "This says that minor child Zoe Briggs is to be delivered to her biological father, Joel Stephen Briggs." He looked at Myers. "You see, Counselor, I have a problem with that."

"What kind of problem?"

"Joel Stephen Briggs is dead."

"Due to a botched raid by the police, a young man lost his life. The baby will now go to his parents."

"I didn't see their names on the order."

"That's because we didn't anticipate the police would kill him."

Cole swallowed fiery words in his throat and answered like the professional cop he was. "Briggs died because he ran. He's a coward and couldn't face the facts. He ran up the stairs to his apartment, and when he reached for a gun, he slipped and fell backward to his death. I think that's called sweet justice."

"It could have been handled differently."

"We handled it according to the book. We had a warrant for his arrest—"

"For what?" Myers fired at him.

"Oh, I guess you haven't read the ME's report. Brooke Bennett died from a blunt force blow to the head, causing her brain to bleed. The fall didn't cause her to die. Joel Briggs did."

The lawyer paled significantly. "I wasn't aware of this."

"We went to arrest him, and then we found out he'd kidnapped Zoe."

"He did not kidnap the baby. She is his biological daughter, and I told him he had a right to her. There's nothing you can legally do about that."

"Did you tell him to take the baby?" Cole was unable to keep his voice from rising.

"My conversations with Joel are privileged."

People were walking by, staring at the group. Nurses and staff were also staring at them. A tech with a cart tried to get past them, and Cole walked to a small waiting area. Myers and the officer and the nurse followed.

It gave Cole time to get his emotions in check. "Briggs broke into my grandfather's home and physically assaulted both him and Grace Bennett and took the baby. They are here now being checked over by doctors. If either one of them has something seriously wrong, I'm coming after you with both barrels blazing. You got it?"

"You can't intimidate me."

"You set into motion a chain of events that killed Joel Briggs. Take a look in the mirror, Counselor. You're guilty as hell. You might want to mention that to Joel Briggs's parents."

"This is smoke and mirrors, Sergeant, and I'm not listening to you anymore. This officer—" he pointed to the officer standing behind him "—is here to see that the baby is delivered to Joel Briggs's parents. Today."

Cole looked at the officer. His name tag said Randall. "Who's your commanding officer?"

"Sergeant Baker, sir," the officer responded.

Cole pulled out his phone and called Baker. He explained the situation.

"The parents' names are not on the order?"

"No."

"It's not legal, then. Tell Officer Randall he can return to the station."

"Will do." He relayed the message to the officer and the man walked out.

"Judge Ramstad will have your head on a platter for disobeying his order," Myers said, anger flashing in his eyes.

"I think Judge Ramstad will agree with me. You can't serve a legal warrant with false information. That I know."

"That baby is going to Joel's parents just as soon as I get another warrant. Don't think you won here today. You haven't."

"I've done a lot of investigating on this case, and it appears that Briggs may not be the biological father of Zoe."

Myers's steely eyes narrowed. "What are you trying to pull?"

"I spoke to Briggs's ex-wife."

"Who?"

"You didn't know he was married before?" It seemed as if Briggs had kept that a secret from just about everybody. "Well, he was, and according to her, she didn't like being hit, cheated on or lied to. She had a lot to say about her ex-husband, and the bombshell was that he'd had a vasectomy."

"I'm sure she's lying. Joel is the father of

that baby, and you're twisting this into something that suits your needs."

"You should know twisting, Counselor, since you do it every day in the courtroom. But I'm giving you facts—DNA testing is being done on Joel and the baby. We'll have it in a few days, and then we'll know for sure who's playing who."

Cole's phone pinged, and he took a moment to look at it. He showed the photo to Myers. "You might want to inform Briggs's parents that he was selling the baby. That's one hundred grand in a carryall. The photo is from Detective Parker, who is handling the case. Two other people were with Joel when we caught him—the buyers for the baby. They're from California and are being held at the police station. Briggs has had them on the hook for about five months now saying that his girlfriend needed time, but he would eventually get her to agree to sell the baby. Warms your heart, doesn't it?"

Myers turned on his heels and walked out of the ER.

Cole took a long breath, turned and came face-to-face with a person he'd never thought he would see again.

"Stephanie, what are you doing here?"

She hugged him briefly. He didn't respond. "I was at the police station, and they said you were involved in an altercation with Joel Briggs. Your friend Bo came in, and I asked him where you were and he said the ER. I came right over. I was worried about you."

"I'm fine, Stephanie, you don't need to worry about me."

She made a face like she'd often seen her do. A face that said she was going to wrap him tight around her little finger—except that was never going to happen again.

"You're still mad, but that's okay. Thanksgiving wasn't a good day for either one of us."

"Stephanie." He sighed and chose his words carefully. "We are over."

She patted his chest. "You don't mean that."

"I do, but let me ask you a question. Since we are such a good couple, why didn't you invite my grandfather to Thanksgiving?"

Her finely arched eyebrows pinched in disbelief. "He's old and wouldn't have enjoyed it."

Her attitude floored him. "He's my grandfather, and he eats, talks and can carry on a conversation like everyone else. He celebrates every holiday, and he's been the center of my whole life. I'm never putting him in a home or any place where I can't see him when I want to. My grandfather means the world to me, and the woman I spend the rest of my life with is going to feel the same way about him."

"Oh, you never said—"

"I did, many times, but you never heard me."

As if he'd never spoken, Stephanie asked, "Was my father just in here?"

"Yes, he was involved with the Briggs incident." That's all he was going to say. Her father could tell her everything else.

"I'm sure he had a good reason."

"Which is only known to Harlan Myers himself."

"Is that her?"

"Who are you—" Cole followed Stephanie's glance to Grace, standing in the ER doorway rocking Zoe and talking to a nurse. What was her fascination with Grace?

"She's not plain."

"I never said she was plain. And what difference does it make?"

"Cole—"

"Goodbye, Stephanie." He didn't feel the need to answer more questions. They were over, and she had to accept it.

He walked toward Grace and met her worried look with a smile. He hadn't said Grace was plain. He'd said she was average. He'd lied more to himself than anyone else. He didn't want to admit how beautiful she really was. Then he would have to admit that he was dating one woman and attracted to another. That wasn't him. But in life there were some things you just couldn't stop. Love was one of them.

AT NINE O'CLOCK they finally made it back to the farmhouse. Everyone was okay, except Mr. Walt was a little grouchy. He was back to his old self, grumbling about everything. Cole helped him to bed, because the hospital staff had given him something to relax him. Grace kissed him good-night and then left the room to take care of Zoe. But she could hear them talking.

"Tomorrow morning I'll give you your pill and watch you swallow it. I'll do the same at night. You have to take your blood pressure medicine."

"Ah, now you're going to be on about that."

"Yes, I am."

"You know, Cole, I could feel your grandma when I was in the ER. It was like she was there."

Cole cleared his throat. "Yeah, you were talking about her...or to her."

"I thought she didn't protect Zoe. Now I think she did. You know, the devil's out there, too, causing all kind of problems."

"Yeah, I think I met him a time or two."

Grandpa chuckled. "Yeah, I was there, too."

"Good night, Grandpa."

Grace took care of Zoe and then went down the hall to the kitchen and started cleaning up the mess they'd made for supper. They'd had turkey sandwiches, so it wasn't much. Grace sat at the kitchen table with a cup of tea, and Cole joined her.

"Would you like a cup?" she asked.

"No, thanks." He stretched his long legs out in front of him. "It's been a long Friday."

"It has to be horrific to watch someone die." She couldn't even imagine that feeling, but she knew the feeling of losing someone you loved.

"Yeah, you never get used to it, either." He scooted forward in his chair as if he was restless. "Everything you told me about Briggs was true."

"And he would've gotten away with it if I hadn't slid off the road by Mr. Walt's house.

I still think about that and wonder how Zoe got to the front porch."

"I guess that will always be a mystery."

He ran both hands through his hair. "But everything turned out okay."

"Not exactly. We still don't know who Zoe's father is."

"Yeah." He sighed. "I had Bo go over and get Colson's DNA so that we'd know how he fits in to the picture. I put a rush on it, so we should have it in a couple of days."

"I'm just worried if Joel's not the father and Colson is, will he want Zoe?" It was constantly on her mind, and she couldn't shake it. But she was stronger now, and she wasn't giving up without a fight. "I spoke to Gabe earlier, and he said he would file a temporary custody order on Monday so I can keep Zoe until this is settled."

"That's the wisest thing to do. Until the DNA tests come back, everyone is in a holding pattern. And a judge is not going to grant any kind of order until that time."

Grace took a sip of her tea. "That lawyer isn't giving up, is he?"

"Myers?"

"Yeah."

"No, but he'll abide by the DNA tests like everyone." He held her eyes. "Even you."

She shook her head. "Don't do that."

"What?"

"Make me face the fact that I may never get Zoe. I refuse to face it. I've had her since she was born, and I just can't let go."

"Grace—"

She ignored his strong voice that held a tinge of reason. "When will my sister's body be released?"

"I'll call the ME's office and tell them where to send the body. Where would that be?"

"I'll call. Just give me the number. I'm really not helpless."

One eyebrow rose. "I never said you were."

She felt guilty for annoying him when all he'd done was help her. But now she had to take control of her life. "I leaned on you a lot these past few days, and I shouldn't have. It's time for me to make better choices."

"Okay. I'll give you the number in the morning."

She got up and put her cup in the sink. "Thank you." Turning around, she said, "I got a text from Frannie. She's coming home on Sunday. I'll probably leave here on Sunday morning. I have to get back to my life."

"Sure." He stood. "I better feed the animals." With that, he walked out of the kitchen, and she heard the back door slam.

Grace leaned against the counter. Cole seemed upset. From the moment she saw him talking to the blonde woman who she assumed was Stephanie, she'd known she had to detach from everything that was happening between her and Cole. They had been together so much in the house and with Mr. Walt, and she had breathed in the warmness of family that she craved. It had been a moment out of the time, but it wasn't real. She had to go back to her daily life, to get in touch with what was real. And she could now, thanks to Cole.

Cole would understand once she was gone and he was back to his regular routine. As she got ready for bed, she kept telling herself that. But somewhere along the way, her heart had gotten involved and she knew she was never going to forget the handsome take-charge cop who'd helped her when no one else would.

SHE WAS LEAVING. That was all Cole could think as he put feed in the trough for the boys. They were bedded down for the night, but they came to the trough to eat. The chickens were bedded down, too, in the hay. He should've just waited till morning. They were fine.

He wasn't. That was the problem. He'd thought Grace would at least stay for another week to give them all time to adjust, but she seemed in a hurry to go, even though Zoe's paternity hadn't been decided. He didn't understand that.

By the outdoor light he'd installed years ago, he found his way around in the barn. He opened the door of his grandpa's truck and got in, staring out at the barn where he'd spent a lot of his childhood. The far right corner was where he and Grandpa had spent every Christmas, except when he was in the Army. Last year he'd told him he was getting too old to spend Christmas in the barn. Grandpa had said Cole would never get too old for tradition. Now that Grandma was gone, he had no idea what this Christmas would bring.

Otis jumped on the hood of the truck and did his cock-a-doodle-doo routine. The light made him think it was morning. That stupid rooster had dementia, but it made Cole laugh. There had been lots of laughs in the barn, too. The beer incident came to mind. After that,

Grandpa had gone to town and bought them beer and let them drink two apiece. And then he and Bo lay on the hay and talked about girls, the Army and freedom. One time they tried to smoke and caught the barn on fire. They'd stomped it out and had scorched their boots. And then there was the time when Cole was twelve years old and his grandpa was teaching him to drive. His job was to park the truck in the barn, which he tried to do, but he'd missed the entrance and hit the barn. He'd thought he was in big trouble. Grandpa looked at the damaged barn and said, "That's not what I meant," and then burst out laughing. So much of his childhood revolved around the heart and soul of this old barn. It wasn't as bad as he remembered. He was never abused. He was never hungry. He was like so many other children—he just wanted what other kids had.

He got out of the truck and headed for the house, the cool north wind nipping at his clothes. He shoved his hands into his jacket pockets, remembering something Grandpa had always told him when things got rough. *There's always another day. When there's not, that's when you need to worry.*

Yep. Tomorrow was another day.

THE NEXT MORNING Cole gave Grace the number of the coroner's office. Grandpa seemed fine. He was busy telling Grace what to cook for breakfast. How was he going to tell him Grace was leaving tomorrow? He thought he would save that until later.

Zoe was in her high chair eating bits of scrambled eggs. He hadn't gone into Grace's room this morning to get her. He thought it was time to let go. That wasn't an easy thing to do.

He poured a cup of coffee. "I've got to go to work. I have a lot of paperwork waiting on me to finish the Briggs case. I don't know what time I'll be back."

Grace glanced at him from the stove. "That's okay. I'll be here."

Her face was healing fast like before, just a little red on her cheek. He had an irresistible urge to kiss it. Man, he was in over his head.

"I'll see y'all later." He headed for the door and Austin to get his mind on something else.

COLE'S ATTITUDE TOWARD her had changed, and she knew why. She was leaving. He had to understand she couldn't stay. She had a job and a house payment. And then it hit her. She was running again from feelings she couldn't face. As she cleaned the kitchen, she made a decision. Before she left, she would talk to Cole and be as honest as possible. Their lives had connected for a brief moment in time, and now they had to go their separate ways.

She made another decision while wiping down the counter. She would also tell Mr. Walt instead of saving that task for Cole. She had to explain to him why she was leaving, and she hoped he understood.

Mr. Walt announced he wanted turkey pot pie for lunch.

"Mr. Walt, I do not know how to make turkey pot pie."

"Don't worry, I'll show you."

That's what she was afraid of. But since this was her last day, she would make anything he wanted. Afterward Mr. Walt took a nap, as did Zoe. Grace sat on the sofa waiting for Mr. Walt to wake up. She dozed off a couple times, and she had to stop that. Taking afternoon naps could become habit-forming.

She thought about Brooke, her beautiful sister, and all the stress she had gone through so she and Joel could become a family. Those beautiful words—a family. Almost every woman wanted one, a home filled with love and laughter. Grace had gotten a glimpse of it during the few days she'd been here on the farm. Even though the Chisholms were an unusual family, she could still feel the love. Saying goodbye wasn't going to be easy for her, either.

Mr. Walt straightened in his chair. "Where's Zoe?" He asked the same question every time he woke up.

"She's asleep in her bed."

"I'll go get her."

"No, Rascal's in there, and he'll bark when she wakes up. I want to talk to you for a minute."

Mr. Walt leaned back. "Okay."

She turned sideways so she could face him. "I wanted you to know that I'm leaving in the morning."

He sat up straight. "What? Why?"

"I have to go back to my life now and face my future. Zoe's paternity is still up in the air, but I can handle it now. I'm so grateful for everything that you and Cole have done for me. But I have to go. Please understand that."

"Zoe will miss me."

She loved the way he phrased that. "Mr. Walt, I promise I will bring her to see you."

He thought about that for a minute. "How

are you going to go in the morning? Your car's not ready."

"I know. I was hoping Cole would drop me in Austin. I can rent a car. I should've done that in the first place."

He pointed a finger at her. "No, you shouldn't have. You were right where you were supposed to be. I know that with all my heart. Cora told me."

She scooted to the edge of the sofa. "Mr. Walt, I've grown very fond of you, and it's going to hurt to leave."

"Then don't."

"Mr. Walt…"

"Okay, I don't understand how you young folks' minds work. It's confusing. But you don't need to rent a car. You can take Bertha. At least I know you'll be safe. You can bring it back when Lamar finishes your car."

"Mr. Walt, that's extremely generous, but—"

He got to his feet. "No buts. Now, what are we going to have for supper?"

The man had a one-track mind, and since it was her last night, she would make him anything. It turned out to be the one thing she didn't want to cook: fried chicken.

While the chicken was thawing, they went outside to check on the animals. She put a jacket and cap on Zoe because it was cool. Rascal ran ahead, barking at the chickens. Otis strutted his stuff and cock-a-doodle-dooed all over the place. Warmth filled her heart, quickly followed by a sting of sadness. She would miss the Chisholms.

CHAPTER SEVENTEEN

IT WAS AFTER four when Cole drove over the cattle guard to the house. It had been a long day and a lot of paperwork, but they were finally able to close the Briggs-Bennett case. He drove into the garage and started to go into the house when he heard Rascal barking. He went outside instead.

Grandpa, Grace and Zoe were at the barn. Rascal ran to meet him and then ran back to Zoe, who was in her stroller, jumping up and down and laughing at the animals. Cole slowly walked toward them and turned as he heard the sound of a truck coming up the drive. The truck loaded with hay stopped at the barn, and a tall, broad-shouldered man got out.

Cole walked toward him and shook his hand. He knew Jericho well. He was one of the Rebel family. A child he had been fostering had gone missing, and he and Cole had worked together to find him. It had all worked out—Jericho and his wife had adopted the boy.

"Mr. Walt ordered twenty bales of hay."

"I'll help you put it in the barn." That's when he noticed three children in the truck. He glanced at Jericho. "You have some of the Rebel kids with you?"

Jericho shook his head. "No. They're mine and Anamarie's. We were planning to wait, but the social worker who handled Dusty's case called us about two little boys who desperately needed a whole lot of attention. They had been abandoned by their mother and were malnourished and had bad infections on their butts from staying in soiled diapers too long. We worried about Dusty, so we let him make the decision whether to visit with them or not. The boys are three and a year old. The moment Dusty and Anamarie saw the boys, it was love at first sight."

"Daddy, can we get out?" A little voice called from the open door of the truck.

"Sure," Jericho called back. "Help Ben and I'll get Logan."

Dusty was about six now and came around the truck holding the hand of a small boy. Jericho got the baby out and held him in his arms.

Cole looked at the boys—they all had dark

hair and dark eyes, just like Jericho. "The boys look just like you."

"Yeah. We took what God gave us, and we got three really good little boys."

"They're my brothers," Dustin said.

Jericho pointed to the three-year-old. "That's Benjamin Francis, and I'm holding Logan McGregor. We call him Logan Mac."

"I'm Dustin Jericho." Dusty shook Cole's hand, and he had to smile at the boy's politeness. It was clear how much he loved his father. "Daddy, can we go look at the animals?"

"Yes, take your brothers." The three of them walked toward the corral holding hands, the baby in the middle. Zoe jumped up and down in the stroller, excited to see kids.

Cole helped Jericho unload the hay. They talked as they worked.

"You named the boys after Francis Mc-Gregor."

"They had first names. Anamarie and I talked about it, and then I called Mr. Mc-Gregor's son to see how he felt about us giving them McGregor middle names. He was pleased. They came to meet the boys, and they're coming again after Christmas."

Francis McGregor was a grouchy old man who'd lived on a ranch across from the

Rebels, and everyone avoided him. He was steeped in the past and out of sorts with the world and took it out on people. Jericho was the only one who ever tried to help him, out of the kindness of his heart. Mr. McGregor had been estranged from his son for over forty years, but Jericho had urged him to talk to his only son. Somehow the old man listened, and before he died he and his son shared the last few days of Mr. McGregor's life. Mr. McGregor's will was a shocker to the town, and it was often talked about. He'd left his large ranch to Jericho, with his son's blessing.

"When are you moving into Mr. McGregor's house?" Mr. McGregor's home had been built in the 1800s and had a southern colonial feel to it.

"I finally finished all the repairs, and it's just about ready. We could move in, but we decided to have Christmas in the bunkhouse and move later. We felt it was better for the boys that way. They're comfortable where they are, and we don't want to disrupt that just yet."

Cole patted him on the back. "I'm happy for you, man."

"Thanks. It feels surreal at times, but when I see Anamarie's face, I know it's real."

Cole could hear the love in his voice. He knew it had been a long road for Jericho and Anamarie to find their happy-ever-after. He glanced toward Grace, who was talking to the boys. He just didn't know if that was in the cards for him.

Soon Jericho loaded up the kids and drove away. Zoe made a face like she was going to cry. Grace squatted and kissed her cheek. "It's okay. You might see them again."

How's she going to do that if you're leaving was on the tip of his tongue. But he didn't say the words. That would make him a jackass.

They made their way to the house, talking about Jericho and the kids. Preparations for supper were everywhere. A chicken was in the sink. Potatoes were ready to boil, and there was corn and green beans in jars. Grace was making a big supper. A goodbye supper. In that moment he realized he was acting like a small child. He'd thought he would have a problem with his grandpa when she left. He never dreamed the problem would be with him. Once he realized that, his whole attitude changed.

"Do you know that Grace is leaving?" Grandpa asked Cole.

"Um…yeah. I'm surprised that you do." He

glanced at Grace and should have known she wouldn't leave it up to him to tell Grandpa.

"She's taking Bertha 'cause she doesn't have a car. She'll bring it back when Lamar finishes her car."

"Uh…okay…"

"There're too many people in this kitchen," Grandpa announced as he pushed past Cole. "I'm going to check and see if *Andy Griffith* is on."

"It doesn't come on until seven," Grace told him. "You're supposed to help me."

"I'm going to check." Grandpa marched into the living room with his mind set on not helping.

"I have no idea how to cut up a chicken." She made a face.

"I'll help you," Cole offered. "Grandpa taught me how to do it years ago. I don't know why, because he thinks a woman's place is in the kitchen."

"He told me if I could cook, I would never go hungry."

They shared a chuckle.

"That's my grandpa."

They worked together in the kitchen, and it felt as natural as if he'd been doing this with her for a long time. And it had only been a week.

They put everything on the table and called Grandpa.

"Did you make a coconut pie, Grace?"

"No, Mr. Walt, I did not make a coconut pie."

Grandpa took his seat. "What are we going to have for dessert?"

"There are chocolate chip cookies in the cabinet," she told him.

"Ah, that's not a dessert. That's a snack."

"Grandpa, if you eat all this food we've prepared, you're not going to want a dessert. Now eat."

A knock sounded at the back door. "Hey, anybody home?"

"Come on in, Bertie," Grandpa called. "We're having supper."

Miss Bertie walked in with a pie in her hand. "Walt said Grace is leaving in the morning, so I made her a pie. Walt said coconut was her favorite."

They shared a glance and, unable to stop themselves, they burst out laughing.

"What's so funny?" Miss Bertie asked.

"Coconut is Grandpa's favorite pie," Cole replied.

"Grace loves it, too, don't you?"

"Yes, Mr. Walt, I absolutely love it."

Cole reached out and took her hand. She squeezed it and smiled. Now he could handle her leaving. It had nothing to do with him. She had to get her life together to move forward.

LATER GRACE AND COLE sat at the kitchen table. She had a cup of tea, and he had coffee. She wanted to talk and explain her feelings, but she didn't want to dredge up those emotions that would make her vulnerable.

"I really don't know how to thank you," she started.

"Then don't. I know how much Zoe means to you."

She traced the handle of her teacup. "Why did you believe me? You said you would check the facts, but the facts weren't in my favor."

"Let's just say I'm a sucker for a pretty woman and a sad story."

"You are not."

He moved uncomfortably in his chair. "I told you I have these instincts, that I can tell when someone is lying. I don't why, but I can, and I knew you weren't lying. But I was hesitant at first, because I didn't know all the facts, and then…"

"We grew closer," she finished for him. "This past week I have leaned on you for support because I was so worried about Zoe. And in doing that, I started to have feelings for you. I knew you had a girlfriend, and I didn't want to do anything to change that."

"I don't have a girlfriend anymore."

"Why? You said something about her not liking your boots. That makes no sense."

"She didn't want me to wear boots to Thanksgiving. It was something her mother wouldn't like since it was a formal dinner. I wore them anyway because that's who I am—a country boy from Horseshoe, Texas. I realized then that we really had nothing in common and ended the relationship."

"I saw her in the ER—or at least I thought it was her."

He moved uncomfortably again. "Yes, it was her."

"I'm not trying to pry," she hastened to reassure him. "But if you still have feelings for her, I think you should work it out. I don't want to get caught in the middle of your relationship."

"Grace." He looked directly into her eyes,

and the blue of his was so warm she could feel it. "You're not in the middle of that relationship. It's over. I can't explain it, but when you came here, it just changed everything. You really are Amazing Grace. Grandpa would eat very little, and he talked to my grandmother constantly. It was unnerving. Now he's eating and can't seem to stop. Zoe brightened up his world and so did you. He's like his old self. You want to thank me? I should be thanking you. I was at my wits' end trying to help him. I thought he would get upset about you leaving, but he's handling it very well. He's even letting you take Bertha."

Grace clasped her hands in her lap. "It's hard for me to leave, too. Mr. Walt taught me a lot of things, especially about cooking. I will miss him, but I really believe that you and I need this time apart to sort through our feelings. I didn't expect to feel anything for you, and now..."

"It's okay, Grace," he assured her. "We've only known each other a week, and we do need time apart. I'll be starting back at my job, and you have to bury your sister and deal with her affairs and Zoe's paternity."

"I know." She got to her feet and put her teacup in the sink. When she walked past his chair, he reached out and caught her arm and got to his feet, wrapping both arms around her. As she nestled close to him, he kissed her cheek and then her lips. She breathed in the scent of him and kissed him back. Pulling away, she ran to her bedroom. She would remember that moment for the rest of her life.

Sunday morning went smoothly. Grace had all her things packed and sitting in the hallway. She and Grandpa took Zoe out to see the animals one last time. While they were outside, Cole loaded her stuff in the car and drove it around to the back door. Grandpa held Zoe as the trio slowly made their way to the car. Rascal jumped up and down trying to lick Zoe's hand as she waved it at him.

Grace tucked her hair behind her ears. "You didn't have to bring the car around."

"I thought it would be better."

She took Zoe from Grandpa and put her in the car seat. Then she hugged his grandfather. "Thank you, Mr. Walt, for letting me stay here and for letting me use Bertha. I will take very good care of her."

"I know you will."

While Grandpa cooed at Zoe, she turned to

Cole, her eyes dark and sad. "Please call me as soon as you hear about the DNA."

"You'll be the first person I call."

Very cool. Very calm. But inside he knew she was hurting, just like he was. Time was ever evolving and measured in seconds, minutes, hours, weeks and months. Was there such a thing as love at first sight? Could that one second amount to decades of love? He wasn't that familiar with the word, but he got a happy high in his chest when he looked at her, when he talked to her and when she smiled at him. It had only taken a second. And then it had only taken a week for him to know that he was caught like a fish on a hook. And that's where he wanted to be—caught in her dark eyes forever. It was up to her to decide if she felt the same way.

She wrapped her arms around his waist and hugged him. He gripped her tightly as the cool north wind blew against them. He kissed the side of her face. "Come back any time you want."

She got into the car, and Grandpa shut Zoe's door. She waved and drove away. Rascal chased the car all the way to the cattle guard. Cole stared until the blue streak disappeared. He drew a deep sigh and accepted that time would tell if she would ever come back. Now he had to deal with his grandfather.

Looking around, his grandfather was nowhere in sight. Oh, no! He probably was in the barn shedding a few tears. Amazing Grace had left the Chisholm men heartbroken.

Rascal slowly made his way back to the barn, and Cole followed. He heard his grandpa's truck crank up, and the chicken squawked. Otis cock-a-doodle-dooed, and the truck shot out of the barn. Grandpa pulled up next to him.

"I'm taking my truck to Lamar to get the muffler fixed. Follow and pick me up."

What? He was stunned for a minute. The sad grandfather he had expected was doing fine.

"Okay." He didn't tell him it was Sunday and that Lamar didn't work on Sundays. They'd figure it out later.

When they got there, Lamar and Dori were backing out to go to church. Grandpa talked to Lamar for a minute and then got into Cole's truck.

"He'll get it fixed," Grandpa said, buckling his seat belt. "I want one of those phones you were talking about a few months ago."

"You mean a cell phone?" Several times he'd tried to get his grandparents a cell phone instead of a landline, but they refused. Grandpa had refused again when his grandmother had passed away.

"Yeah. One of those things. I don't want that internet stuff, but I want one that takes pictures."

"O-okay."

He drove into Temple and bought a cell phone for his grandfather. That brought on the question of if he had enough patience to teach his grandfather how to use it. They sat at the kitchen table as Cole began the process.

"Who do you want to call? I have to put their numbers in here."

"I have a list by the phone." Grandpa handed him the list, and he put the numbers in Grandpa's phone. "Put Grace's in there, too."

"Why?"

"Because I want to know how Zoe's doing."

"Grandpa—"

"Put it in there and stop arguing with you grandfather."

His mind told him to keep the door to Grace closed, but his heart sent him a different message. His grandfather cared for Zoe,

and he and Grace had a good relationship—
who was Cole to tell him who his friends
could be?

"The people on your list are known as con-
tacts in your phone. See." He showed him on
the phone.

"Got it."

Cole went over how to use the phone and
went over it again until he thought his brain
would explode. Why did he ever think this
was a good idea?

"Okay, Grandpa I'm going outside and you
call me."

He went outside and waited and waited.
Rascal rested on his haunches beside him.
He ran a hand over his face, never dreaming it would be this hard. Just then his phone
buzzed and he answered.

"It's your grandpa."

"What took you so long?"

"I had to go to the bathroom."

Cole gritted his teeth.

GRACE WENT HOME to an empty house and an
empty life. She sat on the sofa and thought
about her decision to leave. She wanted Cole
to love her the way a man was supposed to
love a woman and not because she needed his

help and was some damsel in distress. She wanted them to have a full-blown love affair with all the bells and whistles. And of course she could be delusional.

Zoe crawled all over the house, looking in every room. Grace knew who she was looking for: Mr. Walt, Cole and Rascal. In her heart, she looked for them, too. But she really needed this time away from the happy, happy experience she'd had at the farm. And the fight for Zoe wasn't over. She had to arrange a funeral, too.

Zoe climbed onto the sofa and into her lap, and Grace held on to the only person she had left in her life. Zoe's father could only be Joel or Kevin, and she had to be ready to fight whichever one it was.

Frannie arrived home about noon, and just the sight of her made Grace feel much better. They talked and talked, and Grace told her everything that had happened.

"I can't believe all this," Frannie said. "That's not our Brooke."

"I know. He changed her into someone we don't even know. She believed she loved him and wanted them to be a family. I guess Brooke and I are alike—always dreaming of a family."

"Oh, sweetie, I'm so sorry. But you're strong

and you'll get through this. I'm home to help you."

"Thank you." She knew she could always count on Frannie. She also knew that one day she would leave to live with her son and his family. But she had friends, and she would make a better attempt at staying in touch. She would now have the time.

Frannie bounced Zoe up and down on her lap. "She's getting so big. I think she's grown since I've seen her."

"She has. She's almost walking. I wish Brooke could see her." A tear threatened, and she quickly brushed it away.

"She does, sweetie. You can count on that." Frannie put Zoe on the floor, and she darted off to investigate the coffee table. "Now tell me about take-charge guy."

"He's a tough cop with a very soft heart."

Frannie eyed her for a moment. "And you've fallen in love with him." She didn't ask. It was a statement.

Grace didn't lie. "Can you fall in love in a week?"

"Oh, sweetie. You can fall in love in a heartbeat. I fall in love with Tom Selleck every Friday night at nine."

Grace laughed, and for the first time it felt good to be home. She was going to be okay.

COLE MADE NEW plans concerning his grandfather. Cole would drive in to Austin for work and return home every day for now. Miss Bertie would check on Walt at lunch, and Cole would be there to make sure he took his medication. He didn't want his grandfather to be sad or lonely.

On Monday morning Cole left early, and his grandfather seemed okay. By the time he reached the cattle guard, his phone pinged and he looked at the caller ID. Grandpa. This might be a problem.

"What is it, Grandpa?"

"Just wanted to let you know the phone is working."

"Okay."

He was almost into Austin when it beeped again. Grandpa. He gritted his teeth. "What is it?"

"I just wanted to see if this thing would work all the way to Austin. That's a long way."

"Yes, Grandpa, it reaches a long way, so don't worry about it. If I don't answer, you know I'm working."

"Got it."

He expected him to call all morning, but Grandpa was suspiciously quiet. Cole was called into the lieutenant's office and was surprised to see the assistant police chief there. They shook hands, and he waited for a reprimand or something. He was trained to wait for the superior to talk.

"Good work on the Briggs case," the assistant police chief said. Cole relaxed. This wasn't a reprimand about the Briggs case. It was good news. He would continue with his team in missing children, but he would now also work with homicide when needed, as Parker was retiring. He would be busy.

He picked up ribs and sides for supper and arrived home before six. Grandpa hadn't called the rest of the day, and Cole felt guilty because he'd been working and hadn't called him, either. The house was quiet. No one was inside. Cole went to the barn to see if his grandfather was feeding the animals. He wasn't. He pulled out his phone and called him.

"Where are you?"

"In the backyard."

Cole opened the gate to the backyard and froze. A big children's swing set stood in the middle of the backyard. Grandpa sat in one of the swings. What the…

"Grandpa, where did this come from?"

"I bought it."

"Where?"

"From a store in Temple."

"How did you get it here?"

"In my truck."

"Your truck was supposed to be at Lamar's."

"He and Dori brought it back to me this morning so I had wheels. I didn't sit around here feeling sorry for myself. I went and bought the swing for Zoe, and I paid a young boy to put it up because I know you're busy."

Cole sat in one of the swings with a heavy heart. "Grandpa, you do know Zoe's not coming back to stay here."

"You don't know that. Your grandmother said she would, and you know your grandmother. She always gets her way."

He was talking to Grandma again. It didn't bother him like it had before. And if the swing set made him happy, Cole was happy. It was the little things that counted in life. Hanging on to a dream gave a person a strong will. He knew that from experience. His dream of freedom had propelled him to a country far away, where he'd had to grow up fast and become a man. In the dream he never realized he had left the best part of him behind—his grandparents, who had needed him.

Grace had made him see that.

Amazing Grace.

CHAPTER EIGHTEEN

ON SUNDAY AFTERNOON Frannie went with Grace to the funeral home to make arrangements for Brooke's burial. The service would be at ten on Wednesday morning. That evening they sat together going through old photos of Brooke. Grace's favorite was one of them as a family with their parents. Brooke was about three months old, and their dad was holding her. Grace was wedged in between their parents. She was staring at the camera, but her hand was on Brooke. It had been that way most of their lives. She'd been guiding Brooke each day, and she didn't understand how it had turned out so badly. She should have never let go.

On Monday morning she went to the retirement villas to talk to the director and told her that she would return to work on Thursday. The funeral would be stressful, but she had to get back into the swing of living. She couldn't stay home and grieve. She had to be busy.

On Tuesday morning Cole called with the DNA results: Kevin Colson was Zoe's father. They didn't talk long. She did tell him about the funeral, because he had asked about it. She wanted to hold on to his voice just a little longer, but she had to stop leaning on him.

"Do you want me to tell him?" Cole asked.

"No. I'll do that." She now had to handle her own life, and whatever Kevin decided, she had to be strong enough to handle it. On her own.

She found Kevin's number in Brooke's phone, which was in the things the police had given her after Brooke's death. She called him and arranged to meet at a small coffee shop not far from her house. Frannie looked after Zoe.

Cole had faxed a copy of the DNA test, and she had it in her purse. If he wanted proof, she could show him. She was nervous about what he would say, but she didn't bite her nails or run. She ordered a cup of coffee and sat at a small table near the windows so she could see the parking lot. A man of medium height in a multicolored plaid shirt and chinos walked in, and Grace knew it was Kevin.

"Grace Bennett?"

She nodded, and he took a seat across

from her. "You look a lot like Brooke," he remarked.

"Yes. Would you like a cup of coffee?"

"No, thanks. I just want to get this over with. I'm assuming you have the DNA results."

"Yes. You're Zoe's father. Ninety-nine point nine percent." She opened her purse and laid the paper on the table.

"Oh, man." He ran his hands up his face. "I don't understand how this happened. We used a condom, and we only had sex the one time. She was feeling down and I was, too. We drank a lot of wine and it just happened."

"As a doctor, you know it only takes one time."

He stared outside and seemed to be lost in his own thoughts, and then he said in a voice she could barely hear, "My wife gave birth to a baby girl yesterday. The baby was early, and I really should be at the hospital. I just found out I have another child. It's unbelievable. I don't know what to do."

Grace had no words to reassure him. He had to come to terms with his responsibility on his own.

"My wife is a nurse, and she worked years to put me through med school. I can't put this on her. She would not take it well, and she would leave me. I love my wife." His shoulders sagged with the weight of his problem. "If…if I took Zoe into our lives and my wife accepted her, she would not treat Zoe well. I'm almost positive of that. Do you understand that I can't take Zoe?"

She nodded. "Yes. I understand what you're saying, but Zoe is your child, your blood."

"Haven't you been raising her?"

"Yes," she replied in stilted tones. Zoe was not an item to be bartered. She was a little baby who needed her parents. "I love her, and I want her to have a home where she's happy and safe."

He studied his clasped hands on the table. "I'm okay with you raising her."

"Don't you want to be a part of her life?"

He shook his head immediately. "No. I can't do that. I'm sorry, but that's just the way it is."

"That's your plan for Zoe, just to step away and make believe that she was never born, to never acknowledge her existence?"

He ran his hand through his hair. "Yes. That's the way it has to be. I know you'll give her a good life, and that's all I need to know."

Just like that, he shoved the responsibility

for Zoe on to her. She would willingly take it, but it meant Zoe would never know her father. "Are you willing to sign away your paternal rights?"

"Yes." He didn't even take a moment to think about it, and she thought that maybe Zoe was better off with him. Grace strongly believed in family—she wanted Zoe to be a part of a family, because that's what's counted in life. It gave a person roots, confidence and unconditional love. She wanted all that for Zoe.

"Do you want time to think about this? Maybe talk to your wife?"

"No," he murmured.

"I'll have a lawyer draw up the papers, and you'll have until that time to change your mind."

"I won't," he said, getting to his feet. "Call me when the papers are ready, and I will sign them. Do not have them delivered to my home. Once I sign them, Zoe will cease to exist for me, and she will be your full responsibility. I trust you to give her a nice home."

He walked out of the coffee shop, and Grace had to wonder how a man could just walk away from his own child. He already had a wife and kids. But why wasn't there a place in his heart for Zoe? Why couldn't he see her every now and then? Grace would be willing to allow that, but Zoe's father didn't even want her to exist. How was she supposed to explain that to Zoe years down the road?

WEDNESDAY DAWNED COOL and bright, and Cole and his grandpa made it to the funeral home early. People were already gathering inside. A well-rounded lady with reddish hair stood with Grace, as did Amber and Heather. They made their way to the front to see Grace, but he didn't get to say much as people stood in line to offer their condolences. The place was full of nurses, doctors and neighbors. The weary look on Grace's face tore at his heart. It would be a long day.

The service was short, and they made the trip to the cemetery. Again Grace had lots of company, but he still worried about her. She asked that everyone return to her house for lunch. Cole and Grandpa went, because he wanted to make sure she was okay. Zoe was at the house. A lady from the neighborhood had kept her, and Grandpa picked her up just as soon as he could.

There was a lot of talk and chatter as everyone moved around eating and trying to console Grace. People soon began to leave, and Cole spotted Grace in a chair with her feet tucked beneath her. She'd kicked off her heels and sat there like he'd seen her do before, all drawn into herself. He sat on the ottoman in front of her.

"You okay?"

She pushed her hair behind her ears. "I don't know. I'm just going through the motions."

"It'll take time."

"I suppose."

"Did you talk to Colson?"

"Yes." She dabbed at her eyes with the Kleenex in her hand. "He...he doesn't want Zoe. He's signing over his paternal rights."

The way she said it, he knew something was wrong. "That's good, isn't it? Now you can adopt Zoe and not worry about someone taking her ever again."

"He's abandoning her. There's no room in his life for her. How am I going to tell her that when she gets older?"

He reached for her hands and squeezed them. "You will give her so much love that it won't matter. When she finds out about her biological father, she might be curious, but it won't change her heart."

She moved a hand to dab at her eyes again. "I'm going back to work tomorrow."

"Why so soon?"

"I need to stay busy."

"I'm sorry for everything you had to go through to keep Zoe. But you saved her. She's now safe and happy, and you should be proud of that."

"You saved her." A small smile touched her face, and it was all he needed. She would be okay, but it would take time.

LIFE WENT ON. Grace told herself that many times during the next few days. She went back to work, and Frannie kept Zoe. She buried herself in helping other people. It was nearing Christmas, and the villas' residents wanted to go shopping. Mr. Cravey was eighty-four years old and had four children, eight grandchildren, nine great-grandchildren and one great-great-grandchild. He gave them money at Christmastime, and he always wanted her to help him pick out Christmas cards to put the money in. They spent almost an hour looking at cards. He was grouchy—he reminded her of Mr. Walt.

Each resident had a different personality. Mrs. Pearce had her hair done every week, and she wore pearls, a nice dress and sensible heels every day. Mrs. Baranski, on the other hand, wore jeans, T-shirts and sneakers and could care less about her hair. She was a happy person involved in every activity she could attend.

That was Grace's job, planning events that would keep the residents busy and happy, and some days it proved to be a monumental task, since elderly people were known to have opinions and voiced them regularly. Their animated chatter went over her head as she smiled and talked and tried to do her job. By the time a new week rolled around, the sadness around her heart had eased enough so she could think about the future.

Gabe drew up the papers and he and Grace met Kevin at the same coffee shop. He signed away his rights without a word. His name on a piece of paper would allow her full custody of Zoe. Gabe would now start the adoption process. She should be happy. It was what she wanted, but a part of her was still yearning for something more.

COLE SETTLED INTO his new job, and it was very much like his old job. He just had more authority. Grandpa was back to his old self and was enjoying his phone. Sometimes Cole couldn't make it home at night, and his grandpa did just fine. Cole would call to remind him about taking his pill, and that was it. He was back to visiting with his old friends and playing forty-two at the community center. Cole never knew what he was going to do next. Grandpa had survived the grief of losing the woman he loved.

Cole's birthday was a few days away, and since he'd come home from the Army they didn't do cupcakes in the barn anymore. They would go out to eat, and Grandpa always ordered chocolate cake for Cole. It had become a new tradition.

When he arrived home on the day of his birthday, Grandpa seemed a little distracted. "We have to go," Grandpa said. "You're running late."

"I'm right on time." He didn't know what the hurry was about.

They ate at a steakhouse in Temple, and Grandpa didn't order chocolate cake for Cole. He thought that was a little strange, but it didn't matter to him. On the way home, Grandpa tapped his fingers on his jeans, and then he turned up the radio. His antsiness started to get on Cole's nerves, but he didn't say anything.

Grandpa hurried into the house. "I'm missing *Andy Griffith*."

They always had a beer on his birthday. Cole opened the refrigerator and saw beer inside. "How about a beer, Grandpa?"

"In a minute."

A knock sounded at the back door, and Cole went to answer it. Before he reached it, it opened and Zoe toddled to him. He squatted and caught her. She was walking! He stood with her in his arms, and she rubbed her face against his. His heart melted all the way to his boots. His eyes went to Grace, who stood there with a cake carrier in her hand. Now he knew why Grandpa hadn't ordered cake.

"I made you a chocolate cake for your birthday," she said in a soft, teasing voice. Her eyes were bright and clear. She was better. "It's a thank-you. I made it from your grandmother's recipe."

"Cole, are you talking to me?" Grandpa called.

Cole set Zoe on her feet, and she toddled into the living room. Rascal barked loudly, and Grandpa shouted, "Oh, oh, oh, my baby's walking."

Cole turned to Grace. "You look great."

She set the cake on the table. "I'm better. I'm busy with the people at the villas, and that's what I needed. I've come to grips with everything that happened. I just can't understand how my sister could let a man have that much control over her."

"It happens. Briggs's problem was the steroids. That was the cause of the mood swings, the rages and the anger. He couldn't have been a good person to live with, but she stuck it out because she thought she had a child by him and wanted them to be a family."

"Yeah." A sad look revisited her face, and he just wanted to hold her.

"Grace, I'm taking Zoe Grace outside," Grandpa said.

"Why? It's getting dark."

"I just am."

"Mr. Walt…"

Grandpa hurried out the French doors before she could stop them. She stared at the huge swing set in the backyard. "Where did that come from?"

"Grandpa bought it."

She glanced at him, her eyes narrowed. "And you let him?"

"You've been with us long enough to know

that I can't stop Grandpa from doing any-thing. He's as stubborn as that old mule in the barn."

Grace stepped outside. "Mr. Walt…"

Dusk had settled in like an old friend, nice and easy and comfortable. Cole watched as Grace tried to talk to Grandpa, but he was pushing Zoe in the baby swing. Zoe giggled, and Grandpa laughed and paid no attention to Grace.

Cole sat in one of the swings. "Come on, try it," he said to Grace.

"It's getting cold out here, and Zoe doesn't have on her jacket."

"Lighten up. Zoe is enjoying it. Look at her."

Tiny giggles floated through the cool air like bubbles. Grace walked over and sat in the swing next to Cole. As she was watching Zoe, he got up and stood at the back of her and pushed her.

She grabbed the ropes. "Cole!"

He kept pushing, and she kept screaming. "Cole!"

She finally jumped out and chased him around the swing. "I'm going to get you, Cole Chisholm." She chased him all the way into the house. He stopped in the kitchen with his arms in the air. "You got me."

Her face scrunched up, and he thought she was mad, but he realized she was trying to hold the laughter in. She gave up, and laughter burst from her throat in a soft, infectious sound. Then he laughed, unable to resist her. All he could see was forever in her dark, flashing eyes. If he had to wait this long for a good birthday, it was worth the wait.

Grace was worth the wait.

GRANDPA CAME THROUGH the French doors with Zoe in his arms. "Are you two through playing?"

"I'm sorry," Grace apologized to Grandpa. "The swing set is very nice. I was being silly." In that moment, she realized she was almost afraid to live because of everything that had happened. Living brought pain, and she somehow had banked everything down. When Cole was pushing her in the cool air, she'd felt an invigoration that she couldn't explain. She was alive, and a handsome man was flirting with her.

She took Zoe and put her in her high chair, which was still in the same place as when she had left. "Now let's have a birthday party."

She got plates out of the cabinet. Mr. Walt brought the ice cream from the freezer in the utility room.

As they were sitting down, a knock sounded at the back door, and Bo walked in with a six-pack in his hand. "Hey, happy birthday, friend."

Grace grabbed another plate, but before she could put it on the table, Miss Bertie came through the back door with a cake in her hand. She placed it on the table. "Who else made a cake?"

"I did," Grace replied. "I made Miss Cora's recipe."

Miss Bertie waved a hand. "Mine's better, so we'll eat mine."

"Says who?" Mr. Walt confronted her. "Your cake is no better than Cora's. I believe it's the same recipe. Now let's just sit down and enjoy ourselves. My boy is thirty-five years old today."

Grace grabbed another plate and paused as there was another knock at the door. How many people had Mr. Walt invited? A black couple walked in, and the woman had a cake carrier in her hand. Another cake!

She was introduced to Lamar and Dori Jones. It the first time she'd met them. Lamar was tall and thin and wore an old baseball cap. Dori was petite with graying dark hair and a sweet smile. They had to be somewhere in their sixties. "I'm sorry I called so many times about my car."

Lamar removed his cap and took a seat at the table. "You don't have to call anymore. I brought your car over. It's parked outside." He laid her keys on the table.

"Oh, thank you!" She had her own wheels again. She felt like dancing.

"Now, what cake are we going to eat?" Bo asked with a daring look at Cole.

Cole sat in the chair next to her. "I plan on eating a piece from each cake. It's not every day I get three birthday cakes. Thanks, everybody."

Grace served the cake, and everyone took a small piece of each. The conversation became lively as Mr. Walt, Miss Bertie and Mr. Lamar teased Bo and Cole about their childhood. They were good friends and probably had been for a long time. They said what they thought, and no one got their feelings hurt. Grace looked around the room and saw all the pictures of Jamie. She'd almost forgotten they were there. She guessed Cole was right. They didn't bother him. As she sat there and soaked up the conversation and the company, she knew what was missing in her life. This—closeness. Family.

Much later, she hugged Mr. Walt and Cole and got in her car and drove away. And she had to wonder if she would ever return. So much was going on in her head—it seemed as if she had mountains to climb and roads to walk. Would they bring her back here, where she'd glimpsed a touch of happiness?

THE DAYS TURNED into another week, and Christmas grew near. Cole and Grandpa would do something to celebrate the day, but it wasn't going to be in the barn. That time of his life was over. Grace had brought sunshine into his life, and he wished she could see the sunshine was waiting for her here, too, but the sadness was bringing her down. She'd seemed much better on his birthday and he'd wanted to talk to her, but with everyone around, he hadn't gotten the chance.

He came home one late afternoon to chaos. Grandpa had a wheelbarrow in the living room, and all of Jamie's pictures were in it. The wall was bare, with faded spots where the pictures had been. The attic ladder was down, and boxes were stacked in the hallway. What was Grandpa up to? He was speechless.

He cleared his throat. "Grandpa, what are you doing?"

"I'm getting rid of this stuff. Jamie is dead and he's never coming back and I don't need any reminders. All my feelings for my son are in my heart. I don't need to see his picture every day. It's time to let Jamie rest in peace. And now that Cora is with him, I know he's at peace."

Words failed him once again. All these years the photos had been on the walls, and now they weren't. How would Cole live without Jamie's shadow hanging over him?

"Don't just stand there. Come help me."

Cole hurried to do as asked. "Be very sure about this, Grandpa."

"I'm sure. I started a fire out back, and I'm going to burn all this stuff. Everything he has ever owned is here. His clothes, his toys, everything. I saved some things for you on the coffee table."

On the coffee table lay a pocketknife, an Aggie ring, a watch, a fifty-dollar gold piece, a key chain with Cole's picture on it and a photo of a woman with dark eyes and dark hair in a silver frame. He picked up the picture and stared at it. It had to be his mother. He never realized she had dark eyes and dark hair. He must've said the words out loud because Grandpa replied, "Yes, she did. She was very beautiful."

Grandpa handed him a large manila envelope. "More pictures of your mom are in there. I saved them for you."

He sat on the coffee table and looked through the photos of a woman he didn't know. His mother. She had long, long dark hair, almost down to her waist, and she was smiling in every picture. Some of them she was laughing into Cole's dad's eyes. "She looks happy."

"They were."

Cole got lost in the photos of the two people who had created him. A bit of sadness touched his heart. His hand rested on a photo. How he wished he had known her.

His grandfather called him, and he helped carry everything out to the fire. Slowly they tossed things on the fire, picture frames and all. Grandpa didn't want to save them. He was getting rid of all the bad memories. How he had come to this epiphany was a mystery to Cole. But it was something that should've been done years ago. Grandma just couldn't handle living without the memories.

They decided to leave Jamie's baby bed. It was still good and senseless to burn. They kept the high chair, too. Zoe would need it when she came to visit, and Cole hoped that day was soon.

The flames and smoke leaped toward the sky in a blaze of orange and black. The fire licked and gnawed its way to the sky, as if it were cleansing the place of bad spirits. Since everything was old, it burned quickly.

They stood for a long time watching the smoke and flames. Cole took a water hose and watered down the grass around the fire, and it slowly died down. Jamie was gone, and just like that a heavy weight was lifted from Cole's heart. The shadow was gone.

They slowly made their way back to the house. "I bought steaks, and we can do them on the grill. I'll show you how to use it."

"It's about time."

Cole put potatoes in the oven and went into the living room to talk to Grandpa, who was sitting quietly in his chair.

"You okay?"

He waved a hand toward the walls. "Look at that. Now we're going to have to repaint."

"We can do that in an afternoon."

"Let's get it done before Christmas."

Grandpa seemed fine, but Cole worried this might be too much for him. They sat on the patio while they waited for the steaks to cook and talked. Leaves had piled up against the house, and Cole needed to get rid of them. There was lot to be done around the place. Time was a valuable commodity these days with his job. But he had to makc time for his grandpa.

"Your grandma loved you, you know?"

Cole rubbed his hands together. "In a way, I guess she did. She was always trying to protect me."

"Yeah. She was always trying to protect Jamie, too. She just could never let go, and Jamie could never say no to her. He grew a backbone when he met Beth. He told her he was getting married, and she said no, he wasn't old enough. The boy was twenty-two years old, and she said he wasn't old enough. Can you imagine that? He said hc was getting married and she couldn't stop him. She cried and cried and said, 'Walter, talk to him. He's too young.' I told her that she had to let go. He was in love, and he wasn't going to change his mind." Grandpa shook his head. "It was a difficult time when he brought Beth here to meet us. Cora didn't like her, and she didn't make any bones about it. Jamie was as mad as I've ever seen him. He went to his room, packed his clothes and told her if Beth wasn't welcome here, he wasn't, either. And he left. Cora cried and cried for days and begged me to call him. It just went on and on until I finally called Jamie and said we had to work this out."

Grandpa shivered.

"Do you want me to get your jacket?" It was sixty degrees outside and getting cooler.

"No. It just felt like a ghost whispered against my skin."

Cole wasn't sure how that felt. "Maybe we better go inside."

"No. I want you to know how much your parents wanted you and how much they loved you. You were conceived in love. I want you to know there was love in every day of your life, even though it didn't feel like it at times. I want you to know that."

Cole rubbed his hands together again, tears stinging his eyes. "I know that now, Grandpa. You don't have to worry."

"I know I compare you a lot to Jamie, and I don't mean anything bad by that. You're his son, a part of him, but you got all that strong stuff from those other people."

Cole laughed. He couldn't help himself. "Ah, Grandpa, I think I got a lot of those qualities from the man sitting across from me."

"Could be." Grandpa shook his head and got to his feet. "But I'm a lot like Jamie. I could never say no to your grandma." He touched Cole's shoulder. "I love you, son."

Cole stood on unsteady legs and said words he'd never said before in his life. "I love you, too, Grandpa." He hugged his grandfather, and the walls of Jamie came down with a flourish. The past and the bad memories were as cold as the ashes of the fire. He could feel love to the fullest and recognize it when he felt it. He didn't have to yearn for it anymore. He had it. He had everything he ever wanted.

Except for Grace.

CHAPTER NINETEEN

IT WAS NEARING CHRISTMAS, and Grace had long days at the retirement villas. Everyone wanted to be ready for the big event. The place was decorated to the hilt, and there seemed to be an air of excitement. And everyone wanted something done, from wrapping presents to making sure their children would be there sometime during the holiday. That was the sad part. Sometimes the children didn't show up. But everyone at the villas tried to make it as happy as possible for everyone.

Carolers from several churches would come in on Christmas Eve from four to ten in the evening and again on Christmas morning from nine to eleven. She had it planned down to the last minute. Christmas Eve was the big party in the community room. The tree had been decorated in red and silver, and gifts were beneath it. Management always gave everyone a gift; it was usually socks, and it was again this year. It was a small gift, but they appreciated it.

Mr. Walt had called and asked if she could come on Christmas Eve, and she told him that she didn't know. And she didn't. There was so much to do, and she didn't know when she could get away. She promised Mr. Walt she would do her best to be there on Christmas Day. She wasn't working that day. The families would arrive and take care of most of the residents. Those families who didn't show would make it a sad day for some. They could listen to Christmas music and do what they normally did. There would be a big lunch to enjoy.

She was always exhausted when she reached home, but Zoe always brought her joy. She was growing so fast, Grace wanted to keep her a baby forever. She was sitting and playing with Zoe when Frannie dropped a bombshell on her.

"Grace. I know you're busy, but could I talk to you for a minute?"

Grace stared at her friend, who seemed nervous. And Frannie was never nervous. She always faced life head-on. "What's up?"

She pulled something out of her jeans. "Robert sent me a ticket to come for Christmas. I leave at eleven on Christmas Eve. I know it's short notice, but…"

Grace put Zoe on the floor and stood up. "What are you so nervous about?" They'd been friends forever, and there had never been an awkward moment between them.

"I hate to leave you shorthanded. Who will you get to keep Zoe?"

"I'll just take her with me to the villas. She'll be a source of entertainment for those who have no families coming. It should work out, so don't worry."

"There's something else."

"What? If you're not coming back for a few days, I'll work something out. We always work something out."

"Robert wants me to come to Virginia to live, and I'm thinking about doing that. You're strong enough now to handle life on your own."

Grace desperately tried to be happy for her friend. She really tried, and then she had to force herself. She hugged Frannie. "Forgive me if I'm feeling a little sad. I will miss you, but you're right. I'm strong enough now to handle life. Thank you for being my anchor for so long."

"Oh, sweetie." Frannie brushed away a

few tears, as did Grace. "You've been such a blessing in my life. It would've been so lonely without you and Brooke. We don't have to lose touch. We have phones and we can Face-Time—we can do all kinds of things. I will never lose touch with you. I want to see pictures of Zoe almost every day."

"When will you be leaving?"

"After I come back from Christmas, I'm putting the house on the market, and probably around March I'll leave. That will give you time to find someone to keep Zoe—I'm not leaving until you do. I want it to be someone who will take very good care of her."

Grace smiled through her tears. "I love you, Frannie."

"I love you, too, Gracie. And if I don't get along with my daughter-in-law, I will be coming back here to live with you."

Grace laughed. Her last link to family was leaving, but oddly enough, fear didn't grip her or paralyze her. She could handle it. For Zoe and for herself, she could face this new life and whatever came next.

ON SUNDAY AFTERNOON Cole and Grandpa painted the living room in an off-white color. It brightened up the room but made everything else look dirty. That's when they realized they needed to paint all the other rooms.

"This house needs a lot of work," Grandpa remarked.

Cole agreed. "We'll start on that after the first of the year. Let's concentrate on getting through Christmas."

"I talked to Grace and asked her to come on Christmas Eve, and she said she didn't know when she could get off."

There was sadness in Grandpa's voice, and it ignited a bit of anger in his stomach. Why couldn't she come? Grandpa wanted to see Zoe, and Cole did, too. But he had to let it go.

Christmas Eve he came home to find a seven-foot-tall Christmas tree in the corner of the living room. He stared like a five-year-old at the bright lights and the colorful ornaments. At the top of the tree was a star that made him catch his breath.

"Remember that?" Grandpa asked as Cole continued to stare at the tree.

"I made that in fifth grade." He cleared his throat. "You kept it?"

"Of course I kept it. I kept all that stuff we decorated the tree with in the barn. I put them in a plastic box I bought at Walmart and stored them in the attic. It's about time we celebrated Christmas in this living room again."

All the years he'd felt unloved and unwanted came down to this moment. He hadn't felt loved then, but he felt it deeply now. As an adult he was beginning to see that people expressed love in different ways. His grandpa was always there for him, making sure he had things like other kids. His grandmother cooked his favorite foods for him, and she had made his grandfather buy an expensive car so Cole would be safe. Her love was there, but he never recognized it beyond her grief. It seemed as if a sad little boy suddenly stepped into the shoes of the adult Cole. He understood everything. And the pain and the sadness were no longer there.

ON CHRISTMAS EVE Grace was busily getting everything done that she needed to. There were snacks and drinks in the community room, and people were coming and going and visiting with their loved ones. She wanted to leave by two o'clock. She had told Mr. Walt she didn't know when she could get there, but she would try to make it for Christmas Eve. There was no sense in spending Christmas alone when Zoe would bring Mr. Walt so much joy. And seeing Cole would make her Christmas.

Zoe did well in the Pack 'n Play and enjoyed seeing all the people. They oohed and aahed over her. In Christmassy red and white with a big red bow on top of her head, Zoe smiled at everyone. Grace's eyes kept straying to the big clock on the wall. She had to leave soon to make it to Horseshoe by four. Mr. Walt had said that everyone gathered on the courthouse square to celebrate Christmas, and she wanted to be there by then. Zoe would enjoy it. And she would, too.

Just as she was about to say her goodbyes, Mrs. Carroll fell to the floor in excruciating pain. She screamed and clutched her right side. She had recently had hip surgery, and Grace knew something was wrong. She dropped down by Mrs. Carroll as everyone looked on. She called 911 and then the RN.

"It hurts, Grace. I'm scared." Mrs. Carroll was eighty-five and was one of those residents who had no one—her son and daughter rarely visited.

"It'll be okay. Just hold on."

Grace's aide, Nancy, got everyone out of the room while Grace dealt with Mrs. Carroll. The RN arrived and checked her over, and then the ambulance arrived. Soon Mrs. Carroll was carted out on a gurney. Grace hurried to her office to call the son and daughter. As usual they said to do what needed to be done and that they were celebrating Christmas with their families and couldn't come. How could some people be so cruel?

Gwen, the RN, came back in. "She's really scared."

Grace and Gwen had been friends for a long time and usually went out to eat or for drinks, but since Zoe's arrival, Grace's social life had dwindled to nothing.

"I know. Her kids aren't coming. I guess I'll go to the hospital and see how she is."

"Don't you have plans with the hero cop?"

"Yeah, but I can't leave her all alone."

Gwen studied her for a few seconds. "Grace, she's not your responsibility after she leaves here. The hospital will take very good care of her. Go and have a merry Christmas. You deserve a little bit of happiness, too."

Grace thought about that for a minute. "I'll go over and check on Mrs. Carroll and try to make it to Horseshoe by five. I think I can make it work."

"You can't make everybody happy. Take

this time for yourself and go. Mrs. Carroll will be okay."

She wished she could do as Gwen had said. But there was something in her that couldn't leave an elderly person who was scared and alone. Maybe it had something to do with her grandmother, who had taught her to look out for others. Whatever it was, it was there and Grace couldn't ignore it. Mr. Walt would understand if she was a little late.

Luckily there was a girl she knew at the receptionist's desk in the lobby. She asked if she would look out for Zoe while she went and checked on a patient. She happily agreed since nothing was going on.

Mrs. Carroll's bones were porous—the hip was fractured and they had to go into surgery to pin it. She went in to reassure Mrs. Carroll, and she seemed to relax.

Grace waited in the lobby with Zoe until the nurse called to tell her that the surgery was over. The receptionist took Zoe, and she hurried upstairs again. Mrs. Carroll was just waking up. She reached out and grabbed Grace's hand.

"Thank you."

"Everything went fine," Grace told her. "You'll be back to the villas in no time. Just relax and get some rest. I'll try to see you to-morrow."

Mrs. Carroll closed her eyes, and Grace hurried to the lobby once again. Thanking the receptionist and wishing her a merry Christmas, she took Zoe and ran for the front door and Horseshoe.

When she drove over the cattle guard, she noticed it was after seven—too late to enjoy the festivities on the town square. The tree had already been lit and everyone was probably singing Christmas songs by now.

The garage door was down, and the house was dark. She drove around to the back, where there was a light over the back door and at the barn.

She rested her head on the steering wheel. Maybe Gwen was right. She couldn't make everyone happy and she should stop trying. Maybe she should think about herself for a change, but she wasn't that type of person.

The look on Mrs. Carroll's face had said it all for her. She could rest now that she knew someone cared. That meant a lot to Grace. But she'd disappointed people she cared a lot about. She put her window down and breathed in the fresh country air, and that scent of cleanliness evoked a memory of home.

From the second Cole Chisholm had rescued her, there been a connection that she couldn't explain. And after everything they had been through, that connection hadn't changed. Everything she ever wanted was here on this country farm. And she didn't understand why she'd had such a hard time accepting it.

COLE AND GRANDPA made their way home from the festivities in Horseshoe.

"That was a really big crowd tonight," Grandpa said. "I saw people I haven't seen in years."

"Me, too," Cole replied. It was a big event for people who grew up in Horseshoe. He'd seen a lot of people tonight he grew up and went to school with. It was a catching-up time, like a big family reunion, as everyone stood around the big tree, drank coffee and hot chocolate, and ate kolaches and later sang Christmas songs. No liquor was allowed. It was a family occasion. He just wished Grace had cared enough to come.

As if reading his thoughts, Grandpa said, "I thought she'd come. Zoe would have enjoyed watching the tree light up."

"Just you and me, Grandpa. We've done that a time or two." He tried to cheer him up.

"That we have."

He drove into the garage, and they got out.

"You're helping me cook a big meal tomorrow."

"Grandpa, we don't need all that food. We can eat at Miss Bertie's."

"We're not eating at Bertie's. We're cooking dinner just like your grandmother did. That's what family is about. There might be two of us, but were still a family."

Cole groaned as they went into the house and flipped on lights.

"Where's Rascal?" Grandpa asked. "He's not in his bed."

"He probably went—" Cole could hear the dog barking. "He's outside."

"He never goes out this late," Grandpa said. "He must have an armadillo cornered again."

Cole opened the back door, and his heart lifted. There was Grace and Zoe, and Rascal jumping up and down barking at them. They were here!

"Grandpa, come look."

"Nah. Leave that dog outside. He'll come in when he wants to."

"He doesn't have an armadillo. He has

something else, and you have to see it. Come here."

Grandpa stomped to the back door. "I'm ready to sit down. I've been standing all night."

Cole opened the door wide, and Grandpa's tired blue eyes lit up like the Christmas tree in Horseshoe. "They're here! We should have left the door open." He hurried outside as fast as he could, and Cole trailed behind him. Grandpa grabbed Zoe and kissed her cheeks.

"She's cold. I'm taking her inside."

He stared at Grace in the moonlight. He'd never seen anyone more lovely. "You made it."

"I'm sorry I'm so late." She told him what had happened at the villas, and he realized how much she cared about other people. He and Grandpa fit in there somewhere, but he wanted more from her, much more. A tiny part of him was beginning to realize that might never happen.

CHRISTMAS WAS ONE of the best Grace had ever had. Cole helped her carry her things into the house. She carried the diaper bag through the breakfast room to the living room and stopped dead. The diaper bag fell from her hands. She looked around at the freshly painted room with no pictures of Jamie. She glanced at Mr. Walt, who was playing with Zoe in his chair.

"What happened to the pictures?"

"Oh, Cole and I burned them. We burned the stuff in the attic, too."

She ran over and gave him a big hug. "Mr. Walt, I'm so proud of you."

Cole walked in from putting her stuff in the bedroom, and she glanced at him. "It's amazing. The room looks so much bigger."

"Amazing Grace," he murmured.

She smiled and walked to him, hugging him around the waist. "I'll let you get away with that this time." She poked him in the ribs. "Only this time."

After that, everything was magical, but at times Grace could feel herself pulling away, and she didn't know why. They got up early to put Zoe's toys under the tree. Cole explained to her about some of the ornaments on the tree and the star. There were some they had used in the barn years ago. It brought tears to her eyes. There was a miracle happening with the Chisholm men, and it was awesome to watch.

Mr. Walt had bought Zoe a big red wagon

with tall sides, and Cole had bought her a teddy bear that was five times as big as she was. There were other gifts there, too, and Grace couldn't help but think how lucky Zoe was to have so many people love her.

They couldn't get Zoe out of the wagon, so Mr. Walt took her outside to pull her around while she and Cole started dinner. Mr. Walt already had a big hen baking. Cole had talked him out of a turkey, it seemed. Cooking with Cole was so much more fun than with Mr. Walt. They laughed, joked and flirted and she soaked up his presence, his smile, his good mood. It was Christmas, after all.

They managed to get Christmas dinner on the table without ruining anything. It was just the four of them, and it felt like family—the only family she had. It was right there on the edge of her mind, waiting for her to just grab it and hold on to it and never let go. But something was holding her back, and she didn't know what it was. So she went with the mood and tried not to let it get her down.

Later Bo showed up and had his customary beer, and there was more laughter and visiting. Eventually the day came to an end, and she had to return to Austin. She had to check on Mrs. Carroll and…

"Could we talk for a minute?" Cole asked.

They sat at the kitchen table like they had so many times before.

"It was a good Christmas, but I feel you were just partly here. Is something wrong?"

She pushed back her hair. "I don't know. I'm trying to come to grips with Brooke's death, and I'm now getting all this anger inside and I don't know what to do with it." Finally, she'd put her finger on was bothering her. The anger. That wasn't like her.

"Let it go," he told her. "You did everything you could, and there's nothing for you to feel guilty about."

She twisted her hands in her lap. "It's not that easy."

"It is. If you want a life, you have to let it go." He paused for a moment and lifted her chin so he could look into her eyes. "You're the most wonderful woman I've ever met, and if anyone deserves a life, you do. You brought sunshine to this place—" he waved his hand toward the bare walls "—and chased all the ghosts away. That takes a special kind of person, and it's time for you to live your life. And I don't need any more time to know how I feel about you. My feelings are rock solid. I want you to be part of my life. A part of Grandpa's life. The choice is up to you."

"Cole—"

He placed a finger over her lips and stood and kissed her cheek, slowly. She breathed in the scent of him and his masculinity, and it triggered every feminine emotion in her. She loved him. Why couldn't she deal with all the negative feelings inside her about her sister? Why couldn't she just let go and accept what he was offering her? What was holding her back?

DAYS TURNED INTO another week, and the New Year rolled around. Cole and Bo sat in back of the barn, drinking beer and popping fire-crackers. They used to do that as teenagers.

"I think we're getting too old for this," Cole said. "It used to be more fun when we tried to hide it from Grandpa."

Bo set off another rocket that blasted into the air with bursts of lights that lit up the sky. "Like he couldn't hear these rockets going off like bombs."

"He let us get away with a lot," Cole remarked.

"Mmm."

They sat there staring into the moonlit

night, and they could hear fireworks going off down the road. Everyone was celebrating the New Year.

"I don't think she's coming back."

"Why not?" He didn't have to tell Bo who he was talking about. He knew.

"It's just a feeling I have. She's not over her sister's death, and I can't help her."

"Sorry, man. But give it some time."

Time—that ever-evolving thing that never stayed the same.

He went back to work and tried to put Grace out of his mind, but she was always right there. He was never going to forget her. Ironically, Grandpa was fine living his life like he used to. Cole was heartbroken.

They had been like broken stick figures, and Grace had put them back together again. And now she was gone. How was he supposed to deal with that?

CHAPTER TWENTY

DAYS TURNED INTO WEEKS, and Grace just went through the motions of living. Frannie had returned home and was busy packing up her house. She'd put it on the market. Grace had found someone to babysit Zoe. Actually, Frannie had found her. She was a retired lady who lived down the street and was looking for something to do. Grace knew her, so that made it much easier.

Mrs. Carroll went to a rehab center to regain her strength and would be back at the villas in a couple of weeks. Her daughter had finally arrived and was taking care of things. Life settled down at work, and Grace's days weren't so long.

Zoe's birthday came in February, and Grace didn't call Mr. Walt or Cole. She thought it best if she didn't. She had to put distance between them for now. It hurt to do that, but she was trying very hard to figure out how to handle the emotions inside her.

While helping Frannie pack odds and ends for the movers, she came across some photo albums and took a peek before putting them in the box. One of them was of her and Brooke when they were kids. She curled up on the floor and flipped through the pages. Frannie sat on the sofa beside her.

"Now aren't those some beautiful girls?"

"We look a lot alike."

"Not when a person gets to know you. You have a big heart and have a need to help everyone, but sometimes I don't think Brooke cared about anybody but herself. I'm sorry if that hurts."

She looked up at the woman who knew them better than anyone. "It doesn't hurt. I've been trying to understand my feelings about Brooke these past few weeks, and I haven't succeeded. Looking at these photos, I remember all the arguments and all the times I tried to make her see sense, but she had to have her own way. Remember that time she wanted to marry that boy when she was sixteen and he was seventeen? She went on and on about how she loved him and she was never going to love anyone the way she loved him."

"Oh, my, do I remember that. She was going to run away and marry him. And then two weeks later he was killed in a drug deal gone bad. She cried for days."

"Stayed in her room and wouldn't go to school. I thought I'd never get her out of that room," Grace murmured almost to herself.

"All it took was the new paperboy in his souped-up car."

"Yeah, she was running away that morning. She got up early, which she never did. I watched her out my window to see where she was going. The paperboy drove up about that time and pulled to the curb. She leaned in for a long time and talked to him. He pulled away to finish his route, and she came back into the house. And then she was in love with him. That's the story of Brooke's life. She needed someone to love. I loved her, but it wasn't enough. Zoe wasn't enough, either."

"Gracie, you did all you could for your sister, so don't beat yourself up over this. I'd feel much better if you'd talk to Cole. I just want you to have someone to care for you the way you deserve."

Grace got to her feet and placed the album on the sofa. "Yes, I deserve that. I'm going out for a while. Will you watch Zoe?"

"Of course, of course, go and have a good time. Call one of your friends and go out to eat or something. Enjoy yourself for a change."

Grace didn't call anyone. She went to the cemetery. Since it was late February and the weather was cold, she bundled up in her big coat and pulled a cap over her head to stay warm. With the chilly weather, the cemetery was empty. The grass crunched beneath her boots as she walked through tombstones to reach the grave. A morbid sense of futility washed over her as she stared at the tombstones of her parents and her grandparents and Brooke's freshly dug grave.

She drew cold air into her lungs and fought against emotions that she couldn't control. What she could control was her life and how she lived it. She shoved her hands into her pockets. She stood there with the cold wind stinging her cheeks, and it became clear how Brooke had manipulated her over the years. She had to say something for her own peace of mind.

"He didn't love you. He took your life and he didn't love you and no matter what I said you wouldn't listen. Why couldn't you see how bad Joel Briggs was, especially when Zoe was born? You had a child and she should've been your main focus, but the moment *he* called, you ran to him and left Zoe with me because you knew I would take care of her. But she needed her mother. She needed you, and you put *him* before her. That's what makes me so angry and I can't get past it. And Kevin Colson? I can't even put into words how angry I am about that. If you were so in love with Joel, how did that happen? Since you did so much to stay with Joel, I have to assume you didn't know Kevin was the father. For years I've tried to guide you, and you went in all the wrong directions to spite me. Look how it ended.

"If it hadn't been for Cole, Zoe would be living with strangers clear across the country. He risked his job to save a child. Your child. He did it for me. That's love, real love—obviously something you'd never grasped, even though I showered you with love when our mother ignored us. I'm not having any more guilty feelings about what happened. It was your life, and you chose to degrade yourself for a man who used you. That was your choice, and my choice now is to forgive myself and raise your daughter as best as I can. I love Zoe with all my heart just the way I loved you. I'm mad right now, but…but I still love you and hope you rest in peace."

When the tears came, they brought her to her knees, and she said goodbye to the sister she'd loved. "You got in over your head, Brookie, and I guess there was no turning back." The anger left her chest in a swoosh of tears and hiccups. She got to her feet and walked out of the cemetery, feeling free for the first time in months.

COLE HAD JUST helped solve a murder case, and he had two days off. A murder case was draining emotionally and sometimes physically. The seedier side of life always got to him.

He helped Grandpa feed the boys and the chickens and just relaxed being at home. He hadn't heard a word from Grace since Christmas. Slowly she was pulling away from them, and they had to let her go. Their days together were just a moment out of time, but he would remember her always. He didn't think there was a day that went by he didn't think of her and Zoe and wonder how they were doing.

"I think I'll get the tractor out and plow a garden," Grandpa said.

"Why?" Cole asked as patiently as possible.

"Because we need food to eat. Those vegetables your grandma canned won't last forever. Then what will we eat?"

"Those same vegetables are available at the grocery store."

"They don't taste the same."

Grandpa was pushing his buttons again. "Okay, whatever, but I don't have much time to help you."

"I don't need your help. I've been planting a garden since before you were born."

They were sniping at each other again. All of Amazing Grace's magic was for naught. Or he was just having a bad day. Grandpa was still his old self. He was the one having a hard time adjusting to Grace not coming back.

He leaned on the old wood fence and watched as Barney nudged Gomer with his horns. Gently, but not friendly. They were testy, too. Even though it was cold today, there was a freshness in the air that signaled spring wasn't far away. It had been four months since he had found Grace lying on the cold, hard ground unconscious. He couldn't have known how that moment would change his life forever.

Rascal barked, and he glanced toward the lane and saw a blue car coming toward the house. Grace's car! She was back!

She pulled around to the back door and got out, and then she opened the car door to get Zoe out. He blinked to make sure he wasn't dreaming.

He slowly walked toward her and realized he was holding his breath. Sucking in air, he kept walking.

Grace set Zoe on her feet, and she toddled to him with a big pink bow bobbling on her head. He squatted and caught her.

"Hey, smooches."

She planted a big kiss on his cheek with a loud kissing sound.

Cole glanced at Grace.

"She's giving kisses now. Loudly. I think she saw it on a cartoon."

"Cole, where did you…" Grandpa came out of the barn and stopped in midsentence when he saw who was here. "Oh, my, Zoe Grace, my baby, has come home."

Cole kissed Zoe's cheek and pointed her toward Grandpa. She took off as fast as her little feet could carry her, jabbering all the way.

He turned his attention to Grace and stared into her beautiful dark eyes. They were bright and clear, and he didn't see any sadness or secrets. "You look great."

She brushed back her hair. "I feel great."

"Got rid of the demons, huh?"

"Sort of." She caught his eyes. "I'm sorry I needed all this time, but I had to deal with my feelings about Brooke. You helped me so much, and I didn't want my feelings to be out of gratitude. If not for you, Zoe would be living with that couple somewhere in California and I would've never seen her again. Joel would've been arrested, but it would've been too late. Zoe would've been gone, and there was nothing I would've been able to do about it. Joel was the father until you discovered he wasn't. No one would have gone that extra mile. I keep thinking about that, and I guess what made me so mad was that Brooke chose Joel over Zoe and me. That just infuriated me, and I couldn't shake it."

"But you have now?"

"Frannie is moving to live near her son, and we were going through some old family albums. She has lots of pictures of me and Brooke, and as I looked through those photos, I remembered a lot of things I kept stored in my brain and didn't want to verbalize. Brooke always had a penchant for bad boys, even in high school. She would never listen to me, and I realized there was nothing I could have done to get her to listen to me about Joel. It wasn't my fault, and I guess I had to forgive myself. And I had to tell her in person how I felt."

He frowned. "How did you do that?"

"I went to the cemetery and told her things I should have said a long time ago. Afterward, all those negative feelings vanished."

He'd given her the time she'd needed, even though he hadn't been very patient, and it had worked. He took a step toward her. "Remember the day we sat in Grandpa's truck and I told you about my past and you said I needed a big hug to squeeze all the bad memories out of me?" He took another step toward her. "I think I'll take that hug right about now."

"Oh, Cole..." She flew into his arms and gave him the biggest hug he'd ever had. One arm wrapped around his waist and the other around his neck.

"Tighter," he whispered.

They were bound so tightly even cold air couldn't get through. They stood as one. Locked. Forever. Neither said a word as they soaked up the energy from each other. And the heat.

"I love you, Cole," she whispered into his chest.

The soft note in her voice sent his heart soaring. "Not too long ago, Grandpa and I were doing steaks out on the grill and talking. He told me he loved me, and I was able to say the words back to him for the first time in my life. I just never thought that with my childhood, love would be a part of my life. But the moment I looked into your dark eyes, I knew I was lost." He cupped her face, loving the feel of her soft hair against his hands. "Grace Bennett, I love you. Will you marry me?"

"Yes, yes!" Her eyes sparkled through her shining tears.

He took her lips, and the world ceased to exist as they kissed with all the newfound feelings inside them. The heat between them chased away the cold, and Cole held on just a moment longer because he couldn't let go. Finally Grace rested her head just below Cole's chin.

"How are we going to make this work, Cole? We both work in Austin, and we can't leave Grandpa alone."

"Grandpa?"

She lifted her head and smiled. "Yes. I can call him that now."

"Yes, you can. But don't worry. We'll work something out. I want to get married as soon as possible. How do you feel about that?"

"I do, too, and it doesn't have to be a big wedding, but I want to wear a white dress."

"That's…" His words trailed away as he saw a truck coming up the lane.

"You have company," Grace remarked.

"That's Odell. He lives down 77. I'll see what he wants and be right back."

She kissed his lips. "Okay."

Cole walked toward the old white Chevy truck. Odell Willis's family had a vegetable farm. There were eight kids in the family, and Odell was the youngest. He was the "oops" baby, as he had been known to say. Cole and Odell were the same age and had gone to school together. Odell was slow, and kids picked on him. Cole and Bo had always been his heroes, because they took up for him. Cole didn't know a better person than Odell. His heart was the biggest thing about him.

Odell got out and they shook hands. He was a medium height, stocky, with a Dallas Cowboys baseball cap on.

"Hey, Cole."

"Haven't seen you in a long time, Odell."

"My daddy's been sick, and I have to help take care of him." Odell worshipped his dad, and anything his dad said was the law, according to Odell.

"I'm sorry. I didn't know."

"I told you."

Cole frowned. "When did you tell me?"

"When I called you about that woman who hit the tree."

Cole did a double take. "You called me about the woman that slid off the road around Thanksgiving?"

Odell nodded. "Yep. I told you she was dead, and I carried the baby up to Mr. Walt's. I knocked on the door. Rascal barked, so I knew he was home and I could hear him talking. But I couldn't wait. I had to go. My sister had taken my dad to Temple to the doctor, and she called and told me I better get there fast. My dad was real sick."

"You called me?"

"Yeah, and I left you a message, but you never called me back. My dad was so sick that I forgot all about it." Odell pulled out his phone. "See."

Cole looked at the phone. "The last two numbers of my phone number are turned around."

"Oh, dang it, I do that a lot."

Cole put his correct number in Odell's phone. "That happened months ago. Why are you just now telling me this?"

"Because I was in Temple with my dad. He had to have his leg amputated below the knee, and my sister rented an apartment so we could stay there with him. He had a real bad infection. We didn't think he was going to make it, and I would never leave my dad. We came home last week, and he's doing great. I help him with his artificial leg and everything."

Cole patted his shoulder, knowing Odell didn't mean any harm. "I'm glad."

"What happened to that baby?" Odell wanted to know.

Cole pointed to Zoe, who was petting Gomer. "That's her right there."

"You kept her." Odell shook his head. "No, Cole, it was a little baby." He put his hands out to show how little.

"That was four months ago. Babies grow."

"Oh. I'm sorry about her mother."

"What do you mean?"

"She was dead. That's why I didn't put her in my truck and take her to the doctor. I put my hand in front of her nose like my daddy taught me, and she wasn't breathing."

Cole patted Odell's shoulder again. "She wasn't dead, Odell. She was just really cold.

I found her later, and that's her right there." He pointed to Grace standing by Grandpa.

Odell couldn't quite process everything. "Did I do something wrong, Cole?"

"Everything turned out okay, but next time call Wyatt or someone you can talk to and don't leave a message when something is that serious."

"I don't like to call Wyatt. He's always fussing at me for speeding in town."

"Odell, call Wyatt when something goes wrong." His voice was stern, and it got Odell's attention.

"Okay."

Odell drove away, and Grace strolled to him. "What was that about?"

He took her in his arms and smiled into her eyes. "The mystery is solved."

"What mystery?"

"Of how Zoe got to Grandpa's front porch." He told her about Odell's story.

"Are you going to tell Grandpa?"

"Not today. I'm going to let him believe that Grandma or Jamie sent you and Zoe for now. I kind of believe it myself."

"You do?"

"I can't explain what happened on that cold winter day, but I know our two worlds collided in a good way, and I believe it took a little divine intervention for it to turn out the way it did."

She leaned back in his arms. "I love you."

"I love you, too." He kissed her lips gently. "Now let's see how Grandpa feels about a wedding."

Otis shot out of the barn, wings flapping and cock-a-doodle-dooing. Rascal barked. Gomer brayed, and Goober oinked. Zoe's giggles filled the air, and Grandpa's smile was as wide as Texas.

"Welcome home." Cole smiled into her beautiful eyes and wrapped his arms around her, feeling love all the way to his soul. Fear gripped him for a moment, but he knew they were both strong enough to handle the ups and downs of life. They'd been tested and survived. Now the future was theirs.

EPILOGUE

Five months later

"CORA, I THOUGHT I couldn't survive without you and that I had no life left, but I was wrong. I'm moving on now and living. Cole and Grace got married in the little church here in Horseshoe. It was beautiful. Made me misty-eyed. Our boy is happy now. We can't go back and change his childhood, but despite it, he turned out to be a fine young man. I'm proud of him. I know you had a hand in sending Grace and Zoe here to the farm. It was your way to make up for his dismal childhood. Thank you for that. Grace is a kind and loving woman, and Cole is crazy about her. And Zoe Grace just lights up my life. I love her as if she was my own grandchild. And she is.

"There have been some ups and downs, though. They both work in Austin, and they tried commuting and then they stayed at Grace's house, but Grace was worried about me. Bless her heart. Did I tell you what a wonderful girl she is? But I have to take care of the place and the animals. Every now and then I go in and spend the day with Zoe. I firmly believe the young ones need time alone, and I'm doing fine by myself. I go to Bertie's and eat or go down to the diner. I want my boy to be as happy as possible and not worry about me.

"I know you know this already, but everything came to a head last week. Wyatt called and wanted to talk to Cole, so he went in to see him on a Sunday. He was offered a job by the DA's office and the sheriff's office as a criminal investigator. Crime has now come to Horseshoe, Texas, and they need someone with Cole's experience on the team. I thought he would turn it down. He worked for years to get where he is in the Austin Police Department. But it was like a gift from heaven. Can you figure that one out? He's taking the job, and the pay is good. And they're remodeling the house and adding a master bedroom and bath and an office for Cole. The reno should be finished by Thanksgiving. Then we're all moving back into the house. For now we're living in Austin. I thought I would hate the city, but it's not so bad. I take Zoe Grace and

Rascal to the park every morning. Bertie's feeding the animals. She's a good old soul, and we couldn't get through life without people like her.

"That's not all the good news. Grace was also offered a job here in Horseshoe as the director of the community center. We haven't had one in a long time, and she's just the one to plan things to keep the elderly busy. And it will give her more time to spend with Zoe. They'll start their new jobs after the first of the year.

"Did I tell you that Cole's in the process of adopting Zoe? And if the amount of time they spend in the bedroom is any indication, there'll be a new little one coming soon. That might make my heart explode. I never knew it was possible to be this happy. Maybe it's because our boy's so happy. He looks at Grace just the way Jamie looked at Beth. Now, don't get your wings in a knot. It was wrong of you not to accept Beth. I guess you see that now or you wouldn't have sent Grace and Zoe. Thank you, Cora. I won't be talking to you much anymore. I don't need to. I'll be busy raising our grandchild. Give Jamie a kiss from me. I love you. Goodbye."

* * * * *

Want more of Linda Warren's
Texas Rebels?

Watch for Bo's story,
coming December 2020 only from
Harlequin Heartwarming!

Get 4 FREE REWARDS!

We'll send you 2 FREE Books plus 2 FREE Mystery Gifts.

Love Inspired Suspense books showcase how courage and optimism unite in stories of faith and love in the face of danger.

FREE
Value Over
$20

#323 ENCHANTED BY THE RODEO QUEEN

The Mountain Monroes • by Melinda Curtis

When Emily Clark goes looking for true love, she expects to find a cowboy, not a Hollywood writer. But opposites attract, and city-boy Jonah Monroe might be exactly what this rodeo queen wants!

#324 A MATCH MADE PERFECT

Butterfly Harbor Stories • by Anna J. Stewart

Brooke Ardell had to walk away from her family. Now she's determined to right her wrongs with her ex, Sebastian Evans, and their daughter. Are they willing to risk their hearts by letting Brooke back in?

#325 HER SURPRISE COWBOY

Heroes of Shelter Creek • by Claire McEwen

Liam Dale never expected to see Trisha Gilbert again—and certainly not with his baby son! But he's determined to be there for his child...and for Trisha. If only she would let him in.

#326 A SOLDIER SAVED

Veterans' Road • by Cheryl Harper

Veteran Jason Ward is done with adventure, opting instead for new, quieter pursuits, but developing a crush on his writing instructor, Angela Simmons, wasn't part of the plan! Now they both need to decide which risks are worth taking.

ReaderService.com has a new look!

We have refreshed our website and we want to share our new look with you. Head over to ReaderService.com and check it out!

On ReaderService.com, you can:

- Try 2 free books from any series
- Access risk-free special offers
- View your account history & manage payments
- Browse the latest Bonus Bucks catalog

Don't miss out!

If you want to stay up-to-date on the latest at the Reader Service and enjoy more Harlequin content, make sure you've signed up for our monthly News & Notes email newsletter. Sign up online at ReaderService.com.